Conquest

Book 2 in the Conquest Series

By

Griff Hosker

Conquest

Published by Griff Hosker 2023
Copyright ©Griff Hosker

A CIP catalogue record for this title is available from the British Library.

Dedicated to Scout

You were the best of dogs. Your memory is in some of my books as well as our hearts. Know we will never forget you. I shall miss the welcome you gave me each time I walked through the door I will look for you at the foot of the stairs each time I rise. You have left a hole that will never be filled. You were loving and you were loved. Thank you for the time you gave us. It was too short but we will cherish all those memories.

Contents

Real people used in the novel

Duke William, The Bastard, Duke of Normandy
Bishop Odo of Bayeux. His half-brother
William Malet - The Seigneur of Caux (the half-brother of
the fictional Richard Fitz Malet)
Robert Malet - the brother of William Malet and Richard
Fitz Malet
Robert Malet - the eldest son of William Malet
Gilbert Malet - the second son of William Malet
Robert Guiscard de Hauteville - later Duke of Sicily
Robert, Count of Eu
Hugh of Gournay
Walter Giffard
Robert of Mortemer
William de Warenne
Count Enguerrand
Guy of Ponthieu
Waleran of Ponthieu
Gyrth Godwinson - Earl of East Anglia
Leofwine Godwinson - Earl and ruler of Kent and the land
north of Lundenwic
Ealdgyth - daughter of the Earl of Mercia and the niece of
William Malet. Also known as Edith Swan Neck she
married Harold Godwinson in 1066
Edwin - son of the Earl of Mercia upon his father's death,
the earl
Morcar - the second son of the Earl of Mercia and later Earl
of Northumberland.

Prologue

I am Richard Fitz Malet, the result of a liaison between a Norman Seigneur and my mother, the English daughter of a housecarl. I served Duke William of Normandy and had been of some service to him at the battle of Senlac Hill. We had defeated the English, the men of Wessex, but England was far from ours. It had been a hard-fought battle and Duke William had come perilously close to losing it. I was still shaken by the butchering of my mentor, Taillefer, and while others, my friends Bruno and Odo included, celebrated, I looked for simple tasks to do that would take my mind from the slaughter on Senlac Hill. Taillefer had begged the duke to allow him to begin the battle but the finest swordsman I had ever known pushed his luck too far and was pulled from his horse, Parsifal, and hacked to pieces by the English housecarls. The housecarls had fought to the last and had died bravely but all that I had seen was my long-dead grandfather. In their byrnies and helmets with their long axes and shields, they looked identical to how I remembered him. I spent my time with my men and my horses.

I wondered what my future would be. For a week we did nothing and then Duke William sent for me. He would not allow any to honour him with the title King of England, nor would he allow any to refer to Harold as King of England. Harold Godwinson was always called Earl of Wessex. That he had sent for me meant he had a task. He had used me before. He had also used Taillefer. Now there was just me as Duke William's weapon.

The duke had been knocked from his horse during the battle but, so far as I could tell, he had suffered no ill effects. He had remounted and fought on. As I approached he looked as fit as any man. I saw his horses being groomed by his bodyguards and squire. The duke knew the value of good horses and good men to serve him. I had served both Taillefer and Duke William. As such I was considered not to be a threat and I was admitted by his knights and bodyguards with a smile.

He gestured for me to sit on the camp chair, "I have not had the time to speak to you since the battle and I am keenly aware that we have both lost someone dear to us. Others think that they knew Taillefer but, in truth, only you and I can say we truly knew him, you more than me. I envy you that closeness. You should know that he named you as his heir. It brings no land but there is a large chest of coin in Caen. You know it is safe there. His horses, swords and scabbards are all yours too."

I nodded, "I would trade all, my lord, for Taillefer alive and juggling his swords."

He smiled, "As would I and it does you great credit that you would have the man and not the treasure."

I shook my head, "When you have had little then the thought of unimaginable treasure is immaterial."

"Not many would say that." He sat up straighter in his chair, as though he had made a decision. "You have a choice for your future. Your brother is keen to have you in his demesne." I nodded, "I, on the other hand, would like you with my household, as one of my bodyguards. You know, I think, that I would never use my position to take a man from his family. If you wish to serve your brother, then it is perfectly understandable. He is one of my senior leaders and will be rewarded with great estates and lands. If you stay with him then you can expect to be given more land."

My decision was an easy one. I got on with Sir William and his sons Robert and Gilbert, not to mention his brother Robert, but I did not feel the bonds of brotherhood as I did with warriors like Bruno and Odo. Land did not appeal and I wanted to stay close to the man who was so well respected by Taillefer. "I would stay with you, my lord. I know I am not yet ready for spurs and many who are given them early come to regret it. Besides, there is still much to do. We have not even claimed a tiny part of England." I was suddenly aware that I might have gone too far. "I am sorry, Duke William, I meant no offence."

He laughed, "You speak the truth so why should I be offended? Many of my companions think that the battle gave us England. Far from it. There are many times the number of men we defeated still ready to fight. It is another reason for your inclusion in my familia. I need such honest men around me and I need men who can fight. You are one such man." He stood, "You may send your men back to your lands in Normandy. They will not be needed and they have served you well already!"

"Thank you, Duke William."

Carl and the others were happy to be going home, they had profited from the battle, but sad to be going alone.

"I need you three to watch my farm. The conquest of this land will not be quick. I will fight all the harder knowing that my manor in Normandy is safe in your hands."

They left and I became Duke William's man. It was a wise decision.

The South of England 1066

Chapter 1

We were still in the castle the duke had brought over from Normandy. It was functional and, perforce, small. The vast body of men camped outside in hovels and, the lucky ones, tents. I was with the household knights, bodyguards and those who were close to the duke and we enjoyed tents. Each day the Bretons foraged for food. They ranged far and wide taking what they needed from the defeated Saxons. The duke had sent back to Normandy for both men and food as well as horses. The battle had cost others valuable mounts; I knew that I was lucky to have not only Louis and Geoffrey but also the most magnificent of warhorses, Parsifal. After five days the duke decided that he needed to act. The English were not submitting and he was still to be acknowledged as king. William de Warenne, the new Earl of Surrey, was summoned to the castle along with me.

"Earl William, this idleness merely encourages our enemies to think that we fear them. They should know that I do not. I intend to march the army along the Thames and accept the submission of the men who line the mighty river. If they do not, we shall fight and settle this with sword and bloodshed."

William de Warenne was a warrior, and he rubbed his hands excitedly, "Excellent, my lord."

The duke shook his head, "You will be given the opportunity to lead your mesne in battle but first I want Wintan-Caestre and Harold's widow to submit. Take young Fitz Malet with you. He speaks English well and there will be no misunderstandings. I trust you both."

The earl was disappointed, but he was a loyal man and the two of us bowed our acceptance.

"Join me along the Thames when you are done."

I was happy because it meant I would be with my oldest friend Bruno. We rarely saw Odo these days. He led the duke's company of archers. I had sent my men back to Normandy and my horses were cared for by Hugo the horse master. He had twenty men to help him. He liked animals and knew horses. He loved Parsifal and when I said I was taking him he nodded his approval. "When you are seen riding the horse you will be recognised for what you are, a great warrior." He frowned, "Do you go to give battle?"

I shook my head, "We head west to Wintan-Caestre. When we return, I will take Louis and Geoffrey, for there will be battles and these will not be like the one at Senlac Hill where the fates of the high and mighty are decided, but will be inconsequential skirmishes. Parsifal shall be saved for those battles that will decide the future of this land."

We did not have far to travel and all of us were both well-armed and well armoured. We were the best of the Norman army. My grandfather had not been a knight but he had recognised the need for protection when mounted upon a horse. My hauberk was made of tightly knit mail rings. It was expensive and it had been Taillefer's. After the butchery, it had needed to be repaired but was now as good as ever. My conical helmet with the nasal was strengthened with four metal strips and covered my mail coif and ventail. The arming cap had been made in Normandy and was well made. The mittens on the hauberk were fastened around my fingers by leather and it gave me the touch and feel of my two swords. The two weapons were across my back in individual scabbards. They had also been Taillefer's. My shield had my red and white design. One day it would bear my signs and symbols but for the moment was just for identification in the heat of battle. Finally, I had metal-covered boots. I knew others had fully metal boots, called sabaton, but I preferred the softer feel of leather on my foot. With my lance in my hand, we rode off. The lances each had a gonfanon. I knew from some of the prisoners that the flags had confused the English at Senlac Hill. They had taken each flag to be the sign of a lord. When we rode we now used that to make them fear us.

As we headed west, I rode with Bruno who was curious about my family. He had parted on poor terms with my brother, the Seigneur of Caux, "Have you seen your brother?"

I shook my head, "He is an important man and we have passed when he has spoken to the duke." I shrugged, "I am still the bastard but now I am a bastard who has earned their respect. Robert smiles whenever he sees me but Gilbert is still the scowler."

"You need them not, Dick. You are like the comet we spied before the battle. You are in the ascendancy. The duke likes you. Why else would you be here? It is you who will speak to Edith Swan Neck and not the earl."

I knew the reason and it was nothing to do with my position. I said, "I can speak English that is why. Eventually, others will learn the language and I shall be a redundancy."

Bruno laughed, "Knights learn the language of the defeated? I think you are deluding yourself. This land will speak Norman by the time we are done."

We reached Wintan-Caestre before dark and halted before the gates. Would they fight us? William de Warenne turned to me, "Let us try English persuasion before Norman might." He gestured for me to approach the gate. I took my helmet from my head and hung it from my cantle. I slipped the coif from it and rode towards the gate with just my arming cap for protection.

"I am Richard Fitz Malet and my words come from Duke William. Will you hear me or do we dispute these walls?"

An English voice said, "Speak."

The first part was over. They would not send an arrow to end my life. Now I had to persuade them. In many ways that was easy. The burgh of Wintan-Caestre had once been strong but its walls were weak, its ditches were filled with rubbish and, from the sentries I could see, guarded by old men who wore no mail.

"The Earl of Surrey would enter your burgh and accept the submission of the town and of Earl Harold's wife. When that is done you shall be protected by Duke William's men and your lands will be free from raids."

The earl and I had discussed the hint of a threat. I merely couched it in more acceptable terms.

"I will need to speak to others."

"Do not be tardy. We need an answer within the hour." The tolling of the bells of the monasteries and churches within the walls marked the time. I rode back and told the earl what had been said. He asked, "Did you give a deadline?"

I nodded, "An hour. Enough time to agree and not enough time to improve the defences of the burgh."

He laughed, "For one so young you have natural skills."

13

Shaking my head I said, "I do not wish this fine city to be destroyed and if they chose to fight then it would be destroyed."

"Your English blood is still strong."

Nodding I said, "The two bloods struggle within me."

The answer came in half an hour, and we were admitted. Edith Swan Neck was beautiful but the look she gave us was hateful as she glowered at the men who had killed the King of England. We had all taken off our helmets and coifs but we still looked threatening.

The earl spoke and I translated, "Will the burgh of Wintan-Caestre and all its subjects submit to Duke William the rightful ruler of England?" I chose the softest words I could, but the face of Harold's widow winced as though I had slapped her.

The eorledman nodded, "We do, for we have been abandoned by the earls of Mercia and Northumbria." I already knew that there was bad feeling between Edith and those who sought to be the new Harold, Morcar and Edwin, mainly because they had sided with Earl Harold's second wife.

William de Warenne looked at Edith Swan Neck and repeated the question. Once again, I chose the gentlest of words as I could.

"I have little choice, it seems. Were you with the ones who butchered the body of Harold?"

She had not asked me but I answered her question, "I saw his body but my blade did not strike a blow."

"Was the butchery necessary?"

I sighed, "My lady, my grandfather was a housecarl. He told me such warriors fight beyond any hope of survival. Many of the knights who came upon Earl Harold had lost friends to wild attacks. We are warriors, my lady, and when the blood is upon you, it is hard to stop. It was not well done but I met Earl Harold and know that he would not have wanted to survive and endure the humiliation of defeat. He was a warrior."

"You fought alongside him?"

I nodded, "In the Breton war. He was a good warrior and I liked him. Had we met in battle he would have tried to kill me and I, him."

She smiled and shook her head, "I do not understand but I can hear and see that you speak the truth."

14

William de Warenne was tiring of the lack of an answer and he snapped, in English, "What is your answer?"

She stared silently at the earl and then said, coldly, "You have not the manners of your Englishman, Norman and that explains much. Like the burghers of Wintan-Caestre, I have little choice in the matter. I submit to Duke William."

I translated and William de Warenne smiled, "We will leave some priests here and a handful of warriors to see that you are safe."

She added, "And if you send to us again then make it this man, this Richard Fitz Malet. We will only speak to him."

We were close enough to our castle to ride back and reached it after dark. On the road back, the earl said, "You have natural skills, Richard. I can speak some English but you chose words I would not. I shall report so to the duke."

The army had not yet left and that pleased Bruno and the rest of the men. They had all been promised land and estates in England. They could not be given them until their owners submitted. I prepared for the ride across Kent. I returned Parsifal to the horse master. The next day we left to head to Dover. As we gathered Duke William waved me over, "Once more I am in your debt, Fitz Malet. Keep this up and great rewards will be yours."

I smiled and nodded but inside I was thinking of the English family who would have to be displaced to make a home for me.

We were still a large army. We took only mounted men for the duke wanted speed but with banners, standards and gonfanon fluttering we made a regal sight as we headed towards Dover. The English did not use castles. Their burghs were defended towns. All that we found submitted to us. There were simply no men left to fight and while the survivors might still hate us, they were in no position to face us in battle. The men of Mercia and Northumbria were but they were too busy vying with each other to face a Norman army.

Dover was different from other burghs. It was a castle. Taillefer and I had used a ruse to gain entry when we had served with the Count of Boulogne. This time no such ruse was needed. We were admitted and the castle surrendered and submitted to the duke. We also took the cathedral at Canterbury without a fight. The duke was clever. We were taking the important places while Edwin and Morcar squatted in the north. Had they brought the armies of the north to repulse us then who knows what the result might have been, but they were not the Earl of Wessex. I had met them both and knew that they were nothing like the charismatic Harold Godwinson.

It was there that sickness caught up with us. It was inevitable I suppose. We had been in the land for a couple of months. Our diet had not been the best nor had our hygiene. Coming into contact with the garrison at Dover resulted in illness. None died but it meant we had to sojourn there while the men recovered. I was lucky and while others spent hours at the latrines or languished in their cots, I was able to continue to guard Duke William.

The sickness seemed to spur the duke. When all were recovered he roused the army and we marched to Lundenwic. We reached Southwark and the bridge over the Thames. There the men of Lundenwic waited for us. They were gathered before the bridge and the walls of the city teemed with armed men. Duke William did not attack straight away. We had ridden hard from Dover. We made a fortified camp and armed guards formed a barrier in case the men of Lundenwic chose to make an attack. That they did not was revealing. I was too lowly to hear the duke's plan. I stood guard without to prevent any from listening to the duke's words.

Walter Giffard emerged first and said, "When the meeting is over, arm yourselves. Spears, not lances. We fight on foot." Walter was succinct but the few words told us that we would be fighting in an old-fashioned way, with a wedge. It made sense to me for horsemen would not be able to use their spears on such a narrow front. Horses were more valuable than men and the duke would not risk our greatest advantage; our mobility. It would place us toe to toe with the enemy and as we were all mailed I had no doubt about the outcome. Although we all rode with the duke the very nature of our work meant that we did not get to know one another well. This would be a rare opportunity to fight shoulder-to-shoulder with others who were like me.

As soon as there was just the duke within the tent I fetched my spear and slung my shield. A lance was too long to use on foot. Although more effective when used on the back of a horse, the long kite shield did afford a great deal of protection for the left side of a warrior's body. Despite the duke's desire to be at the fore of the fighting, William de Warenne and Earl William Fitz Osbern placed themselves before our men. I saw, behind us, many men with faggots and burning brands. I had expected the duke to try to take the city but then again, as there were just five hundred of us that seemed too great a challenge.

The men of Lundenwic banged their shields and shouted aggressively at us while we formed up. It was their way. They were all bluster. Few from the city had fallen at Senlac Hill. In addition, they easily outnumbered us and, I think, that made them overconfident. They expected us to die when we tried to cross the narrow bridge. I knew that numbers alone meant little. The two earls, both called William, waited until their men were in place and then ordered a charge. It was not a charge as it had been at Senlac Hill. We were on rough ground and afoot but we all moved purposefully forwards, jabbing with spears and holding protective shields before us. Although I was in the second rank I had a target and I thrust my spear at the eager face of the warrior wearing a pot helmet and brandishing a long axe. He might have thought he was a housecarl but he was not. His swing, at the man before me, was loose and wayward. The knight easily blocked it. My spear slid into the warrior's eye and, as he screamed, I twisted and thrust. He died quickly and we moved forward. It was ridiculously easy. They fell back at an alarming speed. When we crossed the bridge and reached the northern bank of the Thames, Earl William ordered the halt and as axes hacked at the bridge, faggots were laid along the side. When the command came to fall back we did so in perfect order and as we vacated the bridge the lighted brands were thrown. By the time the last of us had reached the southern bank, the bridge was on fire. There could be no sally south from Lundenwic for the bridge was burned. Duke William had a plan and he was sticking to it.

We mounted our horses and rode hard to the west of the city. The men on foot were following us and they were the ones building defences. England was being controlled although Edwin and Morcar in the north seemed oblivious to it. When we reached Wallingford the burgh there could not stop us. It was its natural defensiveness that made Duke William halt.

I was asked to hold his horse while he took off his helmet to survey the site. He shook his head and addressed the two earl Williams, "I am just astounded that the English have avoided being conquered before. It is no wonder that the Danish king, Cnut, enjoyed such success."

William de Warenne said, "My lord?"

"Can you not see it, de Warenne? A castle here and Lundenwic is held from the west. With Dover to the south and east the capital of England becomes a prisoner. We will halt here and build a castle. When the men on foot arrive, we shall continue to Berkhamsted and the east of this city."

Now that I am old, men often ask me how so few men were able to control such a vast land and the answer is a simple one. We built castles. While some men foraged, the bulk of us, Duke William included, set to finding a good site and then digging the ditch and raising the mound. I had my grandfather's build and I was sent to the forests with an axe to hew logs. They were split and transported back to the building site. How did we Normans do what we did so quickly? Again, the answer is simple. There were no passengers. If you had two arms and legs you carried, dug, hewed or lifted. By the time the foot element of the army arrived, we had the mound in place and there was an outer curtain of stakes in place. It was the first castle we built in England. The one at Pevensey did not count. We had constructed that in Normandy and carried it on ships.

More of the horsemen who had succumbed to what we now termed the Kentish illness had recovered and we had more than five hundred mounted and mailed men. We spent most of November building the castle and its effect was dramatic. In early December Stigand, the Archbishop of Canterbury, came to submit to Duke William. He had been with the two earls, Morcar and Edwin and his defection told us much. Once again I was an observer for I was tasked with fetching wine for the duke, his brother and the two earl Williams.

"This changes everything."

"How so, brother?" I did not like Bishop Odo. Some men, like William de Warenne, become greater men when given power. Bishop Odo became more corrupt.

Duke William turned and holding his coistrel out for me to fill it he said, "If there was opposition to our invasion then it would be further north where Edwin and Morcar have power and men who have not yet tasted defeat. Stigand was with them and yet he chose now to defect. Do you not see? If the prelate thought that there was any chance of an army facing us in battle then he would stay with them. No, we continue our ride around Lundenwic and then enter. There is no opposition. Senlac Hill was their only chance to defeat us and they did not."

Odo shrugged, "Do we wait for the army to build this castle?"

"We wait not a day. We ride on the morrow. First, we take St Albans and Hertford. The Roman roads of Watling Street and Ermine Street are there. We leave men to guard them and protect us from an attack from the north. I do not think such an attack will materialise but this is not the moment to take chances. Then I enter Lundenwic with the Archbishop and he can crown me in Westminster."

"And, brother, if the men of Lundenwic oppose us?"

"We showed them at Southwark that we have the beating of them. We make a martial march and all will be well."

Stigand slowed us down but not too much. We took Hertford without a fight. Indeed, the presence of the archbishop seemed to help the duke. The burghers submitted. The duke sent his brother to St Albans to accept their submission and then guard the roads while we returned south.

When we reached the northern Roman wall, we were met, not by armed men but by a delegation of the most important men in Lundenwic. King Elect Edgar, the Aetheling and Archbishop Ealdred were there to offer the crown to Duke William. I was not close by his side but even from a distance, I saw the relief in the duke's shoulders. He had the crown if not the kingdom.

The ride into Lundenwic showed us all that we were far from welcome. We flanked the duke and our hands were on the pommels of our swords. It was a ride not filled with threat but a lack of any warmth. Edgar and Ealdred had submitted but the reason was clear. Edwin and Morcar had failed to deliver any hope of an armed resistance. The coronation was set for Christmas Day and we stayed in Edward the Confessor's palace. I knew it from my time with Taillefer. We happily stood night watches in case there was a threat. There was none.

On the day of the coronation, the abbey was filled with Lundenwic nobles and only a handful of the most senior Norman lords were admitted. Duke William had less than thirty men to protect him and we stood without nervously as parts of the Latin service drifted over to us. It was when there was a huge roar from within that some men, not the duke's bodyguard, but the men of Odo and William Fitz Osbern shouted, "Treachery." While we ran into the abbey they drew their swords and began to slay any man that they saw. Some took brands and began to burn the houses that lay close by. When we entered the abbey it was clear that the roar we had heard was merely the acclamation of Duke William as King William the 1st of England. The burning and the slaughter were not a good portent.

Chapter 2

The army arrived along with the horses and men we had left at Pevensey and with their arrival, the king, it was hard to get used to the title, began building a castle in the heart of the city. He used the existing Roman Wall and buildings as the foundation and it was clear that this would be built in stone. I prepared for hard work but was surprised when, as I turned up for work at the building site, I was waved over by the king and William de Warenne.

"The earl told me what good service you did in Wintan-Caestre and I would have you do the same for me again."

I bowed, "Of course, King William."

He smiled, "It is hard to become used to the appellation when most of the kingdom has still to bow the knee. You know the brothers Edwin and Morcar?"

"I met them, my lord, at my brother's home and I hunted with them."

"Then they know you and you can speak English. I wish you to find them and ask them to submit to me. You will go with one of the earl's men and a couple of servants. This will be done quietly. I wish to pursue the path of diplomacy before I resort to the sword."

I already knew before I spoke, that Bruno would be with me once more. "They may not remember me, my lord, I should not like to fail you."

"And you will not." He smiled and that was a rare thing. "I think they just need an olive branch. I could send one of my great lords but that might make the brothers choose to fight. You speak their language and they know you. All you need to do is deliver a message and then you can return here."

I nodded, "And what is the message, my lord?"

"If they submit to me then they keep all their lands and will, in the fullness of time, be rewarded even more."

"And where will we find them, my lord?"

"The archbishop thinks that they will have gone to Tamworth, the ancient capital of Mercia. It is a place to start."

King William was all business and having given his orders he returned his attention to his new castle. Bruno was waiting for me at the horse lines. That he knew our task was clear and that annoyed me. Why had he known before I did? I realised that there had been no question of refusal. I was ordered to do what could be a dangerous task. I put that from my head. Taillefer had taught me to concentrate on the task at hand and that any distractions could prove to be disastrous.

"You have been told then?"

He nodded, "The earl thought that you might refuse but that I should be ready. I knew that you would not refuse and I am prepared."

"There was never a question of refusal."

He shrugged, "I have two pueros to ride with us and act as servants. They are from the earl's mesne and are good lads. Henry is seventeen and keen. Gaston is a little older but already a good warrior. They can handle swords, spears and horses."

"You have done everything that is needed. That is good."

"I have done the easy part. You will have the harder task of persuading the brothers. We will get you there safely but the result will be in your hands."

I chose Louis as the horse was a good one and I knew he would be able to handle the vagaries of the road. We did not take spears as we would not need them. We took blankets but not tents. I spoke with one of the English workers helping to bring the stone for the castle. He told me that it was one hundred and twenty miles or so to Tamworth. That would take two to three days and as we were uncertain about finding accommodation we would just sleep rough.

"The earl has provided us with coins. He said we should pay for what we need."

I cocked a curious eye at my friend, "Very generous of him. Why?"

Bruno shrugged, "He has Surrey which is a rich land. The sooner there is peace the sooner he can begin to profit from the land. I am also promised a manor and my spurs. Your friendship was not the only reason for my participation, Dick. You should begin to look out for yourself as others do. We have thrown the bones and won a great battle. We all took risks at Senlac Hill. Let us profit from them."

I did not answer as we packed the blankets and food onto the back of the sumpter we would take. I still did not feel right about taking my grandfather's land. It was hard to explain, even to myself, but I knew that the journey to Tamworth was not the only one I would make. There would be another one that would take the bastard from de Caux to... I knew not where.

The horse master was more than happy to watch over my horses. After all, I was now seen as someone important. I knew that I was no Taillefer but I felt that the king held me in a higher esteem than many. We presented ourselves to the king before we left. He nodded approvingly, "I have given you nothing of any mark. You will succeed or fail because they know you. Make it clear to them, Richard, that this is their one and only chance to keep their titles and their lands." He nodded towards the ditch and the rising mound, "It is coming on apace, is it not? When we have made more progress we will head north and east to accept the submission of the men of East Anglia. This is how we shall tame this land. Castles and the submission of their lords. It will take time, but it will be worth it."

It was cold and there was dampness in the air as we headed up the Roman Road. I knew that whatever the political outcome my mail would need to be cleaned and oiled when we returned. We were cloaked and cowled against the cold. Our helmets hung from our cantles and our shields from our legs but we had our coifs on our heads. The two pueros rode behind us. They chattered away like magpies. Bruno snapped, irritably, "If you must fill the air with inane nonsense then do it quietly for you make my ears buzz."

"Sorry, my lord."

I smiled, "It does not seem that long since we were so chastised."

"Dick, we would have given our eyes for such an opportunity as they have been given. They need to act more responsibly." He said it loudly enough so that they heard him.

We passed travellers on the road although this was late winter, and it would be summer before there were huge numbers travelling to Lundenwic. The ones we did see spied us and kept well to the other side of the road. We could be nothing else but Normans and we were still the invaders. We passed through burghs and towns. When we stopped, we bought ale and mulled wine as well as food. I am guessing we were charged more than the English, but we had no way of knowing. When I spoke English, they were visibly shocked as though I was some kind of shaman. It depressed me because as soon as I spoke English they ceased talking. It was as though they were excluding me.

We reached the market town of Leighton just before dark. The market was ending and the last thing that they would do would be to keep it open for four Normans. There were no inns or none that appeared to be open. Perhaps there had been during the day but the market was over. I asked if there was a lord who had a hall thinking that might be an option, but there was none. What we did find was a wooden church. There appeared to be no priest and so we entered the church. The four of us made the sign of the cross and Bruno decided that this would be our bed for the night. With just one door in and out we would be as safe as anywhere. The pueros slept behind the door.

As we were leaving, before dawn, the priest arrived. His face affected a look of pious outrage and he made the sign of the cross. "What sacrilege is this? Norman knights allowing their horses to foul God's house!"

He spat the words out in English and I answered mildly in the same language, "Father, there is no mess and I do not think that God would deny shelter to travellers." I reached into my purse and pulled out a silver coin. "If we have offended you then take this coin as payment."

He greedily grabbed it but was not finished with his vitriol, "And what is a traitor doing with the Norman invaders? Have you taken your thirty pieces of silver?"

I mounted my horse and shook my head, "Father, I am half Norman and half-English. No matter what I do I betray someone."

We headed up the road. Breakfast was eaten in the saddle which meant that we were silent. That suited me. Was this how I was to be judged? I knew that there were some in my brother's household who did not trust me. His dead sibling, Sir Durant, had been one. If the English did not trust me then was I to be an outcast?

The wind whipped from the northeast and whilst it was dry it scythed through the wool of our cloaks and we ensured that our cowls covered as much of our faces as possible. It encouraged silence. It was late afternoon and we were just ten miles from Tamworth when my sixth sense began to prickle. I had not known I had more than five until Taillefer explained it to me.

'You see, Dick, the five senses all join together, so some wise men say, to give to some a sixth sense. They tell you what you cannot see, hear, smell, taste or touch. Never ignore that prickle. It is your body trying to save you.'

The prickle I felt made me turn and speak to Bruno. "Something is wrong."

My friend knew me well enough to trust me and he reined in. He said, loudly, "My horse has a stone. Afford me some shelter from this wind while I inspect the hoof."

Henry and Gaston were no fools and knew that there was nothing wrong with the gait of Bruno's horse. They would be alert. As he dismounted, I slipped my cloak from my shoulders and placed it about the rump of my horse. By way of explanation, in case the watchers could hear, I said, "Louis is not a young horse and feels the cold more than I do. While we stop, I will give her some comfort."

Henry said, "You are too kind to your horse."

"You are still a pueros and have yet to be forced to rely on a horse in battle. Your views will change." I was doing what I did not for Louis but to enable me to reach my two swords easily.

Bruno rose from his false inspection. He hissed out his words, "We are being followed. I am unsure of the numbers but they are on both sides."

That made sense. If men were following on foot then the sound of their feet would have been masked by the sound of our horses' hooves.

He pulled himself into his saddle. He would not need to drop his cloak for his single sword hung from his side. It was as he slipped his feet into the stirrups that the bandits attacked. We were ready. My swords were out in a flash as the eight bandits ran from all sides at us. I used my knees to guide my well-trained horse. I was on the extreme left and the bandit with the axe must have thought I was the easiest victim. He swung his axe at my left side. My shield hung there and it was well made. Taillefer's lessons had been well learned and my left hand reacted without being ordered. It slashed down and bit into the side of the man's head. The axe dropped from his lifeless hands; it had not even come close to my shield such had been the speed of my hand. I wheeled Louis as two younger men ran at me with fire-hardened spears. They came from two directions. The blackened ends might have hurt one who did not wear mail but they could not penetrate my hauberk. In contrast, my swords had no such defence with which to contend. The two swords struck between the shoulder and the head of both men. One spear managed to strike my hauberk but it broke.

Wheeling, for there were no more enemies before me I shouted, in English, "Stay your hands or die!"

One of the older men thrust up with his ancient and slightly buckled sword at Bruno. My friend contemptuously grabbed the blade in his mittened hand and then stabbed him in the throat. "A quicker end than you deserved, bandit."

I took in that Gaston and Henry had survived unscathed and there were just three survivors from the attack. One was an older man and the other two were boys, little more than twelve summers old. The man had dropped his wood axe and now held the boys protectively close to him.

Bruno looked at me, "You are the one with the words. Do we kill them now or…"

I shook my head, "I promised them life if they surrendered."

He shook his head, "Banditry is punished by death in Normandy, but I would not have your honour besmirched. Gaston, bind their hands and put halters around their necks. We will see what kind of justice they have here in Mercia."

As they did so I noticed that the boys were barefoot. The shifts they wore would not keep out the cold and they all looked emaciated. I did not know the reason for their banditry, but I could understand that they needed to do something to live. It also made me reassess their ages. They could be up to two years older than I thought. That would make them subject to the justice of the land. I slowed down our pace.

Bruno noticed my action and shook his head, "You are too soft, Dick. They tried to kill us and would have shown us no mercy."

I nodded, "I know but a man cannot change his nature, can he, Bruno?"

"He can try. This is a land that is ripe for plucking. When we have it, we shall need a rod of iron to keep the people in check. There can be no sympathy then. Get it out of your system now, Dick."

I knew I would not heed the words of my oldest friend.

Tamworth was ancient. It had a wooden palisade, not that it would have withstood an assault by the king's men, but it was prosperous. As we neared it, I saw the alarm our horses, mail and weapons generated. We had dropped our cowls and revealed that we just wore our arming caps and coifs but the guards on the gate prickled with anticipation. I saw their knuckles tightening around their spears. We were Normans and all that they knew was that we had slaughtered the cream of their warriors. We were to be feared.

A mailed warrior held up his hand, "I am Aelfgar, the Captain of the Guard and the protector of the earl. State your business."

"We are sent by King William of England, the Duke of Normandy and we seek an audience with the earl."

He had addressed me in English and yet seemed surprised that I had replied in his own language. He looked flustered and then he spied the three captives, "And these?"

"We were attacked by bandits. The others lie dead on the road some miles south of here. We brought them here for the earl's justice."

He was on more familiar ground and he snapped out, "Take these away and keep them safe until the earl can deal with them."

"Aye, Captain."

"If you would follow me. I cannot promise that you will be seen but you have spoken courteously, and I will do my best."

It was an old-fashioned Saxon Mead Hall. The two timbers that supported the entrance had intricately carved dragons and other mythical beasts climbing the trees carved into them. Some earl or king had obviously decided that it was too pagan and crosses had been carved into the pillars. It spoiled the effect.

Leaving the pueros with the horses we ascended the steps. Aelfgar had us wait in the guard chamber with two warriors who wore no mail but carried long axes. Both Bruno and I studied them. One day we might have to fight them and it was as well to search for weaknesses now while there was no danger.

"Wait here."

The two men had muscled upper bodies and I knew that they would be able to wield the long axes for hours. Their weakness was that once they had swung the momentum of the axe head would make them vulnerable to a spear or a judicious strike from a sword.

The door opened surprisingly quickly and Aelfgar swept an arm to admit us. "You may enter but without weapons."

We both nodded and took off our swords. It was to be expected. Entering the mead hall, we were greeted by the blazing light of many candles giving the hall a golden look. A long, raised dais had a table whereon sat the two earls, I recognised them, and their wives as well as senior Mercian lords. Aelfgar gestured for us to move closer and we did so. We bowed. Before I could speak Earl Edwin spoke or rather, he ranted, "What insult is this? Does this Norman duke think that he can send two men who are barely knights to speak on his behalf? Does he try to stir us to war?" He spoke in Norman. There was Norman blood in their family and while he butchered the words they were, at least, understandable.

Before either of us could speak an old white-haired warrior pushed himself painfully to his feet, "I recognise one of them, my lord. It is the bastard from de Caux. It is de Malet's half-brother."

The earl leaned forward and peered at me, "Are you sure, Edmund?"

The housecarl laughed, "Aye, I remember he had courage and that his grandfather was a housecarl. Richard, is it not?"

"It is, Master Edmund, and I am honoured that you remembered me." Until the earl had said his name I had forgotten it.

The earl said, "It is still an insult."

I shook my head, "Not so, my lord. The king," I used the title denied him by the earl, "thought that I would be seen as a trusted emissary for I can speak English and, as Edmund remembered, I am not unknown to you. He wanted no barriers between us to mar our discussion. He offers you the lands of Mercia and Northumbria and the titles that go with them in return for submitting to his will."

Morcar spoke, for the first time, "And that seems reasonable. You fought Earl Harold?"

I took in that he had not given Harold the title of king. Was Morcar a pragmatist? "I did, my lord, and witnessed the deaths of many brave Englishmen that day."

The earl waved a hand, "The hour is late and we have supped. We shall need clear heads to make any decisions. Make a space for our guests and find beds for them and their servants. English hospitality shall not be seen to be lacking."

We were seated with some minor nobles who shuffled to get as far away from us as they could. I smiled. It merely made us more comfortable than they were. We took out our eating knives and platters were placed unceremoniously before us. I carved a piece from the pig and placed it on my platter making sure that there were more of the soggy greens and beans than there was meat. Bruno just carved himself as large a portion of pork as he could. This was England and that meant there was either mead or ale. I chose the mead and I found it powerful. Bruno would have preferred wine but he sipped the mead. It was the wrong way to drink it and he wrinkled his nose. I sighed. Bruno might become a problem.

We ate in silence. Others at the table held mumbled conversations fearing, no doubt, that my knowledge of English might, in some way, betray their masters' intentions. It was uncomfortable until Edmund, aided now by a walking stick, hobbled down to speak to me.

That he was highly regarded was clear from the reactions of the men at my table. He smiled and put his hand on my shoulder, "You have grown and if you were at Senlac and lived then you acquitted yourself well. I hear that was not a place for cowards."

I shook my head, "I saw no cowards on either side that day. It was hard fought." I nodded to his leg, "A wound?"

He laughed and shook his head, "Would that it was but no, it is simply old age. I should have been at Senlac and enjoyed a warrior's death but the earl kept us in the north. To be fair I am not sure that my old joints would have allowed me to stand in a shield wall but, who knows, I might have been able to take out a Norman or two."

"Edmund!" The earl's tones rang out.

"I come, my lord." Shaking his head he said, "Time was I would have been allowed to talk to any but now there is suspicion and men look over their shoulders. It is sad, Richard Fitz Malet, but I trust you more than some of the others on this table." He glowered and glared at the men and most had the good grace to avert their eyes from his fearsome gaze.

When he had returned to the high table Bruno gave me a wry smile, "I did not understand all his words but I know that old man would have emptied saddles before he was taken. He has steel in his eyes."

Before we retired, we visited our pueros and horses. They had been cared for. The animals and pueros had been fed and the pueros were given ale. We re-entered the mead hall with our blankets and found a corner where we could make our beds. Once more men shuffled away from us. It was their loss.

We were woken early for the hall would be where we would breakfast. Dawn had barely broken when we stepped outside into the misty air. Bruno said, as we made water, "I think that we will return to Lundenwic and the king with ill news. There seems to be no hope here of submission."

"And you would have war."

He shrugged, "Better a little bloodletting and then peace can heal the wounds."

By the time we returned, the hall had been awakened and the sleeping men evicted so that tables could be fetched and food prepared. We went to check on the horses and our two men. We told them that we might be leaving soon and they should ensure that the horses were well fed and watered. We had a long ride south ahead of us. We would be leaving, I hoped, as soon as we had met with the two earls. This time, when we were admitted, we were seated at the earl's table but his oathsworn had drawn swords and were watching our every move. Guards kept out others. The bishop was there but Edmund was absent. There were no women. This was as private a talk as was possible.

The bishop blessed the food and said, Grace. We waited until the two brothers ate and then we broke our fast. Edwin did not wait too long before he spoke.

"King William will let us keep our lands and titles?"

I nodded.

Morcar said, "And the taxes?"

I saw no reason to lie and I shook my head, "I know not about taxes, my lord. We are merely the emissaries sent to see that King William's words would be heard as they were spoken. I am guessing such refinements would be negotiated face to face."

The bishop wiped his mouth, "It is the title and the lands that are important, my lord."

The two brothers must have spoken before because, after a mumbled conversation Edwin said, "Then we accept. We will come to Lundenwic within the week and present ourselves at the church of the Confessor. Let all be done well."

The bishop made the sign of the cross, "Amen to that."

Morcar smiled and there seemed to be relief around the table. He clapped his hands, "Admit the others."

The doors opened and the waiting warriors and nobles flooded in.

Edwin leaned forward, "I pray that you keep our counsel until we announce it ourselves."

"Of course."

We ate fresh bread and butter with cold meats, cheese, honey and dried fruits. It was a good breakfast although I saw that Bruno still baulked at the beer and the mead.

Aelfgar approached the table, "My lord?"

The earl of Mercia looked up, "Yes?"

"We still have the men who attacked your guests on the road."

Edwin's cloth came up to wipe his mouth, "You were attacked?"

It seemed so long ago as to be almost forgotten. I nodded, "A few miles from here some unfortunates made the mistake of attacking four mailed horsemen. Most paid the price with their lives but there were survivors."

Bruno had been listening, "We brought them here for justice."

"Then fetch them and we shall show King William's men how we deal with banditry."

The three were, eventually, dragged forth. Edwin, as earl, spoke, "Who are you?"

The man said, "I am Ealdred of Gilling, my lord." I knew that Earl Morcar held the rights to the manor. It meant that they had served the earl but he clearly did not recognise them. That told me as much about the earl as it did Ealdred. "These are my nephews, Edgar and Edward. Their father was slain." His eyes fixed on Bruno.

"Do you deny attacking these men?"

He shook his head, "Of course not, my lord, but my brother led forty men at Stamford Bridge and our orders, after the victory, were clear, to join your brother, our lord and master, in the south and fight the Normans. Who knows? Our presence at that battle might have swayed the outcome but because we had wounded men we were tardy reaching the south and it was over before we reached it. When we saw these four Normans we thought to do that which we had been ordered and we attacked them."

I think even Bruno understood their actions. Certainly, he nodded at the words. Edwin looked at the bishop, "They are guilty of banditry."

The bishop nodded, "And this was not a battle. They were not acting under the orders of their lord. How could they be, you were here, my lord." He looked at Earl Morcar.

Ealdred threw himself to his knees, "My life is forfeit, my lord, and I accept my punishment, but these boys did not lift a weapon. They stood and watched. Their lives should not be taken."

Edwin nodded, "Then you shall be taken hence and hanged. The boys shall be thralls."

"No, my lord!"

Edwin grew angry, "You question me?" I wondered what further punishment he could give to Ealdred.

My voice, when it came, surprised even me, "My lord, if you would give the boys to me then they can become servants." I looked at Ealdred, "Not slaves but freemen. I have land and they can be taught skills. We were the ones attacked and I would not have their serfdom on my conscience."

The bishop descended so that he stood close to the boys. Aelfgar still held Ealdred. The bishop said, "You boys, would you swear to serve this Norman?" He held out his cross, "I have the cross here and you will swear or you shall wear the yoke."

The two boys looked at each other and nodded. The elder, I learned his name was Edward, reached up, kissed the cross and said, "I swear." Edgar emulated his brother.

Edwin smiled, "Then all is done well."

Later, after the boys had been forced to watch their uncle hanged, an unpleasant and distressing sight for any, we headed for the horses. Earl Edwin had ten of his horsemen ready to escort us for the first twenty miles and Aelfgar had procured an old sumpter for the boys to ride.

As we mounted Bruno shook his head, "I know not what made you open your mouth but you have brought us two that we will need to watch for fear of having our throats slit."

I smiled, "Perhaps it was a Christian act, I know not but I know that I could not leave them to be slaves. Remember, Bruno, my life was little better than that of a slave. Something prompted my action."

"Aye, well, they are your problem now. When we reach Lundenwic then I will not have to sleep with a dagger beneath my pillow but you shall."

Chapter 3

Bruno wanted nothing to do with the boys but I felt a responsibility towards them and so I spoke with them. "I meant what I said, I am making you free. When you are old enough to make such decisions you may leave me and find a life for yourselves."

Edward nodded. I was learning that he was the one who was happy to speak. Edgar rarely spoke. "How do we call you, my lord?"

"As you are my servants I would think that master would do."

"And what will be our duties?"

"First, we have to dress you appropriately. You need better clothes and boots."

"Boots?"

I smiled, "Aye, for I remember when I was barefoot. Boots shall be bought for you." I knew that at Pevensey there were many boots for the dead had been stripped before their bodies had been buried or burned. It would not be an expense. "Then, when we are at camp you shall help to tend my three horses, fetch my food and, if we are on campaign, then prepare my food. I shall pay you."

Bruno's head whipped around and his eyes rolled heavenward. He said nothing but he did not need to.

"Squires will attend to the knights and you shall join them serving at the table." Edward nodded but Edgar said nothing.

Having the earl's men as an escort afforded us accommodation at a monastery and, when they left us the next day, we had barely thirty miles to ride to Lundenwic. We were almost at Bedaford when we were found. A column of men wearing the livery of Fitz Osbern found us.

Bruno was relieved, "Well met, Roger." He knew the knight who led the column. "Were you seeking us?"

"No, but rebels, men who opposed us. Have you found two?" He pointed at the two boys who recoiled for they were surrounded by mailed Normans.

I said, "No, they are my servants. Is the king with you for we have been on a diplomatic mission and he will want to know the results?"

The knight called Roger laughed, "Bruno? A diplomat? Here is a tale." He pointed to the south and east, "He is at Bury St Edmunds. We have been accepting the submission of the local lords. It is a slow process. I would that they would fight and then we could get it over with."

I noticed, as we headed for King William's camp, that the two boys kept their sumpter even closer to me. Such was the effect of we Normans.

With the prospect of action in the offing Bruno was keen to report to the king and then return to the Earl of Surrey. I left the boys on their sumpter, Edward holding the reins of Louis. We were admitted to the hall as soon as we were announced.

The king's eyes widened expectantly, "Well?"

"They will be in Lundenwic within a week, my lord,"

"Excellent! Any problems?"

The king would not wish to know of something as trivial as an attack but he would want to know about the earl's requests. "The Earl of Mercia wondered if they would get to keep their taxes."

The king laughed, "That does not surprise me. When we have the land under control then I shall introduce taxes but before I do that I would know what the land is worth. I will smile and agree. I buy the peace, that is all. And now you can rejoin the army. We will secure this bog that calls itself East Anglia and then leave for less pestilential lands when the earls arrive. You have done well." He smiled at Bruno, "You may return to the earl. He has a manor for you in mind."

"Thank you, King William."

He left, "As for you... Richard Fitz Malet, I would keep you closer." He handed me a purse. "Gold taken from rebels. I promise you spurs and a manor but only when this land is mine. You are not only useful but something of a lucky charm." He glanced around, "Do not mention that to the priests. Perhaps it is my Norse blood."

"I have acquired two English servants, my lord. I will need a couple of days to see to their needs, with your permission."

"Of course, but how did you come by them? You have been absent but a short time." I told him of the attack, the trial and Bruno's reaction to my decision. "Your friend may be right we cannot afford to be gentle."

"If we are not, King William, then we will have to fight to hold onto this land."

"We shall see."

I went with my two servants to see the horse master. I wished to ensure that my horses were still happy and they were. Edward took to Parsifal and Geoffrey immediately but Edgar did not. It did not worry me unduly as there were things that Edgar could do for me. I had prevented their thraldom and as soon as they were old enough I would free them. I was giving them a start only. The horse master was also able to point me to Belius who was an older warrior. He had been given the task of collecting all the weapons and serviceable pieces of equipment. My position as a companion of the king meant that, in theory, I should not have had to use my coins but, inevitably, I would for Belius was doing as many other soldiers were doing and making their own profit. I did not mind and I had the coins from the king in any case. I found them boots, cloaks, belts and daggers in scabbards. Bruno would have chastised me for the latter but I knew that it would make the two boys feel safer. That done we found an old woman in the town who, for a couple of silver coins, made the youths clothes that made them look more civilised. Neither were happy when I insisted upon their bathing and having their hair cut but in the heart of a Norman camp the last thing that they needed was to draw attention to themselves. We had to change the water halfway through for the wildlife from their hair and bodies teemed. Scrubbed with harsh soap and their hair combed with a fine bone comb they were free of infestation and soon the blood-spotted bites on their bodies would fade.

Most of the better accommodation had been taken already but I was quite happy with the manger over the horses that the horse master procured. I was pleased that we were eating well. There was a variety of meat and fish, all confiscated from the lords who had refused to submit and fought. Some had died but the result was the same. There was little opposition to King William and he took what he wanted.

When I returned to duty I wondered if the boys would run. If they had it would not have upset me. They would, at least, be free, but I feared that if they did run their future would be bleak. In the event, they did not run and that pleased me.

Riders brought in news of the arrival of the earls Morcar and Edwin as well as the Danish lord, Gospatric, who ruled York and Earl Waltheof, the second son of Siward who had been Earl of Northumbria. That the king was pleased was an understatement. He had already put William Fitz Osbern in charge of Hereford where he would guard the land from the west, and Bishop Odo was lord of Kent ensuring that our supply lines were solid. The arrival of the four men meant that the land had, effectively, all submitted to King William. He had won the country.

We entered Lundenwic as though everyone had won and this was a great victory for England. The four men submitted publicly in Westminster and the feast was a great one. For me, it was a duty. Mine was a harder one than most of the others for I spoke English and was, sometimes, required to translate a word. The brothers spoke Norman, after a fashion, but King William had not bothered to make any attempt to speak English. I was useful. They all seemed to get on and, towards the end of the evening, King William invited his first guests to accompany him back to Normandy where he would celebrate Easter. They agreed and, not for the first time, I found myself admiring this clever man who had grasped the thinnest of straws to claim a kingdom. By taking the four men with him he ensured that the men he left to rule England in his absence would have no opposition and he would be able to strengthen his lands in Normandy. Count Eustace had been an ally but since his return to Flanders, he had begun to plot against the king. So too the Bretons were unhappy. Count Conan had died, poisoned and fingers were pointed in King William's direction. Whatever the truth the reality was that England was more secure than Normandy and so we returned.

This time we did not board from the beach but from the Cinq Ports. It was far more civilised than the beach if not a little chaotic. We had three horses and three sumpters to load and while the three war horses complied, the sumpters did not. It was during the confusion that Edgar fled. Neither his brother nor I realised for a while but when we turned to load the last sumpter, we saw that both youth and sumpter had fled. His flight had been observed by Aimeri, one of King William's bodyguards, and a friend of mine. "I had no horse else I might have stopped him."

"It is no matter. The sumpter was Mercian."

Poor Edward felt awful, "I am sorry Master, I should have realised he would do this."

I put my arm around his shoulder, "It is fate, Edward. He is free and that is something."

"But he stole a sumpter!"

I smiled, "He can have it and welcome." I pointed to the sumpter we had just loaded, "If you wish to follow him then take Janus and I wish you well."

He shook his head, "My brother is wrong, Master. I am your man and swore on the cross. I will not be forsworn. God will punish my brother for breaking his oath. He will not have a good life and his end will be unpleasant." I was learning just how superstitious were the men of the north.

And so we boarded the cog and headed back to Normandy. It was less than a year since we had arrived in England and our journey back meant we had won.

The voyage back was relatively benign but poor Edward did not think so. He threw up a week's worth of food and then spent a day bringing forth white bile. His seasickness took his mind from his brother. Edgar had timed his departure to perfection for there was no opportunity for us to chase after him. Time and tide wait for no man. It seemed a longer crossing to me. I spent much of the time with the horses. There was little I could do for Edward. I seemed to be a natural sailor and while the ride was a wild one I coped. We had been blown off course and would not be able to land at Harfleur. It would mean a longer ride home and a crossing of the Seine. The cog's captain landed us at the tiny port of Ouistreham. The ship had suffered damage and he was far from certain that the ship would make the Seine. We were all happy to depart the vomit-filled ship. Our horses were in no condition to be ridden and so I ate a meal at the tavern by the quay while Edward, grateful to have solid ground beneath his feet, tended to the horses. We walked the first two miles down the road to Caen and only mounted when I was sure that they were ready. I was on more familiar ground. This was Normandy and it was Edward who saw all as new. Caen impressed him beyond words with its huge donjon rising like some prehistoric monolith in the heart of the city. We were on the road from Caen when I broached his brother.

"Do you regret leaving your brother, Edward?"

He shook his head, "Before Stamford Bridge and before Senlac Hill were good times. We had beaten the Norse and we thought we could send you Normans packing. Once we met up with the stragglers from the battle and heard their accounts then life changed. It became harder and the roads we had walked with such ease now seemed harder to tramp. We often went days without food. When we first saw you, it was not only my father's chance to be a warrior but, for me, it was the prospect of taking your food. I would not go hungry again and Edgar will be hungry. He has a dagger and a sumpter but he should have run when we were closer to the north. Your Duke William has secured the south and it is Edgar who will have to hide. I did all that I could to make him accept his fate but, in the end, a man makes his own choices and lives by them. I know that I am on the cusp of manhood as is Edgar and I have chosen my bed." He smiled, "I will see how a Norman one suits."

Edward was bright and had already picked up some Norman just listening to the knights around him. Now I began to teach him as we rode home. By the time we reached my cosy little manor, he could speak to people and understand their replies. He was polite and civil.

My brother's home at Graville was always impressive and we passed that before reaching my more modest home. My men had not been idle since their return from England, and it looked prosperous. They had enlarged their own homes but I saw that my manor had another room added. It was as much as could be done. Any further work would need a second storey and the foundations were not good enough to support such a structure.

I reined in and pointed to my modest hall. It just had one storey but, considering how it had begun life, it was a tremendous achievement, "This, Edward, is my home, Fitz Malet Grange."

"I like it, Master, it seems to suit you."

We were seen as we approached and greeted in the yard next to the hogbog. "Welcome, Master. Is the war over?"

I dismounted, "For the moment, Carl, there is peace. The northern earls have submitted and as they are here in Normandy as the guests of the duke, then there will be peace."

"Good, Master. I hope you approve of the improvements."

"I do. This is Edward. He is English and my servant. I would have him trained to be a warrior. He shall be my pueros when we return to England. I leave his training in your hands."

My three men had been thralls and all were from the lands of the Norse. They could not teach equitation but they could do as my grandfather had done for me and give him the skills with shield, spear and sword. On the road from Ouistreham, he had agreed to become a warrior. He knew it might necessitate fighting his countryman but he showed wisdom beyond his years. 'Whether I like it or not, we now have a king who is not English. The lords submitted to him.' He had shrugged, 'We, the people, had no such say in the matter.' He was practical.

"I know not how long it will be until I am summoned back to the side of the man who is our duke but I intend to make the most of the time we have. I now have money. Taillefer's fortune is mine and it is in Caen. I know that he would wish me to use it well and I shall."

That night, as I ate Heloise's most excellent food, I felt content. I hoped that my grandfather would have approved of all that I had done. I knew that Taillefer would for all that he had done was in support of Duke William. Taillefer had been more than instrumental in achieving victory at Senlac Hill and I knew that I had played my part.

"Any more food, Master?"

"No, Heloise, the whole meal was excellent and I am satiated."

"You know, Master, that you should have a wife. You are well thought of, have money and land and you are a handsome young warrior."

I found myself blushing, "Heloise, I ..."

She smiled, "You do not see it, but I do. You could have your pick of the daughters of any nobleman within twenty miles of here."

I nodded, "Ah, but there is the rub, I am not noble born. I am illegitimate."

"As is the duke and it was no bar to him. You should plant your seed while you are young. Carl and I now have three and there will be more. They will carry on our name and will be there to defend your land when you need them to."

I suppose she was right but I put the thought from my mind. For one thing, it terrified me.

One benefit of our rapid victory and the lack of opposition after Senlac was that breeders of horses in Normandy had speculated that there would be many losses amongst the horses. They had bred so many that the prices were as low as I could remember. I did not need coursers for I had three but I bought four hackneys from Alain, the horse master, at such a low price that even as we drove them home I wondered if I should have bought more. Marie, the mare I bought for Edward was perfect for him. He was still learning how to ride and she was as gentle a horse as I had seen. She would be no good in war but the other three would and Marie would suit. A month after our return I went with Edward and Carl for a journey south. We took the sumpters for I planned on spending some of my money in Caen. We could have gone to Rouen or even Dieppe, but my money was in Caen and I needed to speak to the man who dealt with such things for the duke, Arrius the Greek.

The duke was not in Caen. He was at his hunting lodge entertaining his English guests. King Edward had enjoyed visiting Normandy and Duke William knew how to entertain. He would be building bridges so that when they returned home they would have pleasant memories and be less likely to rebel. I was, of course, well known at the duke's fortress not least because of my association with Taillefer. We were welcomed with smiles. I sent Carl to the market where we would join him. He would be able to find the best prices so that when I arrived we could make purchases quickly. As one of the bodyguards of the duke I was accorded a chamber and, leaving Edward to arrange my clothes, I went to find Arrius.

"I wondered how long it would be before you came to discover your wealth." He had a smile on his face when he said it.

41

I shook my head, "As I did not actually earn it, I feel slightly guilty about the generosity of Taillefer."

He shrugged, "He had no family and he had no land. Who else should deserve the rewards of his life but the man who was at his side at the end? Would you like to see the gold and other treasure?"

I shook my head, "I just need to know how much I have and then I can spend a little of it. I have asked the duke if I can leave my treasure here with his and he seems happy about that."

"Of course, but you should know that there will come a time when the duke takes his treasure to Lundenwic."

I frowned, "But why?"

"Whilst he is here in Normandy, he is a vassal to the King of France. In England, he is king and can do as he wishes. It would be safer if his treasure was beyond the greedy grasp of the French."

"As his new castle is still being built then that will not happen quickly. How much am I worth?"

He smiled and took out a wax tablet. He wrote down the figures. I shook my head, "You have made a mistake."

He frowned, "Where coins are concerned Arrius does not make mistakes."

I tried to take it in. I told him how much I would need. Until now I had had to think carefully about spending each and every coin. I no longer needed to do so.

Arrius smiled, "You are making modest demands of your inheritance. You are wise."

With the coins in a small chest, I returned to my chamber. I took two small purses and filled them with coins. I secreted them beneath my tunic and donned a cloak. Edward now sported a sword and he would be a bodyguard. I did not expect trouble. Duke William kept a tight grip on his capital. Caen market was by the river and was bustling by the time we arrived. "Stay close, Edward."

"Yes, Master."

Knowing the sorts of things Carl had been tasked with buying helped and after a short time I found him by the stalls of the mercier, in English the mercers. He was standing apart watching as people bought various lengths of cloth. We sidled up to him, "Well?"

"Heloise does not want bright colours and that means we will not have to pay as much. That one," he pointed at one mercier, "is the cheapest but the quality is not as good as others. I think we buy from the next one which is only slightly more expensive but the quality will please my wife."

My finer clothes might have made for a more expensive deal and so I handed over one of the purses. Carl took a deep breath and headed for the mercier. The bolts of cloth bought, Edward slung them over his shoulder. We wandered the market for an hour or so buying more of what we needed. We did not have to do it all in one day for we could be there earlier the next day. Poor Edward was struggling under the weight of the cloth and as Carl carried the rest, I was unburdened.

"Let us take food and wine." I headed to a side street where I knew, from previous visits with Taillefer, that the prices were lower and yet the quality of both food and drink were good. It was basic fare but the tripes cooked in cider with pieces of meat and a gravy that deserved the term soup were superb. The bread was rye but was perfectly suited to the mopping of the juices. We drank cider with the meal and that pleased Edward.

It was an optimistic meal. Edward had settled into my manor far more easily than I might have expected. That was largely down to the kindness of Heloise and Carl. The money we had spent would make it a comfortable home and with plans for even more improvements, all was well. We were on our second beaker of cider when Carl broached the subject of the future.

"Duke William will make his home in England." It was not a question. Everyone knew that in England he was free from his submission to the King of France.

"He will. It is a rich country, far richer than Normandy. He will return and he will make it secure."

"You will be rewarded, Master. He will give you land."

"Perhaps."

Carl laughed, "After the service you have done him, he can do none other. What I am trying to say, Master, is have you made plans for Fitz Malet?"

I could see that he feared for his future. "Carl, you are my steward. You and the others came to war with me in England but you will not have to cross the sea to fight in future. If you have to fight for me it will be in Normandy."

Edward had been following the conversation. His Norman was improving but he understood more than he could speak. "Normandy?"

I switched to English, "When England is secure then Duke William will return here to contest with France for lands we feel are Norman rather than French. With the riches of England, Normandy can face France on an equal footing."

Carl seemed happy with my answer and we returned to the castle. There were others in the castle and I let my two men have the rest of the afternoon off while I spoke with them. Some had been with Duke William and the English. Hugh and Aimeri were brothers. Neither was, as yet, a knight. Like me, they guarded the king but unlike me had, as yet, no land of their own. I got on well with them. Their father had an elder son who would inherit the Norman lands. They were William's protectors in the hope of land in England.

"Are the Mercian brothers behaving themselves?"

Hugh laughed, "It all bodes well for the duke. The English, even the brothers, do not trust each other. I think they are here to seek weaknesses in the character of the man who is now their king."

It was my turn to laugh, "They will find none."

Aimeri said, "Make the most of your time here, Richard, for you are needed at his side. It is your skill in English that is needed. Often the English speak it amongst themselves and Duke William fears that they might be plotting."

"They could do little here in Normandy for they came without followers."

"True but someday they will go back and Duke William will return to England to become King William once more. You know how careful he is. We have been given a month off and then we return."

The next day we completed our purchases and even managed to secure a second bolt of cloth for Heloise. One of the merciers discovered that I had been a companion of Taillefer and in exchange for a story or two, we were given a price as low as any in the market. We stayed for one more night and then headed back to Fitz Malet. The ferry was cheap enough but the laden sumpters cost us. In hindsight, we might have been better off travelling to Rouen which was closer to our home and meant we had no ferry fees to pay. My hall grew a little grander and the clothes my people wore became of greater quality. They looked more like the servants of my brother's hall. I enjoyed improving my grange.

It was the younger of my half brothers, Robert, who rode into my yard one late summer's afternoon. I was toiling in my fields with my men, harvesting the wheat we had grown. The field I used was not a large one but we had enriched the soil and the yield was a good one; Heloise was sure that we would be self-sufficient for a year. It had given Carl and me ideas about making another field.

"Well, brother, labouring like an ordinary fellow." He shook his head, "You are a warrior and a man of renown, why labour?"

I smiled for I liked Robert. He had taken my side against Sir Durant and although we had grown a little apart I still felt closer to him than my other relatives. "It is my land and I like to be part of it. Come, let us taste this year's cider."

His squire took his horse and he followed me into the hall. I saw his eyes take in what had been a derelict part of our elder brother's estate. "You have made more of this than I thought possible."

"It was a generous gift and I have done all that I could with it."

We sat and Heloise brought us bread, cheese and cider. "You know that our brother was rewarded with the Honour of Eye?"

"I did not. That is close to Northwic is it not?" When I had found the king in England I learned that my brother was campaigning close to Northwic.

"It is and it is yielding an income already. His son shall be lord of Eye when he is older."

I detected the hint of annoyance in my half-brother's voice, "You will be given something."

"Not until Duke William returns to England and imposes his will as king. This is good cheese, Mistress."

45

"Thank you, my lord. The goats like this land."

"The English cannot make cheese." He chuckled, "They are complaining already that the king has taken their folk land from them."

Edward had explained the concept of folk land to me. While the thegns and gesiths had specific land there were larger areas, woodland, grazing land and the like which were used by the common man. It meant that they could forage for wood as well as food, hunt for small animals and use the land to graze their animals. Taking away those rights would make the common man angry. In Normandy, the lords had long since taken away any such rights.

He wiped his mouth and drank some cider, "I need your help, brother. You have the ear of the king. When he returns you shall be with him and when the English fight us, and fight us they will, we shall take their lands. I would have a manor."

I hid my smile. I had wondered at the sudden appearance of my half-brother whom I had not seen for more than a year. He needed something from me.

I shrugged, "In as much as I ride close to him I shall do what I can. Perhaps our brother will find some land for you. William de Warenne has promised Bruno a manor."

"And de Warenne will deliver on his promise for he has no sons yet. Our brother puts his sons first. I am forgotten."

I now had three half-nephews, Robert, Durant and Gilbert. The eldest was not yet eighteen but he was already a knight. He had been at Senlac but had little to do with the fighting. My half-brother, Robert, had fought valiantly at my elder brother's side.

"I will do what I can, but Duke William is still here in Normandy."

"But not for long. My return was at the behest of Bishop Odo. I have delivered a letter to the duke. The bishop warns the duke of the rising air of rebellion. Make the most of your time at home, Richard. It will end soon enough."

It was September when I was summoned to Rouen. Duke William had enjoyed enough hunting. The orders were to join him immediately and so I bade farewell to my men. "Edward, stay here, for I shall not need you. Better that your time is well spent learning our language and becoming a warrior."

46

I rode Louis with my mail upon a sumpter and by evening was in the mighty castle of Rouen. I stabled my horse and carried my war gear to the warrior hall. Aimeri and Hugh let me know all that was going on. The most important piece of news was that Count Eustace had decided to exploit the absence of the king from England. He had appeared with a fleet off Dover and after being defeated in a sea battle fled back to Boulogne. As Hugh said, it was a warning.

I nodded, "From what my brother said the land is ripe for rebellion. The folk land has been taken from the people and that does not sit well with them."

Aimeri frowned, "It is not our law, Richard. Why should we worry?"

"Because the king has yet to make laws in his new land. There are some lords who will deal with the people much as the king would but there are others..."

We all knew who they were but none would voice their names as one was the brother of the king.

The bodyguards, as opposed to the household knights, did not dine with the great and the good. We stood guard around the hall. We had to be sober and vigilant. The last thing that the new King of England needed was for two of his subjects to have a falling out and shed blood in his hall. Even the presence of the duchess could not guarantee peace. Until she was crowned in Westminster Mathilda was not entitled to be called queen. At the first sign of trouble, two of us would detach ourselves to pour oil on the troubled waters. I saw the reason for my recall. The English nobles had rubbed against each other and tensions had arisen. Halfway through the feast, I saw that Gospatric and Morcar were involved in a heated argument. Duke William frowned and waved a hand at me. I went to the two men. Hugh came with me.

I smiled and leaned forward, "What is this, my lords? Heated words when the duchess is present? This is not well done." I used my voice as a weapon. Taillefer had taught me to modulate it according to circumstances. I used a sing song tone. It had an effect in that both became less violent but they were still angry.

"Why I have to suffer the company of men who did nothing to help Earl Harold is beyond me."

Gospatric snarled, "We were lords of the north when you were still seeking to suckle from Wessex."

I sighed, "And now there is a Norman hand that rules." I lowered my voice, "This is the hall of Duke William and he will not suffer violence. If you cannot sit and speak civilly to one another then we will escort you hence and that would be embarrassing beyond words would it not?" They nodded. "Earl Morcar, I beg you to join your brother. Hugh, escort Earl Gospatric to Earl Waltheof."

I had given them a diplomatic way out of the impasse and they accepted. When we returned to stand behind Duke William he waved me over, "Well done. We will not stay here much longer. I plan to leave for England soon. We will Christmas in Lundenwic."

I stood against the back wall with Hugh. He nodded to the two men we had just parted. "Morcar has been given the land that was Gospatric's grandfather's. Uhtred the Bold, I hear, was a fierce warrior."

I nodded, "So my grandfather said." I gave the slightest of inclines of my head to Copsi, the Dane, "And King Sweyn of Denmark was a cousin of Earl Harold and I hear was offered the crown before the Confessor became king. Harald Hardrada showed that the Vikings still regard that part of the world as theirs. Perhaps they should be kept in prison. That would ensure their obedience."

Hugh laughed, "You have spent less time with them than my brother and I. There are many like these in England. The only way we can secure our new kingdom is to circle them with castles." He beamed and said, quietly, "And that means that we can expect our own reward; a castle, knights to serve us and an income that will make us rich."

I knew the rest of the bodyguards felt the same way but I did not.

Chapter 4

It was Gytha, Harold's mother, and her grandsons that hastened us back to England. She, along with Eadric the Wild had raised a rebellion in the west. Eadric had allied with two Welsh kings and taken the new castle of Hereford. Gytha controlled Cornwall and Devon. There were close links with the Bretons and Duke William decided that he had rested on his laurels for long enough. We sailed and landed back at the Cinq Ports in early December. I still had just Edward as a retainer but his skills had improved so much that I made him my squire. I had yet to be given my spurs but I knew that I was the equal of any of the new knights and the superior of many. I had three coursers and three hackneys. My mail hauberk was newly made and allowed Edward to wear my old one. The number of bodyguards had fallen for Duke William had knighted some before we left Rouen. It meant he had more household knights and there were fewer of us as pure bodyguards. I did not mind for the twelve of us were, in my view, the best.

Fitz Osbern was heading for Hereford to deal with Eadric and the Welsh threat but we went to the last refuge and stronghold of the old Godwine family. While Harold's sons gathered supporters in Ireland, Gytha, the Queen Mother, was attracting an increasing number of rebels to Exeter. There was a Roman fort and a burgh there. Unlike Wintan-Caestre, it had been improved and stone towers built. It would also take us as long to reach it as travelling north to the Roman Wall.

There was a subtle change when we returned to England. Once we landed we addressed William as king. In Normandy, he was the duke but this was his kingdom and he began to rule as one. He had brought with him churchmen to be appointed to the many vacant bishoprics. It was a clever strategy. Some of the other bodyguards did not understand it. As we waited outside the church at Canterbury where they were anointed and appointed, Aimeri and I explained it to them.

"The church is above the nobles. They can do little in terms of marriage and the like without the church. By appointing his own men the king controls the church."

Aimeri nodded, "Remember the papal banner we carried at Senlac? The pope supports King William. The new bishops may not have to fight but they will be another weapon in the king's armoury."

One or two of the bodyguards looked confused, "Weapons?"

"The bishops control the priests and it is the priests that the ordinary people speak to about their sins as well as their hopes and fears. Those priests will now have Norman voices instructing them." I shrugged, "There are only a handful now but as we head deeper into England and more positions become vacant so will the church become a shield for us."

We headed for Lundenwic where there were men waiting for us. I saw Malet men. They were led by my half-brother, Robert. He nodded an acknowledgement as we passed. I knew, from his visit to the grange, that he would be seeking his own land. As we headed along the Roman Road that led to Exeter, we picked up more men. The great lords, the king's companions, were largely absent. The king would lead this conquering column while they would ensure that those parts we already had remained in our hands.

We stopped at Wintan-Caestre where the king spoke with Edith Swan Neck. The next day, as we headed into the land that was, as yet, untouched by Norman hands, he waved for me to ride at his side.

"You impressed Lady Edith, Richard. She found you well-spoken and sincere. My choice of diplomat swayed her to my side. Once again, I thank you. I may need your honeyed words when we meet Lady Gytha." We were passing another small burgh which, at our approach, had yielded and submitted. "For the moment we will leave these strongholds but when we have subdued Exeter we need to give thought to putting Norman masters in place and building castles. One day I shall give you you better spurs and you shall be such a lord. You shall build a castle."

I shook my head, "I am not ready, yet, my lord. My land in Normandy, Fitz Malet, allows me to learn to be the master of people. I was not brought up to do so."

He laughed, "Nor was I. I was destined to be a warrior. You, too, are also a warrior. Taillefer saw it and others have spoken to me of your conduct at Senlac. I know there is little glory in guarding my standard and my body but it is the task of a warrior and not a noble seeking land."

As I rejoined my companions I had another insight into the complicated mind that was William the Bastard. I looked at the other bodyguards. None of them had any likelihood of land from their own families. Indeed, a couple were like me, either bastards or they were the sons of men who had lost their land.

When we reached Dorset the royal progress changed. We camped and bands of knights led horsemen to take the towns and villages. Most fell quickly. The ones that did not were reduced by the arrival of the army. We reached the town of Dornwaraceaster. It was at the end of the road the Romans had built from Lundenwic, the Portway. The sea was just a few miles away and the king had the small fishing port there occupied so that we could be supplied by sea. We built a camp,

Once more I was summoned to the king's side. Sir Roger de Corcella, was there. He was not one of the king's companions but he had often dined with us and was an old friend of Bishop Odo. He was one who sought land. His squire was his son, Turstin.

"I need you to be an emissary again but as we are deep in the land which has yet to submit, Sir Roger will take his men as an escort. Your message to Lady Gytha and the Exeter rebels is simple, yield and live. Fight and they shall die."

Sir Roger nodded, "The message will be delivered, my lord."

There was little to add and I left with the knight and his son. He had twenty men at arms on horses as well as ten light horsemen. I did not remember them at Senlac and knew that they were new to combat in England. The knight looked at me once we were in the daylight and said, "Are you English?"

"No, my lord, although my mother was."

"I hear that you were Taillefer's man."

"I was, my lord."

He sniffed, almost imperiously, "I could never understand the man. He had money and yet he never sought land or position. Now he is dead his fortune is… where?"

I said nothing. Sir Roger would never understand a complicated man like Taillefer.

"Do you know the way to Exeter?"

I shook my head, "All that I know is that this road we travel on was built by the Romans and if we stay upon it, we shall find the burgh."

His face told me that he had little experience of travelling through what was, in essence, enemy territory. If he had he might have asked me questions. As it was he just said, "Then let us be about it."

One advantage of my upbringing was that I had been taught Latin. Father Raymond had been a hard taskmaster and his work paid off. I spied the milestones and knew that we had more than fifty miles to go to get to Isca Dumnoniorum, the Roman name for Exeter.

"My lord, we cannot reach the town in one day. We will need to camp." Edward and I had food and we had ale skins. I had looked at the saddles of the men with Sir Roger and knew that they did not.

"Hmph, then we shall have to take what we need from the villagers."

I was far too lowly to argue with the knight although I knew that he was wrong. I merely nodded. The settlements in this part of the world were small. It was a fertile land but the areas that were cultivated were like islands amidst a sea of trees. We stopped by the coast at a village we learned was called Cernemude. There were just twenty houses and most of the people made a living from the sea, although there were three ploughed fields and an area cleared for meadow. There was no opposition for there were no warriors. Sir Roger rode in and evicted the headman from the largest house. I knew it to be a mistake. He compounded his error by having a bullock slaughtered to feed us. He did not even use me to translate for him.

Edward and I did not use the houses but a shed used for the drying of fish. It stank but it was a shelter and as it was unoccupied, we offended no one. We did not share in the beef that was cooked but Edward and I gathered shellfish and made a stew with samphire and some of the ham we had brought. It was tasty fare. Our fire was by the beach and when we heard footsteps on the shingle behind us we both grabbed our swords and whirled. It was the priest from the village. He held up his hands and spoke to me in halting Norman.

"I mean no harm, my lord."

I answered in English, "You will shorten your life, Father, if you try to sneak up on Norman warriors. I pray you sit and share our food. It is not ready yet but it soon will be."

We had spare bowls and Edward went back to the fish shed to fetch one. The priest said, "Have you offended the knight, my son? You sit alone and eat here on the beach when they eat the finest of meats."

I smiled, "No, Father, I am an old campaigner. Sir Roger should have brought food and taking the beast was a mistake. I am content." Edward had returned and taking a spoon to taste the stew nodded. He began to ladle it into the three bowls. "This will be tasty and not having taken food from the mouths of the women and children of the village will make it taste even better."

"I do not understand. You dress like a Norman but you speak in English and you sound like a priest. You are a conundrum."

I laughed and sipped the stew. The salty samphire had been the perfect seasoning but it was still too hot to eat, "I have been called many things, Father, but never a conundrum. I have a Norman father and an English mother." I made the sign of the cross. "I serve King William and I am here to speak to Lady Gytha and the men of Exeter."

He sipped the stew and nodded his approval, "Had your lord been of the same mind then your journey west would have been safer. I came here to learn from you but having spoken to you I will give you a warning. This," he waved a hand at the settlement, "was not well done and there will be opposition."

"Thank you, Father. Your warning was unnecessary. As soon as the throat of the bullock was slit, I knew that we would have to fight before we reached Exeter."

"Our new king, what can you tell me of him?"

"That he is the rightful King of England." He paused with the spoon in mid-air. I explained, "I was there when Earl Harold swore that he would support Duke William's claim to the crown and even more importantly, I was there when King Edward announced that Duke William was his heir. I regret the deaths at

Senlac and those since but King William has the right to the crown."

"The people hereabouts like not kings. They prefer the local leaders. They are more comfortable with the men who led the defence of this land to the Danes. Men like King Ethelred did little to help them. The idea of a king ruling them and controlling their lives will be hard to take."

"What I can say, Father, is that the king will bring order to the land and people will be safer. There will be law."

"What is your name?"

"I am Richard Fitz Malet and this is my squire Edward."

"Then I will pray for you. I can see that I should not judge all by the same standards."

I rose early and roused Sir Roger and his son. Neither was happy. "My lord, I think we should leave early. The slaughter of the bullock will not have endeared us to the people. We need to be on the road sooner rather than later."

"We are not here to endear ourselves but to rule."

I sighed, "My lord, we have a handful of men. Do you really need a battle?"

That decided him and we mounted and left just as the sun was rising behind us. I had hoped that my words and warning might make him and his son wary but they soon lapsed into the manner of men making a pleasant ride in the country. His men also displayed their lack of experience and they rode without keeping their attention on their surroundings. The exception was their sergeant, Ranulf. He, like me, gave every tree the close scrutiny it deserved.

At one point he rode next to me. "What do you know of this?"

By 'this' I took him to mean the danger. I saw no reason to be less than honest with him. "The priest came to me to warn me that the villagers had taken the slaughter of the animal badly and he feared we might be attacked."

He sniffed, "Aye, that would make sense but I have seen little to make me fear any warriors. They look to be farmers armed with billhooks."

"And billhooks can pull mounted men from saddles. Have these men fought before?"

His head whipped around, "They have been at battles."

"But not fought."

"They were not needed." He added defensively.

"Then let us hope that when danger rears its head, they are ready."

Had the men of Dorset been more martial and cunning then they might have ambushed us. As it was they had simply sent word overnight and raised the local hundred. Thirty or so of the men of the area had created a barricade across the bridge over the River Otter and with strung bows they awaited us.

I was just pleased that the wisdom of the sergeant prevailed, and Sir Roger kept his men beyond arrow range. "We need to shift them, my lord."

Sir Roger stroked his war horse's mane. It was an expensive animal. "If we charge them then some of the horses might be hurt. The last thing we need is for us to be afoot. We will fight in a wedge."

I stayed mounted as they dismounted, "We can try to outflank them, my lord. The river does not look to be deep and we can ford it and Exeter lies just up the road. We need not fight."

He snorted, "If you think that my banner shall retreat and flee before a rabble of peasants then it shows you have no honour. Dismount and follow us."

I shook my head, "My lord, you do not command me. I am the king's man."

His son snorted, "Then you are a coward."

I gave him a thin smile, "When this is over and if you live then you can repeat those words and we shall settle the matter over unsheathed swords."

Sir Roger waved an airy hand dismissively, "When this is over and you have served your purpose I shall have you punished as you deserve for your impertinence."

It was only Ranulf who showed me any sympathy as they tethered their horses and formed an inadequate-looking wedge.

"Edward, with me. You shall guard my left."

I turned and headed down the river. I saw what looked like a shallow patch of the river some half a mile upstream from the bridge. As we rode towards it I heard the jeers from Sir Roger and his men. His son shouted, "Coward!"

I ignored both and concentrated on the river crossing. I had crossed a river before but Edward had not. As it turned out, when I approached the water I saw that while men on foot might struggle to cross it a horseman would only need to swim for a pace or two. I shouted, as we entered the water, "Trust your horse, Edward. She can swim. Just hang on to the reins. If you need to then slip your feet from the stirrups and follow my precise line."

"Aye, my lord."

The bridge was hidden from us but I heard the cries of battle and then the clash of arms. I prayed that the mail of Sir Roger's men at arms would protect them but I feared that men would die and it was so unnecessary. Sir Roger did not need to fight. We made the other bank and I waited for a moment while the horses shook themselves and Edward regained his stirrups. He had a spear and I had my lance with the gonfanon. My shield was a long kite shield and his was a smaller, rounder one. It was larger than a buckler and easier to hold than a kite.

"My intention is to attack their rear, Edward. You guard my left and your job is to stop any of them from getting to me."

"Master, there are too many of them."

"And none wear mail. I am neither a fool nor a glory-hunting squire. I want to hurt as many of them as I can and weaken part of their defences to afford Sir Roger the opportunity to break through. When I give the command, we fall back and rely on our horses to help us escape. If we fail the first time, we can repeat the action. At the very least our distraction might enable Ranulf to break through."

"Sergeant Ranulf?"

"He is the warrior. I am counting on his skill and not that of his lord. Now follow me." I hefted my shield to hold it tightly and rode Louis up the bank to the road that led to the bridge. This was not a Roman Road and was made of compacted earth. It meant we made little noise as we galloped towards the bridge. We had been forgotten by both sides and all the attention was on the battle. Arrows flew and rattled into shields. I had no idea who was winning. The local road joined the Roman Road thirty paces from the western end of the bridge. I reined in. Edward had heeded my command and the head of his horse was level with

Louis's rump. I lowered my lance and spurred Louis. He leapt forward and after lowering his spear Edward followed.

The English archers were standing back from the barricade and loosing their arrows blindly over the top. Men stood on top of the barricade with axes and spears. I did not think that they would do much damage but they would be a distraction. I rode directly at the archers and had lanced one before they even knew. As the other five turned, Edward jabbed his spear at one. I lanced a second and then stood in my stirrups to make Louis rear. It takes a brave man to stand and endure the hooves of a war horse. As his forehooves clattered into the back of the legs of an archer who was trying to get away, I lunged with my lance and speared a warrior standing on the top of the barricade, swinging his Danish axe. He fell and my gonfanon fluttered above the barricade. It told the others that I was there. Men turned their heads and weapons to face us and I shouted, "Edward, back."

Even as I wheeled, I used the lance's head to make men fall backwards. One was a little slow to do so and the line scored across his cheek showed just how sharp it was. We clattered over the bridge and I reined in at the small road we had used. The English on the bridge had a dilemma. They could not catch us but they dared not simply ignore us. They compromised and three archers and two spearmen waited at the western end of the bridge. Our attack had been successful. Not only had we killed and wounded men but the distraction had allowed Ranulf and some of the men at arms to climb to the top of the barricade. With no arrows to annoy them, they used their mail, shields and superior weapons. The English fought hard. I decided that it was time to gamble.

"Edward, we will charge the men sent to watch us. Keep your shield tight and stay to my left. Your hackney may not be a warhorse but she will terrify the men. When you strike with the spear then punch as though it is a fist."

I heard nervousness in his voice, but he said, "Aye, master."

We were close enough for the archers to have loosed arrows at us and their lack of enthusiasm told me that they did not trust their skill. The horses were rested and when I shouted, "Now!" and dug my heels into Louis's flanks he leapt forward, leaving Edward in my wake. In half a dozen strides we were within lance range and by then the three archers had loosed their arrows and fled. One ran back to the barricade and the other two threw themselves into the river, seeking the shelter of the abutments. The two spearmen stood their ground but my lance was longer. I rammed it into the neck of one of them and as he fell his spear cracked across the face of the other. Louis's shoulder struck him and he fell towards the river. The fleeing English archer must have shouted a warning and the inattention as men's heads turned allowed Ranulf and his men to slay those on the top of the barricade. The survivors fled.

Edward had joined me and I backed our horses to the side, "Let them go. There is no pleasure in spearing fleeing men who have just done their duty." For their part, the men who fled had no wish to risk the wrath of the two horsemen. By the time they had fled, the barricade was down and Ranulf appeared next to me. He pushed back his helmet and shook his head, "Mad as a bucketful of frogs but you have courage, Master Richard." He looked over his shoulder where Sir Roger and his son were mounting their horses to join us. He said quietly, "You were right but I will not argue with the hand that feeds me. Expect no thanks for this."

I nodded, "I know and if nothing else, this day has shown you which men are worthy, has it not?"

"That it has."

The attack and the proximity to Exeter meant that Sir Roger did not want to push on. He tacitly ignored me and said, "Ranulf, we will make camp here. Search the bodies and then sling them in the river. I would not have their stink disturb my sleep."

"Aye, my lord. The wounds to our men were slight." Ranulf deliberately drew Sir Roger's attention to the wounds for he had ignored his own men.

Edward and I camped away from Sir Roger. That was the knight's doing. It was their loss. Edward had slung lines in the river as soon as we lit our fire and we had a couple of river fish on the fire to go with our ham and cheese. The others did not fare as well.

The knight and his son chose not to speak to us. We rose the next day and headed for Exeter. That some of those we had attacked must have fled there was obvious. The question in my mind was, would it bode well or ill for us?

As we saw the walls of the mightiest burgh west of Wintan-Caestre hove into view, I reined in and turned. I lifted my helmet, "Sir Roger, I have been sent on a mission from the king and I will fulfil it. It would be easier with your cooperation but I intend to ride to the walls and deliver my message. It might look better if a knight rode with me."

I saw him wrestling with his dilemma. Eventually, common sense prevailed, and he nodded, "Very well."

"Good. Then have the men remove their helmets and lower their lances. It is a sign that we wish to speak and not to make war."

To be truthful it would have been obvious that we had no intention of fighting but I had learned to observe the niceties.

"Remove your helmets."

We headed towards the closed gates and watched, while we drew closer, as the ramparts filled with defenders. Sir Roger was determined to show that he was in command and he began by demanding, in Norman, that they open their gates and admit us. The Norman words echoed unanswered and I saw the twitch of his eye. He was becoming angry.

I ignored him and spoke, this time not only in English but also in a respectful tone, "We have been sent by King William to ask Dowager Queen Gytha and all those who reside in the western march to submit to the will of King William. He has been appointed in Westminster and the earls of Mercia and Northumbria have both submitted. If you do so then your freedom is guaranteed and your lives will not be forfeit."

This time there was an answer, "We accept that others may have submitted to King William but you should know that this was an ancient kingdom and even in the time of King Alfred we received special treatment." There was a pause. "Allow us some time to debate the matter. Return at Nones and you shall have an answer."

The bell for Sext had sounded as we had approached. We had three hours to wait. I nodded, "We will return." Sir Roger had clearly not understood a single word and he frowned. "We are to return at Nones for an answer."

As we headed back, he snorted, "They will not submit. We will have to reduce this burgh."

"Perhaps but have you seen their defences? They have a good garrison and it will not be easy. The king would prefer a diplomatically engineered solution."

Once again Edward and I sat apart and ate. It gave me the chance to study the walls. I suspected that King William would not be happy with the answer he received and we would have to fight. He would want to know how to take the walls. They had used Roman foundations and the existing legionary fort as the basis for the burgh. They had added towers to the corners and the gatehouse was well made. At least the Norman fleet could cut the burgh off from help. In my experience, starving out defenders saved the lives of attackers.

We returned before the appointed time and the same faces were there. The man who had spoken to us was accompanied this time by an elderly woman I took to be Lady Gytha. The man's tone gave me the answer before he had finished his statement, "Let King William know that we will pay him the tribute which we paid the old kings but we will swear no oaths and we will not receive him in our walls."

I translated for Sir Roger who snorted and shouted, "Then you will all die!"

I quickly spoke, "I think that what Sir Roger means is that the king will be less than happy with such an answer but we shall return to him with the message."

"Hold!" It was a woman's voice and I guessed belonged to Lady Gytha, "What is your name?"

"I am Richard Fitz Malet."

A purse was thrown down, "I thank you, Richard of Malet. At least one Norman knows how to be courteous. The burghers and I will pay tribute but it is a reluctant payment. While my grandsons live there is hope that a Godwinson will rule England once more."

I dismounted, bowed, and retrieved the purse. As we headed back to our men, I told Sir Roger of her words. For once he listened and did not try to show his superiority. "I think, Sir Roger, that they are just buying time. Even as we ride back they will be laying great stores of food and making the defences even stronger so that we will have to bleed upon their walls."

Chapter 5

The ride back was uncomfortable. Sir Roger and his son avoided us and if Ranulf or one of his men spoke to us then there were barked orders. I was glad when we reached the camp and could report to the king.

He listened to Sir Roger's account and then looked at me, "What did you learn, Richard?"

"That they want you to besiege them and they want our army to be weakened."

"Then we shall oblige them but if they think it will be just Normans who climb the ladders they are wrong. I will summon men from all the shires that have submitted. The lands of Dorset, Devon and Cornwall will pay a heavy price for this insolence." He turned to Sir Roger, "Thank you for this service, Sir Roger. There will be a reward for you."

"Thank you, my lord." Without any acknowledgement of me, he left.

I was about to leave when the king said, "What did you make of Sir Roger?" I hesitated. "You are oathsworn, Richard, answer."

I sighed, "He is reckless and arrogant. He fought a battle he had no need to fight and he does not heed advice."

The king frowned. We had not told him of the village and the bridge. "Explain."

I did so and he idly played with a parchment. "That does not sound like a leader I can give a fine manor to." He tapped the parchment, "This is the deed to Shepton. I had thought to give it to Sir Roger but now... perhaps I should give it to you. You have done me greater service."

I shook my head, "As I said, my lord, I am not yet ready. There is no haste."

He gave a stern look at the parchment, "The lord of this land fell in battle. I need a hand there that can win around the locals and yet be a firm one. From what you say that is not Sir Roger. You would have done a good job although I would have lost a valuable warrior."

"My brother, he would make a good lord there."

"Sir William? Shepton is too small for your brother and besides he has the Honour of Eye."

"No, my lord, my other brother, Sir Robert."

"Ah, I remember him. Aye, you are right and Sir William's family have ever served me well. Thank you. It is sage advice and I shall heed it."

I returned to our camp pleased that I had been able to do what I had promised Robert."

It took some time to send out the summons for men to come to the muster. During that time Robert was informed of his gift and he came forthwith to thank me, "Richard, I know not how to thank you. Other men offer promises and deliver nothing. You make no such promise and yet here am I, lord of Shepton. I am in your debt."

"We are family, Sir Robert."

He sighed, "And yet you were mistreated by Durant. It is not right and I would that we could undo that which was done."

"Grandfather once told me that the past was a puzzle that was already finished and if you tried to change it then the puzzle would be no more. You cannot change the past, Robert. You learn from it. I think we have both learned."

When he left I threw myself into the preparations for the campaign in Dorset. King William would be at the fore and I needed to be prepared. Edward had done well in his first encounter and I felt more confident about leaving him to follow the king's banner. However, I also remembered that Taillefer had never been satisfied and so I practised with Edward every day. His skills with a sword improved. I smiled as I found myself not making the strike that would end the practice. Taillefer must have done the same for me. I was carrying on a tradition. It was as we were sparring that Turstin, Sir Roger's son, arrived. He was not alone although Edward and I were. Turstin had with him another five squires. He strode directly up to me, "You are a bastard and you have robbed me of my birthright."

I turned and put the tip of the sword in the soil, "What?"

"I have heard that you persuaded the king to give Shepton to your brother. It was to have been mine."

"What the king does is his business."

"You are a coward."

63

My eyes narrowed, "You called me that once and I let it go but now, before these sycophants who hang on to your cloak, I will say take back those words or face the consequences."

"These are true friends. These are real Normans and not some bastardised half-breed." He drew his own sword. The other five did the same.

Edward said, "There are six of you."

I drew my second sword, "And they are attacking one of King William's bodyguards." I swept my second sword before their faces, "Those who survive will have a lot of explaining to do."

Two of them looked at each other and sheathing their swords turned. One said, as he did so, "He is right and besides I hear he has Taillefer's skills."

"Cowards!"

I smiled, "For a man who has yet to make a strike in anger you bandy that word around too much. Well, do we touch swords or are we just filling the air with empty promises?"

It was Turstin who came at me. He had a shield and a sword. I just had my two swords. The practice with Edward had ensured that my eye was in and as he lumbered towards me, flailing his sword like a farmer winnowing wheat, I blocked his sword and hooking my right leg behind his left, used my left hand to punch him to the ground.

Edward laughed. Two of Turstin's companions came at me. They came at two sides at once. Perhaps they thought that I would merely stand and wait for their attack. Taillefer had taught me better than that and my battles at Senlac had honed my skills. I struck at both of their heads at once. It was almost laughable for they raised their shields and swords at the same time.

Suddenly I heard, behind me, "Master, watch out!"

I heard the clash of steel as Edward blocked the blow from the last squire. It was one thing for me to be in danger but Edward was barely trained. I punched with my right hand at one squire. He had just lowered his shield and the crosspiece of my sword broke his nose. He dropped his shield and sword to stem the flood of blood. Spattered by the blood the other squire just stared and then swung his sword down. I blocked it easily and brought my knee up between his legs. I had yet to meet any who could stand after such a blow.

I whirled around as Turstin, now risen like Lazarus, advanced with the other squire to attack Edward. "I thought to teach you a lesson but, Turstin, this is dishonourable beyond words. You shall pay with blood."

Even as I brought my sword down Ranulf's voice pleaded. "I beg you, Master Richard, spare his life. This is ill done."

I halted my sword a finger's length from his unprotected throat, "Ranulf, if I see this whelp again, he dies."

"Come Master Turstin, you have been given your life. Do not spurn the offer."

The other squires had sheathed their swords and were backing off. Turstin had little choice and he reluctantly did as he was commanded. He left but with no grace.

Ranulf smiled, "I have only seen such skills in knights, Richard Fitz Malet. You will be a great knight and I thank you for sparing his life." He left.

I turned to Edward, "That was bravely if foolishly done."

"I could not allow him to strike you from behind."

"Aye, well we have practised enough for now."

We left two days later. I discovered that the king had heard of the encounter as we neared the bridge where we had chased the English away. As we watered our horses he said, "Richard, I need you as my protector, not teaching six callow squires a lesson in swordsmanship. From now on you draw your swords at my command. Is that clear?"

"Yes, my lord."

The king was ruthless on our way west. We captured every burgh, town and village in Dorset. The survivors fled to Exeter where they told the tale to the burghers. The bodyguards did not even have to draw a sword as King William used Englishmen to take the settlements.

When we reached Exeter they were ready for us but King William took no chances. The whole town was surrounded by a mass of camps and the fleet was summoned to block support from the sea. That the burghers were terrified was clear and the nobles from the city, the thegns who ruled there submitted and begged King William for mercy. Five hostages were taken while negotiations took place.

The king himself went to the gates to speak to the Dowager Queen, "Gytha Thorkelsdóttir, will you submit yourself to my mercy and enjoy the safety of my camp?"

"King William, I am safe here for I am amongst Englishmen whom I can trust. I will stay within while words are bandied without."

Baldwin Fitz Gilbert was placed in command of the camps while King William discussed terms with his hostages. That night the burghers of Exeter and Lady Gytha decided the fate of Exeter. Men sallied forth and slew some of Fitz Gilbert's men while the mother of Harold escaped in a boat to join her grandsons. I thought I knew King William as well as most men. What he did next was typical of the man. He was angry with the men of Exeter but that anger was a cold one. There was nothing personal in his actions. He had the prisoners brought forward and, just out of arrow range of the gates, he walked along the hostages. He did not even look at the man he chose but merely said, "As punishment for this betrayal, this man will be blinded and returned to Exeter. The others will await my pleasure." The man, Ælfhheah, hung his head. He had been betrayed by those within the walls but he could do little about it. After his punishment, he was led to the gates. They were opened and he was admitted.

It was a calculated act by the king. It showed that he could be draconian and the presence of the blinded man within Exeter's walls would be a constant reminder of his power. Other hostages whose right to be treated well might now be forfeited by the actions of those within Exeter. It was a threat from the king. The effect was to show the English that *he* was a force to be feared. He placed himself as close to the siegeworks as was deemed safe. We, his bodyguards, were given the task of ensuring that the stones and arrows sent from the walls did not come close to him. He went about his work bareheaded so that all knew King William was on the prowl.

He stood with Baldwin Fitz Gilbert and pointed at an apparently randomly chosen tower. It was not. We had walked the circumference of the walls first and he knew exactly which tower was the weakest. "We build a mine there. Our archers and crossbows will keep up a steady shower of bolts and arrows. I care not about the cost of ash and goose feathers. I want their will to fight to be broken."

"It shall be done, my lord."

We were at the mines every morning as the dawn broke and that too was deliberate. Many arrows were wasted as they tried to kill King William. We took it in turns to shelter him with our shields. The rotation was necessary as the shields were soon laden with bolts and arrows. They became too heavy to hold. We had relief at noon when we retired but even then King William's will was to be seen. We ate, beyond the range of missiles, freshly cooked food. The smell drifted to the walls making them even hungrier.

A fortnight passed and soon the mine was deep under the tower and ready to be fired. We rose at Lauds as the bells from the cathedral chimed. We breakfasted and then donned our war gear. King William wore his helmet and Aimeri carried his banner. The men of Exeter would feel the wrath of King William. The men with the faggots entered the mine completely undetected. When they emerged brands were brought. They were seen but our archers were ready and even as white faces appeared over the walls so arrows rained down. One brand bearer fell but the rest made it and after they had dragged their wounded comrade back to the surgeons, we watched as smoke poured from the mine. The construction of the tower was like the ones at home. There was an outer wall, an inner wall and an infill between. It meant that as the faggots burned and then lit the timbers supporting the mine, so heat and smoke were drawn up through the infill. I saw smoke oozing all the way up the tower. As the fire took the heat increased. Valuable water was used to try to slow down the heat but to no avail. The first sign of success was when a thin crack appeared at the base of the tower and began to zig-zag up the wall. It looked innocuous at first but when I saw men leave the fighting platform I knew that, inside, it was worse. I could only imagine what was happening inside the mine. The wooden timbers were now gone and the mortar used to bind the stones of the tower was drying and cracking.

It took an hour or two but when there was an ominous and audible crack the king said, "Prepare!"

The tiny crack became a fissure as wide as a man's arm and the tower split in two. No matter what they did they could not repair the tower. When, in the early afternoon, stones began to tumble into the ditch we knew that we could assault.

King William was in no mood to wait until the timbers and stones had cooled. He would attack as soon as he could. Baldwin Fitz Gilbert prevailed upon the king to allow men to be sent with long poles to dislodge some of the stones. When the king saw the wobbling stones he agreed. Ordinary soldiers poked and prodded with their long poles and were rewarded when two-thirds of one side of the tower tumbled down to make a sort of glacis. The interior of the tower was exposed and we now had the means to attack. We had swords and axes. I had exchanged my kite shield for Edward's round one and some others had done the same. As King William pointed his sword we moved towards the debris from the destruction.

The king was in the midst of his household knights and, closest to him, were his bodyguards. As we advanced we held our shields, not to protect us but to prevent arrows hitting the king. Progress was not swift for the ground was uneven. The stones which had fallen threatened to turn beneath our boots. Arrows hit our shields and stones were hurled but the cries from the battlements showed that our archers and crossbowmen were reaping a harvest of the hardier souls in the city. Once we reached the tower four of the king's knights headed for the now-exposed gate that led to the city. They were the best of knights and the door was torn asunder and they stood within the city itself. The four fought off the opposition until more and more knights joined them to make an enclave into which the king could emerge. The advantage we held was that the king had used the best of his men to make the assault. No one within the walls could cope with our skills.

As soon as the king emerged he organised the men and made two lines of the household knights with himself in the centre. Four of his bodyguards were before him and four after. I was one of those before him. Another four guarded his standard.

"Advance!"

The men of Exeter were brave and they threw themselves at the wall of metal that advanced towards them. It was in vain.

They had too few men with mail and they were driven inexorably back. While their numbers diminished we clambered over their bodies and our line grew as more men were fed through the breach. The defence lasted barely an hour before the last of their warriors fell and most threw down their arms to plea for mercy.

I was still wary and kept my sword unsheathed. I saw that there were some mailed men left alive but, rather than heading for the king, they headed for one of the other gates. That struck me as unusual. Housecarls were tough men. We learned, much later that the fall of Exeter began the trickle of warriors who left England to fight for other masters. Many of them headed for the empire of the Byzantines where they joined the Varangian Guard. If there had been any leader who could have rallied the warriors of England then they might have stayed. The only thorn that now remained was Eadric in Hereford and he was not of royal blood. That blood stained the hill at Senlac.

King William did not do as many expected. There were no further blindings. The one he had ordered was sufficient. Instead, he set to building Rougemont Castle. The castle and the west of England were to be the reward for Baldwin Fitz Gilbert. We stayed just long enough for our army and the impressed men from the town to complete the first level of the donjon. The king then left to head for Hereford. Before we left he gave Cornwall to his brother Robert. That part of England would be a bastion.

We marched towards the Severn and took town after town. The king had proved to the English that he was not afraid of them and so he did not need to prove himself in battle. We were spectators as his nobles competed to earn estates. Those who battled well and defeated the thegns were given their lands. It was encouragement enough.

Eadric proved elusive and cunning. Every time we thought we had him he fled back into Wales with his increasing band of followers. Each victory for us swelled his numbers as the survivors inevitably joined the last rebels in the west. By the end of February, the king was tired of the campaign. His wife was in Lundenwic and the king decided that it was time to have her crowned. With his household knights and bodyguards, we headed east to Westminster and the coronation that would seal the king's position in England.

The Saxon palace at Westminster would be our home. There was room for all of the king's household although his bodyguards, being the lowliest of them, were given the meanest quarters. None of us objected. We had all done well from the battle for Exeter and the subsequent conquest of the southwest. His bodyguards were normally the ones sent in to secure the king's quarters and we became adept at discovering where the English hid their treasures. The household knights had benefitted for many of them had been rewarded with lands in the fertile Severn Valley. Newer young bloods took their places but our numbers remained constant and that helped us for we were closer to one another. The attack up Exeter's glacis had been successful but that was down to the discipline of the king's men.

Once more the coronation saw the household knights and the bodyguards outside the church. Inside were the English lords who had submitted and wished to keep their lands. The notable absences were the lords of Mercia, Northumbria and the north. It had been a subtle departure. One moment Edwin, Morcar, Gospatric and Edgar the Aetheling were at William's Court and then they were not. The king did not seem to mind. Eadric in the west was still nuisance enough.

The coronation feast was a real celebration. When the king had been crowned the time was not right but now with the east and the west largely subdued the king and his queen could celebrate their new kingdom. It was as we stood guard behind the king and queen that I saw, intermingled with the Norman nobles, the English lords who had chosen to support their new king. There were more of them than I had expected. The king had not been the monster that they had all expected. His most controversial decision, to take the folk lands as royal land, had little effect on the lords and they did not mind. The ordinary people might object but they were, at that time, leaderless. It was, as we came to realise, the calm before the storm. The flames of rebellion were about to be fanned.

Chapter 6

York became the centre of the rebellion. Word came from the courts of Europe that the lords of the north had sent to Scotland, Wales, France and Flanders seeking allies to fight the Norman invasion. The king prepared to move north to meet this opposition. As we prepared to travel with the king, Hugh, Aimeri and I spoke of the situation.

Hugh was particularly dismissive, "The English do things a strange way, Richard. They could have done this when King William was first crowned. Then the West and the East remained free. To wait until we have half the country subdued and after the queen's coronation seems wrong."

They thought of me as half English and used me as a sounding board for their ideas. I nodded, "I agree but perhaps it is because the queen has been crowned the flames of rebellion have been ignited. I think that the queen is with child. An heir to the throne would secure the king's position."

Aimeri held up his fingers and counted, "The king has children: Robert, Richard, and William. There is even a daughter, Adela."

Hugh shook his head dismissively, "She cannot rule."

I smiled, "This is England. The Aetheling, the heir to the crown, must be born in England. King William has it by right of conquest but a son born here would have the legal right, in the eyes of the people, to be king. That may be the reason for rebellion."

They both saw the wisdom of my words, "Anyway, whatever the reason it is the chance for conquest and, perhaps, a manor."

I looked at Hugh, "You are ready for one?"

"When you secured Shepton for your half-brother I wondered why you did not take it for your own. From that moment I have thought what it would be like to be a lord of this land." He gestured towards Edward. "You have shown that Englishmen can fight for Normandy and you have shown me how to speak to the people. I could be a lord now. The north, I have heard, has many large manors. I will have one."

Aimeri added, "The king has said many times that our courage means we deserve reward. We are getting no younger and I would like to be married and have my seed inherit the riches I did not."

They seemed convinced. I was not so sure.

The armies were mustered and the lords who had been thus far rewarded were summoned to bring their mesne to support the king. I met with my half-brother, William, for the first time since Senlac. I was also reunited with a Bruno. I greeted my brother first.

"You have done well, my lord, the Honour of Eye is an important position."

He smiled and said, "You have shown greater nobility by giving our brother that which was yours by right. Why did you do so? I cannot think of another who would have done as you did."

"It was clear, my lord, that he wanted a manor more than I did and besides Robert showed me greater kindness than any in de Caux."

"And for that I am sorry. I was wrong." He stared at me as though he was emphasising his words. I nodded and smiled. "And now we go north. These are your grandfather's people, Richard. Will they fight?"

"Taking away the folk land has given the nobles an army that will fight. They are not afraid to fight but they are badly led."

He stroked his beard, "Morcar and Edwin are my kinsmen, yet they seem to lack any nobility. They bent the knee did they not?"

"They did."

"And yet now they raise the standard of rebellion. The king needs to use an arm of iron."

I did not comment. I knew the king far better than my half-brother. We had stood close to him in battle and that gave me an insight that William, despite his friendship, did not enjoy.

My meeting with Bruno, Sir Bruno now, was uplifting. He was clearly pleased with the knighthood but he had a generous spirit. "You should be a knight too, Dick. I have spoken with the household knights and they tell me that you are the most important of the bodyguards. You are the one to whom the others look. You must stop being so selfless. You need to think of yourself."

"And I will."

He nodded and then leaned in, "And I am married too."

"Married?"

He smiled, "Aye, Margaret is the daughter of a Saxon thegn. He died at Senlac and she lived with her widowed mother and young brother in their manor at Romfort. It is a small manor but the earl gave it to me. I see great potential in the manor and I hope it will grow and bring me a fortune."

"But married?"

"She is pretty and she seems to like me. Her mother encouraged us and we were wed within a month of our meeting. It is early days and I have no men at arms but soon I shall. I hope that this campaign will yield me the coins I need to pay men."

"So you are a banneret?"

"I am but my ambitions do not stop there. I would be a baron. They are the men with power. A banneret merely serves barons. I am lucky for I just serve the earl and he seems to like me."

It was north of Northampton that I came across Odo. It was some time since I had seen him but when I did I saw that he was doing well. We had camped and Edward and I were heading for the river to water our horses when I found the camp of the archers. It was clear that Odo was their captain. He had grown in girth since the last time I had seen him. It was all muscle and he looked like an archer.

His delight at our meeting touched me, "Dick! I see you wear the colours of the king. Your star is on the rise."

I smiled, "Yet look at you, Captain of Archers."

"And it suits too, Dick. I like my feet on the ground and not atop a horse. You are close to the king, will we fight?"

"That depends on the English. If they do not march to meet us then we will just take town after town."

He looked glum, "And we shall not be needed. It seems the English are not all like you or your grandfather, Dick. They have let us have this rich land too easily."

"You know that Bruno is a knight?"

"I did not but I am pleased."

73

"Perhaps but we are young, are we not, and have much to learn?"

"That we have and I have seen nothing thus far that can stop us."

On the march north, I did not see much of Bruno, Odo or my half-brother. Until we neared the enemy there was no need for a council of war and the king kept apart from all, seemingly deep in his own thoughts.

The English chose Warwick to meet us and they were arrayed for battle. This time there was a council of war. As soon as the enemy was sighted the king sent Hugh, Aimeri and myself to scout them out and ascertain their numbers. It was, I suppose, the measure of the trust the king had in all three of us but especially me as it was to me that he addressed his instructions.

"I need to know not only their numbers, Richard, but also the constituents in each unit. Take no chances. I need the information and not three empty saddles."

"We will stay safe, my lord."

I rode Geoffrey. Louis was getting too old. He was still the most comfortable of my horses but I would not risk his life on such a venture.

The English had no scouts out and that was not a surprise. They spurned horsemen. Sometimes a noble would ride but they did not use light horsemen to scout and to use as piquets. It helped us for it meant we could close to within long bow range and give a truer account of their numbers. I took off my helmet to give me a better view and as I identified the leaders I spoke aloud. If anything happened to me the king would have a true report.

"I see the standards of Gospatric, Edwin, Morcar, Edgar the Aetheling as well as the banners of the Danes who live in the five boroughs."

"Danes?"

"Aye, we are close to Danelaw and they will fight any who threatens what they see as their land." I shaded my eyes, "I estimate that there are more than ten thousand men and at least two thousand are mailed."

"That is more mailed men than we have seen thus far."

"The Danes use byrnies. They may be old but they will still stop arrows and blades. I see, perhaps five hundred archers and no crossbows."

We rode a little further to the east in case there were more men to be seen but there were not.

"They have chosen a position which is defensive. They are on the north bank of the Avon and have a bridge that they can fire if they choose." I pointed to the east of the bridge, "but that looks fordable by horsemen. Come we have seen enough."

The king heard our report in private and then summoned his nobles. We three were his only bodyguards who were present at the meeting. The hall he had commandeered was barely large enough to hold the earls and barons he had summoned.

"My scouts have reported that the enemy await us on the far side of the river. They outnumber us and yet I do not think that they will attack. Senlac Hill burns in their memory. My scouts have reported that there is a place to the east of the bridge that we can ford. William de Warenne and William de Malet will place themselves at the ford. Captain Odo and the archers will rain death upon the bridge and the main attack will be on foot across the bridge at the same time as our horsemen cross the river and make a flank attack."

"And who leads the attack across the bridge?"

We all knew that Bishop Odo was keen to gain more glory but the king had planned already, "William de Comines will have the honour of leading that attack."

The early evening was filled with the sounds of swords and lances being sharpened. Some of those with William de Comines had chosen axes and sparks flew as edges were put on the wicked weapons. We were all in position before dawn. The king and his household stood just behind those who would assault the bridge. Until the sun illuminated the battlefield then my brother and the Earl of Surrey, along with their mailed horsemen, would be hidden.

I saw that my friend Odo looked easy in command. He walked along his men cajoling and joking with them. He was the best of archers but he did not make the mistake of boasting of his prowess. He used his skill on the battlefield. I noticed that none of them had strung their bows but as well as arrows rammed in their belts they had also planted a few in the ground to make for a speedier draw.

It was when dawn broke and the English saw our dispositions that there was movement. Captain Odo ordered his men to string their bows and loosely nock an arrow. English horns sounded the alarm and I saw the leaders, conspicuous for they were mounted, gather a little way beyond the bridge. The body of horsemen upstream had clearly worried them and there was a hasty council of war.

The king nudged his horse next to his brother's. We were close enough to hear the words, "We have, it seems, upset their plans by sending men to the ford. What think you brother?"

"They will detach men to guard the crossing. It bodes well for our attack, my liege."

In the event, nothing of the sort occurred. Instead, with bare heads Edwin and Morcar rode towards the bridge. They wished to speak to us. King William turned to his bodyguards and brother, "Brother come with me and we will speak. I just need my oathsworn. Richard, stay close. You know the brothers better than any, I think."

It was as we rode through the archers that I watched the flight of the other leaders and then the army followed. They were leaving Warwick and there would be no battle. The exception was the part that was Mercian. They stood. King William said, "So, we intimidate them. Come, let us see why Mercia waits."

When we reached the Mercian army the two brothers, Edwin and Morcar, had abased themselves and their men had laid down their arms.

It was Edwin who spoke, "We submit to your will King Wiliam. Forgive us our mistake."

Bishop Odo was next to his brother and snorted, "Hang them, King William, and be done with them."

King William shook his head, "They, too, could have run but they did not."

Bishop Odo was clearly not happy, "They have delayed us. Had they fled too, my lord, then we could have ridden them down and ended this rebellion. As it is they are free to fight us another day."

King William was always patient with his brother. It may have been because he recognised what a force he was on the battlefield. "Then we shall find them again. I forgive you but your lands, Morcar, are forfeit. You and your brother can return to Mercia. Use your men to help Earl William defeat Eadred and when I return from the north we shall see if you are still loyal."

It was too late for pursuit and so the king stuck to his original plan. We secured Warwick and King William sent men to begin work on castles at Nottingham and Leicester. That done, we headed north. Our army was smaller, having left garrisons at the three castles we were building. Even so, we were still too strong for the English to try to defeat in open battle. None of their burghs were strong enough to withstand our attack and even when their soldiers halted to hold some river crossing, the sight of King William and his banner made them flee. We reached York and all of us expected some spirited resistance. The city was a fortress but they admitted us and then their leaders and the archbishop submitted. It surprised me for the town had many with Viking blood and I had expected them to be more belligerent.

The taking of York ended our campaign. King William appointed William of Comines as Earl of Northumbria and we built the first of two wooden motte and bailey castles in York. By the time we left to return south to our home, York had a garrison and Robert of Comines led his five hundred mailed men north to Durham where the last resistance to Norman rule had gathered. Gospatric, Edgar and his mother had taken refuge at the court of King Malcolm. We headed south in triumph.

We had barely reached Mercia when we received the news that Harold Godwinson's sons had landed close to the Severn and were raiding. We changed our line of march to head there but by the time we reached Oxford, we found that we were too late. The Irish led by the three sons of Earl Godwinson, had raided but an English lord, Eadnoth had met and defeated them in battle. Although Eadnoth had been killed in the fighting the raiders had fled and that part of England was safe. As we headed to Lundenwic King William was quite pleased. The threat had been dealt with by Englishmen rather than Normans. Eadric the

Wild still held Herefordshire but other than that the England of Harold was under Norman rule.

The reason for the king's return became clear when we reached Westminster. Mathilde was close to her time and would give birth. Many men wondered at King William's concern however we, his bodyguards, saw all and we knew that he loved his queen but there was more. King William and King Edward had been close and King William knew that his heir could not be a child born in Normandy. If his wife gave birth to a boy then the succession was assured. For the last month of her confinement, we stayed close to home. There was no hunting and his appearances at court were brief. When Henry was born there was a great celebration. The queen was hale and the baby healthy. The king held a feast but he did not invite his nobles. It was just his household knights and his bodyguards. I had never felt as honoured. King William was telling the world what he thought of his oathsworn.

The next day I wondered what changes there would be and, to my surprise, the first was when I was summoned to his palace and with the Archbishop of Canterbury and the Earl of Surrey in attendance, I was given new spurs by the king. He had them specially made. There had been no indication of the honour and I was speechless. That seemed to amuse the king.

"I would have thought, Sir Richard, that your time with Taillefer would have given you an answer to anything."

"I am sorry, King William, but this is so unexpected that I fear I might suddenly wake up in my chamber and find that this has been a dream."

"No dream, Richard, but a new reality. Eadnoth showed me that the English can fight for their land and it came to me that I need more men like you. You have shown a skill with words and an understanding of the English that is as valuable as an army of knights. I am giving you a manor. I have my clerks searching for a suitable one. When one is found you shall become a lord of the manor. Until that time you will serve with my household knights."

My old comrades, Hugh and Aimeri could not have been more delighted. That was understandable, for my elevation to lord of the manor brought theirs closer but none of us had any time to enjoy my new rank. The news came from the far north that Robert of Comines and all his knights were massacred at Durham. This was a disaster. So far we had not lost a battle. Now the men of the north had destroyed five hundred men. With just a tiny garrison in York, the north revolted once more and Gospatric and Edgar had taken York. Leaving his new son in Lundenwic with ten of his household knights, the rest of us joined an army that included my half-brother, Earl William. This time it was not a leisurely march up the Roman Road. It was a forced march. I think that the king realised he had been as merciful as could have been expected. He had forgiven Morcar and Edwin but had he been more ruthless in his pursuit of his enemies, then he might not have lost a good friend and five hundred knights and men at arms.

The gates at York were Roman in construction and therefore stronger than the ones built by the English at their burghs. Tunnelling was out of the question. The king did not bother with siege machines for they would have taken too long to build, instead, his lords were commanded to have ladders constructed. This would be an escalade.

I would fight alongside the household knights. Some had been bodyguards like me. The difference was that they had yet to be given manors. I knew not which my manor would be but I would have a home. In many ways that affected the way that I fought for I knew I had my reward already. The night before we were due to attack Edward and I prepared our weapons. He would follow me up the ladder. In the last year, Edward had grown both in body and in mind. He now spoke Norman fluently. There was an accent but he rarely used English. He had a mail hauberk and a good sword. He sported a kite shield and he could fight as well as any squire and better than most. If an enemy met him they would assume that he was Norman.

"Tomorrow, Edward, it will be your initiation into the world of war. You have fought before and have saved my life, but tomorrow we ascend a ladder where all manner of objects and weapons will be used to end our lives. Once we reach the fighting platform we will be outnumbered."

"I am ready, my lord."

"Your task is to watch my back. We shall be the last of the knights to ascend and behind you will be the men led by the Earl of Surrey. They are good men and your back should be safe. When you strike, then make your blow a killing blow. A wounded man, like an injured boar, can still kill."

"I will do so. I do not know the men who defend these walls although my father and uncle came from the land to the west of here. These are Gospatric's men. These are wild men and I will not underestimate them."

I was content. That night I prayed, as I always did, and spoke not only to God but to my grandfather, mother and Taillefer for I believed that they were all in heaven and heard my words. I knew that in the heat of battle, my life could hang by a thread. Having allies in heaven could not hurt my chances of survival.

We rose before dawn and were blessed by bishops. King William placed great faith in the support of the church. We stood beyond bow range and waited. As the sun rose the command to loose arrows was given. King William had seen the value of arrows and Captain Odo and his archers cleared the walls. The horn sounded and we raced forward, holding the ladder. The ones without ladders held shields above their heads but I did not use my shield. I relied on my helmet, coif, and ventail along with the faith that God would watch over me. The ditch had not been well-maintained nor was it deep enough. The ladders reached the crenulated wall and Sir Guillaume led the assault.

I was halfway up the ladder when Sir Guillaume's body was hurled from the walls. It did not deter me but spurred me on. I was the fifth one in line on our ladder and when I reached the top I saw that just two others had survived. I had to step on Sir Jocelyn's body. My two swords had been sheathed in my ascent and that had enabled me to use two hands to thrust myself through the gap. Sir Jocelyn's body almost made me slip but I had quick reflexes and I regained my balance and drew my swords. The two knights who had made the walls before me ensured that I had a few moments to do so. Sir Henri was struck on the side of the helmet with a club and as he slid to the fighting platform, my left hand darted like an adder's tongue and skewered the clubman. I swung my right hand at the next man to allow Edward to make the fighting platform.

I had learned that fighting a man with two swords confused most warriors. The defenders of York were no exception. While a shield could be used offensively, the whirling edges of sharpened swords were deadlier. Taillefer had taught me well and my hands were quick. I no longer thought about what each hand was doing. It was as though they had a mind of their own. I made my way along the fighting platform. Edward stood to my left, his kite shield protecting my open side. The crenulations protected my right. I moved confidently down towards the next ladder where the Earl of Surrey's men were trying to gain a foothold. I saw that two lay dead, one half hanging over the wall. As the next knight rose I saw that it was Bruno. He held his shield before him. His right hand gripped the stone and the warrior who swung the axe at the shield thought that he had added another Norman knight to his tally. My left arm swung in a wide arc and hacked into the man's back. It grated along his spine. As I pulled out the blade a spear came from behind the dying man. Edward punched with his shield to deflect it and then hacked down with his sword to sever the spearman's arm. With two men disposed of Edward and I now had the room to step beyond Bruno and allow him and the rest of the earl's men to ascend. A flurry of blows from men maddened by our skills were easily blocked for these were neither knights nor men at arms. These were York burghers. Their ancestors might have been Vikings and they had good weapons but the skills their forefathers had were no longer in evidence.

Bruno took charge for it was his men he led, "We have numbers, Richard. You and your squire have done your work well. Now it is time for fresher blades."

I knew that Edward was new to this so I stepped to the side and Bruno and four of the earl's men made a block and began to advance down the fighting platform. Protected by shields and with swords wielded by well-trained warriors, they easily pushed back the defenders. The resistance became weaker and by the time Edward and I had reached the stone steps that led down to the street level, Bruno and his brothers-in-arms had managed to make a killing zone that allowed the rest of us to descend safely. I stepped between Bruno and a knight with a war hammer.

Edward tucked in behind me. When another three knights had joined us, Bruno shouted, "Forward."

I knew that all along the huge circumference of York's walls others would be doing as we were. It was like knots of mailed men, well protected, insinuating their way through men whose skill was not up to the task. Many took to ships and boats when we reached the river and fled. York was well connected to the sea. A considerable proportion of those we had defeated had relatives in Denmark and they would flee there. Others would simply escape the killing machine that was the Norman army. The result was that by noon the city was ours. The killing halted, Edward and I joined Bruno and his brothers-in-arms to search the dead we had slain for treasure. There were rings and even a torc or two. There were weapons. I had killed two men in byrnies and while the metal was not of the best quality, the weaponsmiths who accompanied the army were happy to pay Edward and me silver for them. They would reuse the metal and make better hauberks. The same was true with the helmets. The swords and daggers we took we kept. The king had promised me a manor and I wanted to be able to arm my people. We slept that night in the safety of a city guarded by Norman warriors. I slept well.

20 miles

Chapter 7

The king sent his brother with half of our men towards Durham. The rest he kept in York. Gathering his senior lords he made an important announcement. "Earl William is to be the Sherriff of Yorkshire and the guardian of the north." All eyes went to my half-brother. This was a most important position. York was the capital of the north. Holding it would give him both power and a serious income. The Honour of Eye was as nothing compared with this. My nephew Robert visibly grew when the announcement was made for he was the heir and his future was assured.

The Earl of Warenne and Bruno were close to me. The earl said, quietly, "An honour but one I am glad was not accorded me."

Bruno asked, "Why not, my lord?"

"We have yet to fight a battle here in the north. We took York too easily and as the Scots are eager to support rebellion I fear that Richard's brother will have more fighting than we will."

My brother had never shied away from fighting but I realised that with our other half-brother in Shepton, it would be his young sons who would be his crutches. Were they up to the task?

"I have also decided to give the manor that formerly belonged to Earl Morcar, Eisicewalt, to Sir Richard Fitz Malet in recognition of the service he has done us." He nodded to my half-brother, "And he will be close enough to the earl so that they can continue to strengthen their family ties."

Bruno clapped me on the back, "It may just be a northern manor but it is a start. Congratulations."

"Thank you." My first thoughts were to discover where the manor was to be found.

Belisarius was the senior official brought by the king. He was a wise and well-read scholar. I sought him out as soon as was practical. "Brother Belisarius, where is Eisicewalt?"

He smiled, "You should know, Sir Richard, that the king asked me some time ago to find a manor for you. When he told me that your half-brother was to be the Sherriff then Eisicewalt leapt to the fore of my mind. It is a few miles north of here, on the road to Durham. It was an ancient royal hunting lodge and the Earl Morcar used it when he was Lord of Gilling which lies to the west of here. There is neither wall nor fort but it is a profitable manor. Many travellers halt there on their way to York. The fields are fertile and yield good crops, but I am unsure of the people. That will be down to you, my lord. Like the king, I am happy about your abilities. This is something you can do but it will take care and you will need the ability to lead people."

"Thank you. Is there a church in the manor?"

"There is not. Earl Morcar liked the manor for it had good hunting and gave him an income. It is not a heavily populated place."

"A church is needed."

He nodded, "I agree but a priest would be a start. Leave that with me, Sir Richard. There are priests who came over with the king in the hope of a place. Most want a good church with a large manor but there are some whose ambitions are lesser. The king will stay here until the castle is built and then he is anxious to return to the queen and his new son."

Before I left for Eisicewalt I had a meeting with my half-brother. His position was important. Yorkshire was a large county and was probably the second most important place in England. He was busy learning about his new office but he found time for me.

"I am pleased, Richard, that you have been rewarded. As I told you once before, Robert told me what you did for him and it was both selfless and thoughtful. I know it is a little late to make the offer but I would have found you a manor."

"The king promised me one after Senlac, my lord, and I am content with this one."

"I am only sorry that I cannot offer you men to fight for your new manor. The loss of five hundred knights at Durham was a sore blow. Until more men come from Normandy we will have to make do. I have to defend York with just my own retinue and it is not a large one."

"I know the scale of the task."

"What I can do is ensure that my patrols go as far north as Eisicewalt so that you are not isolated. If you need anything then tell the patrol when they visit with you."

Edward and I, with laden horses and sumpters, headed north. I had a parchment in my saddlebags but that might mean nothing. We rode mailed and helmed. Bishop Odo was heading north and that should have ensured that the road was safe but who knew what dangers awaited us on the road north? We passed through the northern gate of York and saw small farms that bordered the road and farmed thin strips of land. Those people eked out a living but knew that if there were raids and wars they had the security of the walls of York close by. That was the pattern for some miles. No villages but clusters of homes. The only village we passed was Shipton and after that, the dwellings by the side of the road ceased. The forest grew perilously close to the road and both Edward and I felt threatened by the land. We had just twelve or so miles to travel and having left early in the day, reached my new home well before noon. The village appeared to be little more than a dozen houses but the manor house was more substantial. We reined in so that I could observe it. I saw that it was set back from the road and there was a green area with animals grazing. That was folk land and I knew I would have to tread carefully around the villagers in that regard. The manor house itself, from a distance, told me what a generous gift the manor had been. It was a substantial building. It was Saxon in build but I could see, even from across the folk land, the influence of the Danes. It was single storey and it reminded me of the hunting lodge I had visited with Duke William and Taillefer when we had stayed with King Edward. On a smaller scale, it explained why Earl Morcar liked it.

"Well, Edward, our next adventure begins."

We spurred our horses and trotted towards the hall. There was no gatehouse and no ditch. I frowned as I saw that. The times were too dangerous to leave the property so vulnerable to attack. As we clattered into the cobbled yard, heads and faces appeared from the various outbuildings. Before I dismounted, I took off my helmet and surveyed my new home and lands. Both dwarfed Fitz Malet. There was a bakehouse some twenty paces from the house. There were two buildings which might be barns or stables and there looked to be a smaller house that lay beyond the hogbog. That the hogbog was new was obvious. It had been recently added and had fresh mortar. The entrance to the hall had two oak pillars and the carvings showed both dragons and the cross. I knew from my three men in Normandy that the Danes used such carvings. This had been Danelaw even before the coming of King Sweyn and King Canute. I had been given land that was not truly English. This was Anglo-Danish.

The faces and heads became bodies and I dismounted, handing my reins to Edward. "Keep watch." I was no fool. There were at least three men and two youths, if they disputed my right to the land then I would have to fight and a mounted Edward gave me a better chance of survival. I took the parchment from my saddlebags and walked towards the carved pillars. I saw that the men stood to one side while the woman and the two youths occupied the doorway. I saw the face of a child, a girl, appear between the youths.

I took out the parchment and unrolled it. I spoke in English, "I am Sir Richard Fitz Malet. King William of England has given me this land which formerly belonged to Earl Morcar, and I am the new lord of the manor." I knew not what else to say. When I had been given Fitz Malet it had been almost an afterthought from my half-brother. This seemed more formal.

The woman set the tone. She curtsied and said, "I am Benthe Berntsdotter, and my husband and I were the stewards for Earl Morcar. You are welcome, Sir Richard, but your sudden arrival has taken us unawares." She swept a hand behind her, "We have lived in the hall for a year or so and we will have to vacate it for your lordship."

I smiled, Taillefer had told me that a smile was a passport into the hearts of strangers, "There is no haste, so long as Edward, my squire, and I have a bed that will suffice. Before we enter I would know the names and titles of those who dwell here."

She nodded, "These are my sons, Aethelstan and Alfred." She smiled, "My husband, Eadwine, God rest his soul, was a proud Englishman and named his sons after two great English kings." She moved the girl from behind her apron, "This fey young hart is my daughter Birgitte. My husband let me name her although, as he was taken at Gate Fulford, he never saw her grow. The three men you see work your land, my lord: Lars, Drogo and Gandálfr." Each nodded and bowed when she said their name. Their names were of Danish origin and that told me much.

"Know that I am half English and half Norman. My half-brother Earl William is the new Sherriff of Yorkshire. I am here to make the lives of those in Eisicewalt safer and better but it will take me some time to get to know the land and its people. I will need your help."

"And you shall have it, my lord, for we have been neglected for the past two years. The manor needs a hand and, for my part, I care not if it is Norman, Saxon or Danish so long as it is a firm one. What you should know, my lord, is that few in the village call it Eisicewalt. There are two settlements. This one is better known as Uppleby because it is better land and the other part, the one on the lower ground, is Lessimers. So called because it is leased waterlogged land. Upple was the Dane who settled this land. The dozen houses you see are Uppleby, and Lessimers is hidden further north for it is low ground." She smiled, "I thought you should know for there are many here of Danish blood. My father's people came with King Cnut and he was given a farm not far from here."

I breathed a sigh of relief. The barriers I had assumed would be there were not. "Edward, fetch our gear. It is Lars is it not?" The man nodded, "Have our horses taken to the stables and groom them. I will apportion tasks when I get to know you. Mistress, if you would take me on a tour of my new home."

"Of course."

I looked at the boys, "And if you two would care to help Edward, I am sure he would appreciate it."

The two youths were no longer boys but had not yet attained the frame of a man. I knew that they would need careful handling but, remembering my own mind at the same age, I knew that they would enjoy handling the weapons that were on the backs of the sumpters.

I had to duck under the lintel. It was then I realised that I was taller than the three men who worked for me. The hall had been built when men were smaller. Inside it was dark and I knew that I would need to invest in candles to brighten it. There was a small room through which we passed. I guessed that in the past it had been a guard room of some description. The door led to an open space and there were doors leading from it.

"This, my lord, is where they used to dine." She opened the door and I saw a chamber with a table that held ten people. It was larger than I had expected. By way of explanation, she said, "When this was a hunting lodge then it held feasts after the hunt. It has been many years since Lord Morcar availed himself of the lodge." She led me through a small door and said, apologetically, "This is the way to the kitchens, my lord, and I only take you this way to show you all that is yours." It was a narrow passage and led to a kitchen that was much larger than the one at Fitz Malet. There was an open fire and a chimney. Pots, pans and spikes to suspend meat were fixed, neatly, to the wall. This was something unexpected for it was grander than I had expected. She opened a door and said, "This is the larder." I saw some hares, squirrels and game birds hanging there as well as a round of cheese. What I did not see was any ham. She opened the back door and I saw the hog bog. "My husband built that before he went to war. We still have fowl but the pigs were stolen."

"Stolen?"

"After the battles of Gate Fulford and Stamford Bridge, my lord, there was much lawlessness. My sons were young and the three men you see now were originally five. Two died trying to stop the thieves from robbing us. They came from the village up the road, Tresche. Bad men live there, my lord." She shrugged, "Now you see why I am happy to see a warrior, any warrior, come to this hall."

The tour of the rest of the house revealed four sleeping chambers and a room that had a fire and looked cosy enough to use as a sort of solar despite the fact that there was no wind hole. It needed none for the chimney took the foul air up and into the skies. There were two seats there and I said, "Mistress, take a seat and let us speak." She looked doubtful but obeyed, "What you should know, Mistress Benthe, is that I was brought up almost as a thrall. I expected nothing like this. I have a small farm in Normandy but it is tiny by comparison. I will need all the help I can get and I would have you as a friend."

Birgitte had seated herself on her mother's knee and looked content. Benthe stroked her daughter's hair and nodded, "I have Danish blood in me, my lord, and while I am a Christian, I still have some of the old ways in me. The volvas of my people set great store in feelings and in fate. The three sisters who were said to spin webs were tales I liked as a child. I have known you less than an hour and yet I can hear in your voice and see in your eyes that you have a good heart. We have expected a new lord, but I confess that we feared a cruel Norman. I think that King William has chosen well, and we will do all in our power to help you make this a safe and secure land."

"Good. I am not a wealthy man nor am I poor. Whatever coins I have will be used to make this comfortable. I will buy pigs to replace those that were stolen. What else do we need?" I gestured to the walls. Heloise had taught me much. "Wall hangings would make the rooms warmer in winter and brighten them up."

"There are women in the villages who would welcome an income sewing for the lord of the manor."

"Good, now sleeping arrangements: Edward and I need but one room each. You and your family can have the other two and then the three men can use the other dwelling."

She looked relieved but said, "Are you sure, my lord? We do not mind living as we did the last time Earl Morcar came. It was cramped but we managed."

"There is no need to manage when we can live comfortably. This suits. Now we cannot have just you labouring in the kitchens for I have a squire and there may be visitors. You know those in the villages. Find two young women and I will pay them to help you in the kitchen. I dare say the income will please their families."

"That it will."

"And that brings me to the matter of the income from the manor. What do we produce?"

She cast her eyes to the ground and shook her head, "Not enough, my lord. Lars planted barley and oats but we have two fallow fields."

"You do not grow wheat? Beans?"

"This is too far north for wheat my lord and beans… we should."

I saw the problem. Benthe had been holding together what she could. This wasn't her fault. I was just glad that my half-brother was so close and that there was peace in the land. We had a chance to rebuild the manor.

I smiled, "Tomorrow we shall begin anew. Edward and I will ride the land and in the next few days, when I am happy with what I have seen, I shall ride to York. I will use what little influence I have with my brother. This is well met, Benthe."

She beamed, "It is, my lord." She rose, "And we have much to do, Birgitte. We will put food and ale on the table, my lord, and then I will go to speak to two girls who might suit your purposes."

Alone in the room, I felt comfortable. I had but a few moments alone before Edward peered into the room. "Where do I put our sleeping gear and clothes, my lord?"

"There is one large bedroom and a smaller one attached to it. The larger is mine and the smaller is yours."

His face lit up, "A chamber to myself? I thought I would be chamberlain."

"No, Edward, it is not only my life which has been changed but yours also. I will help and then, we can enjoy the fare of my new home."

The two of us had surprisingly few clothes to hang on the hooks on the wall. The hauberks and coifs were our normal attire. When we visited York I would need to buy cloth for clothes for Edward and for me. Once they were hung we went to the hall where there was a platter with freshly made rye bread and runny cheese. As we ate and with the door closed, I said, quietly, "What did you make of the boys?"

He smiled, "They have good hearts and they are keen to help. Their father was a hero to them. He fought for Earl Morcar at Gate Fulford and died, so they say, well."

I knew what that meant. The survivors had told the tale when they returned to assuage the grief of the family. The reality might have been that Eadwine had been butchered by the Norse but the story had clearly inspired the boys.

"We shall train them as warriors as well as the three men."

The three labourers would be a different problem. They had Danish blood but that did not make them warriors. I would have to find their stories. I knew I would not be as lucky as I was with

91

my three Danish thralls in Normandy but I would work with whatever I could.

The meal, that night, was a simple one. The game that the three men had trapped was cooked in a stew enriched with the addition of the lees from the beer that Benthe had brewed. It was tasty. I insisted that the family and the three labourers join us. They were, at first, reluctant but they bowed to my will. I wanted to get to know them. I learned that I was correct in my initial judgements. The three labourers were workers and not warriors. That was not to say they could not be trained but they would not be archers and that was what I needed. They knew how to use a wood axe and so I would train them to be axe men. The two boys, in contrast, were keen to learn how to use a sword. Benthe, surprisingly, approved when I suggested that they be trained by Edward with such skills. The atmosphere became relaxed. Birgitte said little but she kept staring at both Edward and me; I knew why. Our clothes and lack of beards were in direct contrast to the three labourers who had long hair and unkempt beards.

Before we retired, Edward and I went to the stable to see that the horses had been attended to. As it had been a hunting lodge there was room for more horses than we had and that was a good thing. The roof was a good one and it would need no work. When we went to our chamber I found that the bed was a good one. The pillows had been stuffed with goose feathers and I slept as well as I could ever remember.

The cock in the hogbog woke me well before dawn but I did not mind. In Normandy, I was a tenant of my brother. Here I was the lord. I wondered if my mother and grandfather were looking down from heaven. If they were then I knew that they would be proud and I was determined to be the kind of lord and master that my mother had deserved.

When I entered the kitchen Benthe shook her head, "I will have that cock in the pot, my lord. He cannot tell the time!"

"It matters not. I am anxious to see my land."

Edward burst into the kitchen looking flustered, "My lord, you should have woken me."

Laughing I said "I thought the cock had done that. No matter. We will breakfast and then ride my land and the two villages."

Benthe apologised for the plain fare but it suited. There was oat porridge with honey and berries as well as the stale bread from the previous day toasted and covered in homemade butter. It was a good breakfast.

Before we left I said to Lars, who was clearly the foreman, "I will speak with the three of you when I return. We have much to plan."

"Yes, my lord. It will be good to have some direction. We do our best but..." Gate Fulford had been a battle lost and in its loss, many men had died. The manor had lost its helmsman.

We mounted and, bareheaded and without mail we rode from the hall down the road through the two settlements. We rode slowly so that I could see the state of the dwellings. Most were poorly made. I guessed that in winter the wind would whistle through the gaps I could see in the daub and wattle. This was especially true in Lessimers. Whenever a face appeared I spoke, politely, to them to let them know who I was. One woman, emptying her night water into a large wooden tub bowed and said, "Your lordship has just taken on my daughter Agnetha. I hope she gives good service but I am grateful for the coins."

I took a guess, "You are a widow?"

She nodded, "My husband, Ethelbert, died with Eadwine at Gate Fulford. Times have been hard since then. I help my brother Ned and I earn a little from him but the coins you will pay Agnetha will be more than welcome."

"Now that I am lord I hope that they will be better. Do not be afraid to ask for my help, Gammer. Just as the villagers owe me service I have a responsibility from both God and the king to care for my people."

"We need a priest, my lord. I am getting too old for the walk to York."

"I will see what I can do."

The differences between Uppleby and Lessimers could not have been more marked. Lessimers had houses that were little better than hovels and I knew that the people would struggle for food in winter. The king's edict about folk land would hit them hard. I would have to see what I could do to make their lives easier.

When we had passed the last dwelling I headed east and rode towards the woods that lay there. They were an ancient woodland. I guessed that when the Romans came north they would have seen the same trees that I did. I sought and found a path that meandered between the trees. This would be the land used for hunting. As we rode through I saw signs of deer and wild pigs. I also saw signs of men; there were footprints and evidence of trees being copsed. As the forest had not been used for hunting for some time then these were men who were taking advantage of the lack of a lord. I would have to deal with that. It was not that I might begrudge men the chance of meat but if the land was overhunted then that might destroy all the wildlife. I needed a bailiff to manage my wood. I saw where timber had been taken. That too was an issue. I would have to organise the copsing of the trees to enable all to have firewood for the winter but also to ensure that we had trees for the future. This was all new to me.

It was almost noon when we arrived back at the manor and my three men were making willow hurdles. It was a necessary task. There were a few sheep on the farm and the hurdles would be a way of containing them for both their wool and their slaughter. Leaving Edward to see to the horses I gathered them around me. Agnetha, one of the two new servants, brought out a jug of beer. The men all had their coistrels hung from their belts but Benthe had sent out a fine beaker for me. We sat on the willow logs that had been hewn. They would, in the fullness of time, be made into firewood.

"I will give you my vision of the manor and you can let me know the skills you possess that will enable my dream to become a reality." They nodded. "First, I need a bailiff to manage the woods and forest. Secondly, we need to buy and then rear animals for food. We have sheep but how many?"

Lars stroked his chin, "One tup and ten ewes."

I shook my head, "That is not enough. Do we have goats?"

Gandálfr frowned, "Goats, my lord? Why should we need goats?"

"Cheese, my friend, and goats can graze and eat where a sheep cannot. Do we have cows?" They shook their heads. "Animals to pull a plough?" Again they shook their heads. I sighed, "Then we need two oxen and some cows. We will have to wait to buy a bull. The fallow fields, what did they produce?"

Lars said, "Beans, my lord."

"Then they will be fertile. They should be replanted. Why is there not a growing crop of beans?" Their gaze shifted to their feet. "Come, I demand honesty. I cannot make lives better if I know not the root of the problem."

"Coins, my lord. We have not had any silver to buy beans. Earl Morcar had not been here since, well since he asked the men of the village to fight at Gate Fulford. He seemed occupied with other matters."

I knew only too well what those matters were. He had been trying to gain power.

"That is in the past. I will go this week to York. Can you ride, Lars?"

"After a fashion, my lord."

"Well, a trip to York and back should improve those skills. We will buy what we can. Now, a bailiff."

Lars said, "We are farm labourers, my lord. It has been many years since there were hunters here but as I recall Earl Morcar brought his own men with him and they acted as beaters and gamekeepers."

Drogo said, "Ethelred."

I looked at him, "Who is Ethelred?"

Drogo said, "The last house in the village, the one that looks as though it is about to fall down, is Ethelred's. His sons died at Gate Fulford and his wife of a broken heart, it is said. He is a poacher. He knows the woods better than any man."

"If he is known to be a poacher then why is he not stopped?"

Lars gave a sad smile, "Ethelred was one of the few men to return from Gate Fulford unharmed. It is said he slew ten Vikings and Northumbrians when his sons fell. He is not a man to be crossed. Drogo is right. If he was the bailiff then there would be no poaching for all men fear him. He especially hates all those he believes have Norse blood in them. We are of Danish descent but he sees us as Vikings."

Edward had returned and I said, "Tomorrow we visit Ethelred the poacher." He gave me a strange smile. "I will explain later." Turning to the other three I said, "You are my men and, as such, I expect you to defend my land. Edward will take you to the room we have designated as our armoury. He will equip you with weapons. Each day you will spend the first hour of the day with the two of us. We will do our best to make you into warriors." I rose. "And now I will see Alfred and Aethelred."

The two boys were in the kitchen helping their mother. From the flour on their hands, I deduced that they had been making bread. "Mistress Benthe, is this a good time for me to speak to your sons?"

"Of course, wipe your hands and mind your manners."

They rushed outside to the water trough to wash their hands and by the time I emerged were wiping their wet hands on their smocks. They were still young and unused to speaking to a noble. I took them to the stables. Parsifal snorted and stamped the ground as we entered. This was still strange to the war horse and he was exercising his power. The two youths looked at him in awe.

"Your father was a warrior." They both nodded. "Would you two like to follow in his footsteps?"

They chorused, together, "Yes, my lord."

"Then Edward and I will train you but I warn you it will be the hardest thing you have ever learned. You will have bruises in places you thought impossible and your muscles will ache and scream long into the night. We will also teach you to sit on a horse and use a spear. I know your father did not have that skill but we Normans bring new ideas to the battlefield. You will learn to ride by mounting a horse every day and your buttocks will become sore and bleed. You will curse both Edward and me if you heed our words, then one day you shall be able to stand in a shield wall, much as your father did and have a chance of survival."

Their faces told me that they accepted my warnings. I had begun to be a lord of the manor.

Chapter 8

I knew that my first task involved Ethelred and the next day we headed, on foot, to his home. It was the last house in Uppleby and set back from the road. Even before we reached it, I heard snoring. The door to what was little more than a tumbled-down shack was hanging from its leather hinges and did not stop us. We entered what was barely a hovel and my nose was assaulted by the stink. The house stank of piss, the stench of an unwashed body and the reek of ale. The man was a drunk. I went over to him and touched his body with the toe of my boot. He moaned.

I shouted, "Ethelred, wake up. I wish to speak to you."

I was partly expecting his reaction but Edward was not and he was taken by surprise. The man leapt violently to his feet. There was a staff next to the man and he grabbed it and swept it blindly at us. I guessed we were just two threatening shadows. I jumped up and over it but Edward stumbled back, hit the door and ended up outside the dwelling.

I spoke firmly, "Ethelred, I am Sir Richard Fitz Malet and this is my land. Do not make me chastise you."

He opened his eyes. They widened when he saw me. He recognised my garb as that of a lord. He struggled to his feet, "Sorry, my lord, but woken harshly like that…"

I shook my head, "I have heard that you were once a mighty warrior and men fear you still. I just see an old drunk who lives in his own mess." His eyes narrowed and his fingers clenched. "Make no mistake, Ethelred, if you even think about violence I will have you punished and driven from the village. Go outside and wash yourself in the trough. When you pass him apologise to my squire."

As he stepped outside, he mumbled, "Sorry, young sir."

Others who lived close by came from their dwellings to see what was going on. I was well aware of their scrutiny and everything I did was calculated. We walked to the trough and I said, "Take off your smock." He whipped his head around. "Do it." He did so and I saw the wildlife crawling about him. I said, quietly, "Is this well done, Ethelred? What would your sons think? You had vengeance for their deaths but now you have dishonoured that glory." I added a little louder, "Edward, ask Benthe for some strong soap and fetch some of my old clothes from the slop chest."

"Aye, my lord."

As he ran off, I was aware of the attention from the ones who had peered out of their homes. My actions thus far had shown them that I was not a man to be crossed but Ethelred, from Benthe's words, had been a warrior and he deserved his dignity, "I am sure that all of you have work that you could be doing. When King William comes for his taxes…" I let the threat hang. The heads disappeared.

Ethelred began to wash himself. I took a ladle from the trough and poured it along his back. I used my hand to sweep away as much wildlife as I could.

He said, "You do not know what it is like, my lord, to have your family taken from you."

"I do indeed, Ethelred. I watched my grandfather be unfairly blinded and then sink slowly into an early grave. He did not have the glory of a death with his axe in his hand so I understand your grief, but what I do not understand is the way you are coping. Poaching and then drinking yourself asleep are not the way for a warrior to live. Better you had died at Gate Fulford."

His eyes had widened at my story and he nodded. "And I wish I had." My words suddenly sank in, "Poaching?"

"That is what they call taking animals from the lord of the manor without consent is it not?" The punishment for such a crime could be blinding, the loss of a limb or both. He became silent as he washed. He plunged his head into the trough and I saw the nits as they tried to escape a watery grave. Edward arrived and he handed Ethelred the soap. He placed the clothes in a neat pile to the side.

"When you have washed then dress in these clothes." Edward produced a nit comb. I guessed that was Benthe's doing. "Use this comb and when you are groomed and dressed we will talk about your punishment." The threat silenced him. When he was dressed and groomed, I said, "We need your hair to be cut but this will do for the present. Ethelred, you are one of my people now. Your home is on my land. So far as I can see you do nothing for either me or the village. Indeed, you are seen by many as a threat and they walk in fear of you. I intend to change that." He looked at me fearfully. "I would have you as my bailiff and gamekeeper. I want the wildlife in my lands to be managed for the good of all and not a drunken old man. You will repair your home and, in return, you shall be paid. If that is not an acceptable offer then leave the village and we will say no more."

"You wish to reward me for poaching, my lord?"

"No, I wish to change you and redeem you. I would have you become the man you were and not the one you have become. The punishment will be that you will have to work hard and do so under my close scrutiny."

He smiled and dropped to a knee, "I accept, my lord."

"Good. Come to the hall later this afternoon and I will give you your first payment."

As we walked back Edward said, "Payment?"

"The man has not eaten well and has drunk more than he has chewed. His first payment will be food. I will have Benthe make him a pot of food and give him bread. Tomorrow, he can begin his work."

Benthe more than approved. She was delighted. "Ethelred and my husband were shield brothers. He was a good man before his sons died. If his wife had not died too then his life might have been different. You are a good man, my lord, and I was right, the three sisters sent you here."

The visit to Ethelred meant that my trip to York needed to be delayed. By the end of the week, I had made enough changes to warrant a visit to York. I had spoken to all the villagers and told them what I expected of them and what they could expect of me. When we rode to York I also took Alfred and Aethelred, as well as Lars. The ride would be a good chance to teach them more skills. We left well before dawn to be at the market when it opened. I had a bag of gold. I knew that I would have to send to Caen for more but I had enough for the present.

We left early with cloaks wrapped about us to keep out the cold. We all sported swords. The two youths were particularly proud to be doing so even though the short swords they carried were little better than seaxes. As we headed down the road Edward and I continued to teach the three of them how to ride. It was easier doing so on the road where we could ride behind them and correct their posture and their hands. The youths learned more quickly than Lars but he did well enough. He would never need to be a good rider but if the youths were to become pueros then they would.

The road to York was busier than I expected and the last mile or so our pace slowed. My spurs and my horse accorded me some space but it took longer than I thought it would. We went first to the market where I bought cloth for Benthe as well as sacks of seeds: beans, cabbages, turnips and oats. We sought the animal market. The pickings were not what I might have hoped but I managed to buy a sow and a boar. Neither was as large as I would have liked but they were relatively cheap. The oxen proved a problem and I found none that were suitable. Instead, I bought two bullocks. They could pull a plough and when they were no longer needed could be slaughtered for their hide and meat. We bought three goats, a billy and three nannies. The goat trader explained that the normal sheep trader was absent but he lived towards Malton, to the east of us. He suggested I might visit there.

We now had livestock and the drive home would take forever. I still had some coins and so I sent Lars to buy a wagon to transport the cloth and the pigs. The goats and the bullocks would be able to move faster. He returned with one half an hour later. Two of the men from the wagon makers helped him to push it. Leaving Lars and the youths to load the wagon and hitch two sumpters to pull it, Edward and I headed for the castle and my half-brother. While going around the market we had heard dire warnings of disaster. I did not like gossip and decided to ask the Sherriff.

The second castle was far from finished but it was defensible. The hall had been built and my brother, along with his sons were there with the senior captains. I was recognised and admitted.

"Ah, Richard, you come at a propitious time. I was going to send a rider to warn you of danger but your timely arrival means I can speak face to face."

"What has happened, my lord? I heard the word disaster when I was in the market."

He snorted and put down the stylus he had been using on the wax tablet, "There has been no disaster but Bishop Odo got no further north than Northallerton. He had desertions and he chose to return to Kent. I do not know what the king thinks of it, but I am less than impressed. It means the men I command are the only warriors to face any threat from the north."

"And is a threat imminent?"

"We chased Gospatric and Edgar north and there lies King Malcolm. He could come south to make mischief in the hope of enlarging his country at the expense of England. Yours is now the most northerly Norman outpost. I do not have the men to waste in patrols. If you wish you can come to York."

It took but a heartbeat for me to make my decision. I could not leave Benthe and the others to be attacked, "No, my lord, I took the manor and I will bear the burden."

"Belisarius is about somewhere. I think he found you a priest." He stood and held out his arm for me to clasp, "Good luck, my brother."

"And you."

Belisarius was not in the castle but men told me he was at the minster. Bishop Wulfstun had recently died and Belisarius was helping with the entombing of the prelate. When he saw me, he stopped what he was doing and told the men with him to have a drink break. He waved over one of the labourers and came to me, "Sir Richard, this is Gregory. He is a priest who seeks a church."

I looked at the man who was stripped to the waist and looked to be the least likely priest I had ever seen. His hands were those of a labourer and he had a muscled chest.

He bowed, "My lord, I would dearly love to be your priest and minister to the people of this land."

"We have no church as yet."

"What does it say in the Bible? '*Where two or three are gathered together, there is a church.*' Whatever you have shall suffice."

Belisarius smiled, "Get your gear, Gregory. Work will be slower without your broad back but Sir Richard shall need you, I am sure." As he went off Belisarius said, "Gregory is English and has rubbed the Archbishop the wrong way. He means well but he has a habit of speaking his mind and that does not sit well. He will be perfect for you. I know what you are like and you will get on."

"What about the dangers from the north?"

"You heard about that?" I nodded. "You will be in danger. If I can find any warriors then I will send them to you."

"Will my brother not need them?"

"He will but there are some men who might not be suitable for him but perfect for you. Leave these matters in my hands."

Belisarius was the sort of man who made empires function. Gregory returned and he had his bundle about his back. Now wearing a brown shift he looked more priest-like. We headed back to the market. I had left money for my three men to enjoy food and drink from the stallholders in the market and they had done so. The freshly cooked pies looked appetising so I bought three for Edward, Gregory and myself. While we ate, I was able to make the introductions.

I wiped my mouth and finished the coistrel of beer. "Gregory, you can ride on the wagon with Lars. I will speak to you when we reach the manor. Tether the bullocks to the rear of the wagon." I saw that they had managed, somehow, to put the four goats in the wagon. Had the pigs been bigger that might have proved impossible. It meant the bolt of cloth was used as an improvised cushion for the two driving. It was noon when we left. The wagon forced its way through the throngs. I now knew why so many people were on the road to York. There was danger from the north.

Edward and I rode at the rear allowing the two youths to have the honour of leading the wagon north. "I had thought, Edward, that we might have enjoyed more time to make our home defensible but Bishop Odo has made that impossible. We shall have to improve the defences and train men at the same time."

He nodded, "How many men do we have, my lord?"

I did not know and I shouted, "Lars, how many men are there to defend the village?"

I smiled as I watched him hand the reins to Gregory and then use his fingers to count. Eventually, he said, "Twenty men and boys, my lord."

"Boys?"

"Those like Aethelstan and Alfred."

"And weapons?"

"Tools, mainly, my lord: billhooks, hatchets, axes, most men have an axe. A couple, like Ethelred, have a sword."

"Do we have archers?"

"Some of the boys can use a bow and Gurth was an archer but he is old now."

I was silent and Edward said, "I am new to war, my lord, but that does not sound enough."

"It is not. We need a weaponsmith, a bowyer and a fletcher. Those are skilled crafts and I cannot see us finding any before danger arrives. I fear, Edward, that you and I will have to bear the burden of fighting." Edward's silence was eloquent. "It is not as bad as it sounds, Edward. In my experience if you can discourage an attacker early on then they often seek easier targets but, no matter what the case, we have to do what we must. We cannot abandon the village. We have a duty to protect it."

The journey back was longer than the one south but we arrived in good time and the animals were secured in willow-bound pens. We had, as yet, no home for Gregory. After introducing him to Benthe and the servants I was at a loss. Edward saw my dilemma and offered a solution, "My lord, my chamber is large enough for two. If Father Gregory does not mind sharing a chamber until we can build him a home…"

I looked at Gregory who beamed, "I would sleep on a floor so long as I can serve God. I thank you for your kind offer, Master Edward, and willingly accept."

There was little point in being coy or secretive and so, while we ate I told them of my fears and plans. "The English to the north of us and, perhaps, some of their Scottish allies will seek to make mischief. We need to make this manor a fort. There is neither a wall nor is there a ditch but the latter would be useful to prevent the flooding Lars told me that the manor suffers. We will spend a week making a good start on the ditch. We plant the spoil with whatever wood there is. We use hazel, willow, as well as brambles and wild roses. We make a barrier around the ditch that will slow down an attacker. If we make life hard they may seek other targets. We will make a bridge to cover the ditch." I saw them nodding. "We also need to build a home for Father Gregory and a chapel."

"That is not necessary, my lord. There are more urgent matters."

I smiled, "I am not being altruistic Father Gregory. I thought to build your chapel and home adjacent to the stables. We can then make a small wall to join that to the hall and we have a second line of defence."

He nodded, "I can see that you have studied war, my lord."

"Let us say that I was younger than Alfred here when I first went to war and with my friends we helped to take a castle. If you know how to attack then it is easier to make your defences. I fear that we will all have to work hard and I will also need to speak to the men."

Father Gregory said, "Today is Friday, my lord. We work tomorrow but what say I hold a service on the folk land on Sunday? I can meet those to whom I shall minister and you can speak with them. I do not mind holding a service in the open air. Our Good Lord did so."

Benthe nodded her approval, "And I know that would please those in the two villages, my lord. Having a priest is a comfort. Many of the old died without the comfort of a priest to give absolution."

"Good, then all is settled. Tomorrow, we rise early and begin to labour as we have never worked before."

Benthe said, "And I will go amongst the villagers and tell them of the plans for Sunday."

My prayers that night were the most earnest for many years. When I had prayed before Senlac my thoughts had been on me. Now I had the souls of Eisicewalt to worry about too.

The next day we began early. I used my sword to mark out the line of the ditch. The priority was to get the ditch dug and worry about the planting of the timber later. I also marked out the foundations for the chapel and the wall. That done I stripped to the waist and the eight of us began to dig the ditch. The mound of earth grew as we moved our way around the hall. My back soon complained. Father Gregory was a revelation. I had seen his muscled back in York Minster but now he dug like two men. When we stopped for an ale break and honey cakes I asked him his story.

He smiled and held out his hands, "Aye, these are not the hands of a priest, are they? I was an orphan taken in by monks at St Mary's Abbey in York. The abbot decided that we needed to have a place further north where monks could reflect beyond the temptations of York. It was close to Kirkby Moorside. The church was called St Gregory's and I was named after the saint. I went there and laboured for ten years building the church and the cells for the monks. When the work was done I returned to St Mary's where I was ordained." He shook his head, "I am not sure they ever thought I would be a monk. I cannot write well and my hand is better suited to hammering in nails than spending hours copying beautiful pictures. The archbishop thought I was too rough to be a priest and he made my life hard. I took it as a penance from God to make me a better priest. It was Belisarius who saw my potential. When I was loaned to the Minster to help with the building of the tomb he spoke of you and said we would get along. Thus far he has been proved to be correct. This feels like the home I never had."

At noon Ethelred appeared with a spade in his hand, "Mistress Benthe told me what you planned, my lord. As you now have a priest, perhaps labouring next to such a holy man might help to save my soul. Besides, hard work might rid my body of the effects of the drink."

The extra man made all the difference and by the end of the day, the ditch had been laid out halfway around the hall. When we finished laying it out there would still be many days of work left to make it an obstacle. The foundations for the chapel, Father Gregory's home and the wall would need far more work. When Ethelred had arrived he had brought with him a couple of hares he had trapped. He did not dine with us but Benthe gave him a pot of the stew she had made and a freshly baked rye loaf. He was a happy man. Having a priest say Grace and bless the food made it taste better somehow and the pot was completely cleaned by the time we had finished. The more useful bones had been kept and would be cleaned and made into needles and other tools. We wasted nothing.

Father Gregory was up so early that had we had a church bell it would have sounded Lauds. He went to the common, the folk land so that he would be there before any came. We rose and ate a quick breakfast before we marched in procession down to the open-air church. It was Sunday and we all wore our best. Birgitte's hair was plaited and Alfred and Aethelstan had been groomed by their mother until they complained.

There were many people there already. I saw that Father Gregory was to the side and it was clear that he was hearing confession. It had been many months since most people had been able to confess. When he saw me he made the old woman he was listening to his last confession. He stood and held up the cross he had brought from York. He did not speak in Latin. He had told me that while the archbishop might not approve he wanted this first service to be one that involved the people. "When we have a church, then I will use the liturgy. What we do here, my lord, is unique. Let us make up our own rules."

I saw now why the abbot had not known what to do with this priest. He was a free thinker and not bound by rules from Rome.

Father Gregory spoke well and the service made us smile and think at the same time. When he finished, he said, "When Sir Richard has spoken to you then I will hear more confessions. From tomorrow I will be at the manor where any of you may speak with me," he smiled, "However, there will be a cost. You shall need to labour." He gestured, "Sir Richard."

I was tall enough so that all could see me. "I have spoken with all of you and you know that I have plans for Eisicewalt. Events, however, have conspired to make me alter those plans. The Sherriff of Yorkshire believes that men will come from the north and try to cause mischief. I am making the hall into a fort. When danger comes then all of you can bring your families and animals into its walls. I have weapons and each Sunday from now on, when Father Gregory's service is over, we will hold an old-fashioned wapentake. The men of Eisicewalt will learn to fight as one." I looked at the faces and saw no dissension. "I do not ask this of you, I demand it. I shall lead you in battle but I do not intend to die. I want the men of Eisicewalt to become feared by our enemies. What say you?"

To my delight and relief, they all cheered. I turned to Edward, "Take our men and use the manor cart to fetch the weapons." As they headed off I said, "Bring whatever weapons you have and we will spend an hour or so today getting to see what we can do."

We did not have enough swords to go around. In fact, we had but five for I had given two to my pueros. However, by giving daggers and spears we ensured that everyone had a weapon. Ethelred came with his shield, sword and helmet. He no longer looked like a man at death's door but a warrior who would hasten his enemies to theirs. Edward had brought out mail, helmets and shields. I wanted things kept simple.

"If an enemy comes to take what is ours then we shall fight from behind the walls of my hall. Spears will be the order of the day and I want every man to go to my woods and cut himself a good length of ash for his spear. Until we can find spearheads they will be fire-hardened. I want every boy," the boys who were not part of the wapentake stood to one side looking enviously at the weapons in the hands of their fathers and brothers, "to get as many stones as they can for with their slings they will be our best and strongest defence." It was the right thing to say and they all swelled with pride at the compliment. "If we have to fight in a battle, and that day may come, then we fight as one and that is what we shall practise this day. We will use a wedge."

I saw Ethelred and some of the older warriors nod their approval. Others looked blank. "We will take it step by step. Edward, stand behind me to my left." He did so. "Ethelred to my right." He looked surprised but pleased. I was counting on the old memories coming back to the warrior. I then looked for the older warriors who had shields and placed the next three behind Edward and Ethelred. I had my three men along with Aethelstan and Alfred at the rear. If they were disappointed it could not be helped, I would explain later. I did not think we would use this formation but its importance, as my grandfather had explained to me, was in the discipline it taught.

"Those of you with spears poke them out so that we are like a hedgehog. If the fox comes to take us he will find he has to break our spines first. Next, we need to march as one." I remembered my training and how some men did not know right from left. I turned so that I could see them and I began to beat the pommel of my sword against my shield. As I did, I shouted, "Sword foot stamp. Shield foot stamp." It took some time for them to get into the beat. Edward and Ethelred helped me by banging their own shields. "Keep stamping." I retook my place. "On my command, we march forward using our sword foot." We banged and then I shouted, "March!" I knew I had the easier task for there was no one before me but I prayed that the others would not trip. I counted forty steps before I shouted, "Halt!"

I turned and saw a grinning wedge behind me. They were together and they all cheered.

"That was well done. Now let us form a single line, a shield wall and when I shout '*wedge*' I would have you take up your positions in the wedge." The shield wall went well but when I gave the command it took longer than I would have liked to reform into a wedge. I was patient. I saw Ethelred scowling but we had made such progress that I forgave the errors. By the time the sun was at its zenith, they could manage the formation easily. Stomachs were rumbling and men were hungry. I dismissed them. Benthe and our servants had gone back to the hall for they did not need Father Gregory's ministrations. They could see him any time. When we reached the hall there was hot food waiting for us.

There was an ebullient mood around the table although when Aethelstan addressed the problem of them being at the rear it cast a slight damper on the mood, "Why, my lord, were the five of us at the rear. Do you not trust us?"

"Quite the contrary. You five will have the benefit of daily training and by the time your skills are needed then you will be the best men in the company. Edward, Ethelred and I will be the edge but you five will be the backbone that holds the rest steady. You will be the best armed and will stop men fleeing." I saw the smiles that told me I had said the right words.

Father Gregory arrived halfway through and he had a glow about him. "I know why I was sent here. The people need a priest. There are babies that need to be christened and marriages that need to be blessed. I have heard more confessions in one morning than in my life thus far." He began to eat and after a couple of mouthfuls said, "My lord, I know that it is presumptuous of me but we need a chapel sooner rather than later. I cannot hear confessions in a field when the snow falls and the wind whistles."

I nodded, "I know that Sunday is a day of rest but if you are willing, Father Gregory, you and I can labour."

Lars said, "And so can we."

In the event, more than half of the men in the village came to help us when they saw what we did. By the end of that first Sunday, we had the foundations for the house, chapel and wall completed and we had found stones for the base of the walls. As lord of the manor, I could not have had a better day and I just hoped that any attack would wait until we had our defences up. I felt more optimistic than I had a right to considering we were the Norman limb just waiting to be chopped off.

Chapter 9

We also had a stroke of luck. When we were searching the outbuildings, we came across what had been a sort of armoury when the manor was used as a hunting lodge. The door to the store had seized up and we had to break it down. Inside we found a tangle of spiders' webs and rotting covers. Underneath the covers we found treasure. There were half a dozen boar spears, twenty javelins and four bows. There were also fifty hunting arrows. They had obviously been from the time it had been a royal hunting lodge. I kept four javelins and four boar spears but gave the rest to the men who trained with me each Sunday. The difference it made went beyond what might have been expected. It was as though I had given them a mystical sword that had lain long forgotten in the ground. Our training reflected that improvement.

While not every man in the village helped to build our defences, every one of them gave some time during the week and even the women came to do what they could. They stripped branches from the stakes for the palisade. The smaller branches we did not use were then made into faggots for their fires. We wasted nothing. Even Ethelred joined in, but I asked him to use his time wisely. "I would have you estimate the animals on my land. How many can we cull? And while you count them look for signs of enemies scouting and approaching." I did not think that they would have begun yet but it is better to be forewarned.

"Yes, my lord."

Such was the keenness of everyone to have things completed that we took to working after dark. In a perfect world, we would have built the chapel from stone but that would have taken time, not to mention a mason. We used timber from my wood as well as wattle and daub. The only stone we used was the huge boulder that we uncovered when digging out the ditch. It was almost as tall as Birgitte but there was a natural bowl at the top and when we discovered it Father Gregory took it as a sign from God. "This shall be the font, my lord. It is perfect and coming from your land can only be a good thing."

It took a month of the hardest work I could remember but we finally finished the ditch which was five feet deep. The crude palisade was taking shape but it would not have pleased my brother. It was uneven, however I was happy with it. It was a barrier and that was what was needed. The gate was an important piece of construction. We used trees for the posts at the side and we had a small fighting platform over the gates themselves. The gates were well made and I had Lars and Drogo make a sturdy pair of locking bars to secure them. When we had the time we would have two small towers but for the present it ensured we could bar our gates and fight behind our walls. When the chapel and Father Gregory's humble house were finished Father Gregory was happy. It would hold just four or five people but it did not matter. The priest could hear confession and I could use it as my own chapel when the church we planned was built.

Ethelred had seen no signs of any scouts but he had established that there were too many deer. "There are three stags, my lord. The older one looks to have a broken antler. He will find it hard to win a fight but he might injure a younger one. We should hunt him. There are also three females that look either to be injured or too old to bear young. If we were to hunt them now we would have food for at least three months."

I looked at the palisade, "When we have finished the palisade and a gate, if we are not attacked, then we will hunt."

"Good. We will make a stronger herd by doing so."

I had not asked him about the wild boar but his silence on the matter meant he had yet to make a decision. If you employed a gamekeeper, it was as well to trust him.

With the chapel built and the font installed, Father Gregory took on the task of christening all the babies and children that needed it. I was asked by many of the mothers to be present and I was honoured. The children and babies all had names but, in the christening, most of the boys had the name Richard added. I was flattered.

The men's training had come on apace. Whilst we still had but three archers the eight boy slingers had shown great skill. They were adept at hitting pigeons in flight. It was the hunting of pigeons that set my mind to thinking and I had a dovecot constructed. The same boys that hunted pigeons fetched eggs from the nests of doves. They took just one egg from each nest and we reared them. It would not yield results for a year or so but we would have a supply of both eggs and meat in the future.

When we went to hunt I took Edward as well as Aethelstan and Alfred. I was not confident enough in my skill with a bow so I took spears. I had a boar spear as well as three throwing spears. Ethelred also had a boar spear and a throwing spear. The other three just had fire-hardened spears. I hoped that they would not be needed. I let Ethelred instruct the three of them and he impressed me with his patience.

"You need to be silent. We shall not need speed. Watch where you place your feet and make not a noise. I will lead us so that they do not smell us, and their eyesight is not the best. If we are charged then stand behind his lordship and me. Hold your spears before you and pray that God watches over you."

We headed into the woods with the three of them behind Ethelred and me. I was in his hands for these were his woods. Even when he had been at his lowest ebb he had clearly been able to hunt and keep himself fed. He had ascertained the wind direction and knew where the animals were to be found. It was not yet rutting season and so the first target, the stag with the damaged antler would be alone. The females could wait. Ethelred had told me before we had left that the old stag had a favourite place to graze. There was a bramble bush that he found attractive and we headed for it. I heard him before we actually saw him. His head was brushing the bushes as it sought those berries that had ripened the most at the top of the bush.

Ethelred nodded to me and stepped to one side. I was the lord of the manor and it was my right to have the first attempt at a kill. I handed the boar spear to Edward and two of the throwing spears to the two boys. We moved closer and I heeded the advice given to the three by Ethelred. I watched where each foot was placed before I moved on. I saw the stag and he was clearly enjoying what would be his last meal. I stopped at the edge of the thin saplings that had grown up around the rowan tree. I set my feet apart and lifted the spear. I hurled it. The old stag had not survived this long without acquiring instincts that kept him alive. Even as the spear headed towards him he lifted his head and then raced at the threat. The result was that whilst the spear hit the beast it was not a killing strike. It would slow him and in the fullness of time he would bleed out but he could still kill. Ethelred was no coward and he stepped before me and held the boar spear so that the stag, lowering its head in an attempt to kill us, ran onto the spear. Such was its power that it knocked Ethelred to the ground. It raised its antlers to finish off the fallen man. In an instant, I drew a sword and as the stag lowered its dying head to gut Ethelred, hacked through its neck. It lurched to the side and did not pin my gamekeeper to the ground.

I sheathed my sword and held out my arm which he took. He shook his head, "I owe you my life, my lord. You made a good strike but he was a cunning old beast." He patted the head, "You had a good death, old friend."

I turned to the other three, "Gut the beast and then cut a sapling so that we can carry it hence."

Having taken the head, I carried it and Ethelred took the guts. The three boys struggled under the weight of the carcass. The meat would need to be cooked slowly but it promised a tasty feast. It was still early when we reached my hall and we hung the carcass in the pantry. Benthe would put the guts on to cook. We returned to the wood.

This time the boys were better prepared. As we neared the woods Ethelred said, "You have seen how it is done. You each have a throwing spear. When his lordship throws then you can do so too. You will recognise the prey for they are old deer and two of them limp. Throw true and if you can, give them a quick death, but his lordship has shown that his hands and his sword are the best of executioners." I took the compliment.

This time we sought a herd. There was a dominant stag watching but we could smell the herd before he could smell us. The animals were in a clearing. The three old animals were easy to spot and I chose my target, I picked the nearest one favouring a hind leg. It looked as though she had been injured and the wound had not healed. The range was not perfect, they would be twenty feet from us, but with four throwing spears I hoped for some success.

I was aware that this time I was flanked by the brothers and my squire. I balanced my feet, pulled back and threw. I was lucky. The spear entered the side of the doe's head and she fell

113

like a stone. Edward's spear hit her flank. The two brothers also hit the target they had chosen, the other limping doe, but neither were killing strikes. The stag led the rest of the herd away while the injured deer took off through the trees.

Ethelred shouted, "Follow the blood!"

The blood trail was clear. The doe was leading us away from the herd. Even in her dying, she was trying to save the others. We hurtled down the path after her. I say path but she did not bother with the path and instead just fled through the undergrowth and we followed the newly created trail. Inevitably that slowed her down. By the time we reached her, she was almost out on her feet. Ethelred took his boar spear and said, "You have had a good life." He thrust the spear into her ear and she died quickly.

It took longer to gut the animals and put a stake through them. By the time we reached the hall, it was dark. Ethelred took a haunch of venison along with the hearts, kidneys and liver as his share of the kill. He was a happy man. The three animals hung in the larder and a pot collected the blood. It would be used to enrich stews. There was no haste to butcher them. They were all old beasts and needed to be hung. Benthe's sons were full of the hunt as it was their first real kill. They had brought pigeons down as boys but this was different. I saw a change in them; they were moving from being youths to men. The hunt had tired me. I was not used to walking so much but I felt better for the exercise.

I was woken early, before Lauds, and it was Ethelred who knocked on the door. He had with him one of the village boys. "My lord, I am sorry to wake you early but this boy came to my house an hour ago. Tell your tale, Egbert."

The boy was no more than eight summers and he wiped his nose with the back of his hand before he spoke. "My lord, last night I was out hunting roosting birds in the small wood to the north of Lessimers. I had sneaked out and my mother knew not that I had gone. I enjoy the excitement of being out in the night. I had taken two birds when I smelled woodsmoke. I travelled through the woods and it was there I saw the camp. There are warriors camped four miles from here."

"You are sure? This is not a dream you have had?"

"No, my lord. I heard them speak and there were Scottish voices mixed with the English."

I looked at Ethelred. He knew the boy better than me and he nodded, "My lord, Egbert is a truthful boy. He barely knew his father who also fell at Gate Fulford but he has his father's nose. I went with the boy and although I did not see the camp I saw sparks in the sky from their fires and smelled their smoke."

I took a decision. Edward had risen as had Aethelstan, Alfred and Father Gregory and I gave my orders. "Rouse the villagers and have them bring their animals and families within these walls. If this is harmless then I will live with the criticism but it is better I am laughed at than we lose a single person." They nodded, "Ethelred, Egbert do the same. This was well done, Egbert, and we all owe you a debt."

They raced off and I turned to see Benthe and Birgitte, "The enemy may be at the gate. I will rouse Lars and the men. I have sent for the villagers. We shall be overcrowded for a while."

She smiled, "We planned for this and we are ready. Come Birgitte, today you shall be my right hand."

I woke Lars and the others. "The women and the children will be housed in the barn. When the men come put them on the ramparts. The boys who cannot see over the stakes can climb on the roof. Spread the spare weapons out and prepare yourselves."

"Aye, my lord."

I went to my chamber and dressed for war. The padded gambeson had not been needed for some time, nor had the mail. I slipped them on and then my scabbards and belt. I ensured the mittens covered the back of my hand. I pulled on my boots and then donned my arming cap and coif. I carried my helmet and let my ventail hang. I grabbed my shield and headed to the gate. The gates were open and I used the ladder to ascend to the small fighting platform. I placed my shield next to the wooden wall and hung my helmet from one of the stakes. Already those who lived nearest to the hall were pouring through the open gates.

"Head for the barn. Men and boys, join me when you have seen to your families,"

I knew that, thanks to the battle at Gate Fulford, there were fewer men than women in Eisicewalt. There were, however, boys and youths who would grow into warriors. If we survived this visitation then it would make us stronger for the future.

There was silence as the people passed beneath me. It was new and fearful to them all and I could understand that. By the time the sky began to lighten, the last few were heading through the gates. Ethelred was the last through and he had with him his haunch of venison and weapons. He stopped and looked up. "The village is empty. I took all that I had in my hovel, my lord." He held up his haunch of venison, "They shall not have this."

"Good. I want you at the north wall." I wanted Ethelred's sturdiness there.

The enemy would come down through the village and the two places that were vulnerable were the north wall and the road wall. I cupped my hands and said, "Lars, watch the south wall. Drogo, take some men and guard the east wall. Gandálfr, join Ethelred on the north wall. Alfred and Aethelstan, you are with me. For the rest spread yourselves out along every wall. Edward, saddle your horse."

"Aye, my lord."

Father Gregory arrived and I saw that he had strapped on a sword, "And me, my lord?"

"I would have your comforting presence everywhere but as that cannot be, choose your own ground."

Edward appeared below me and I shouted, "Open the gates." As the gates were opened I said, "Edward, ride to York and warn the Sherriff of the danger." I paused, "Do not try to return. Stay in York."

"But I am your squire, my lord."

"And you obey my orders. Now go and ride like the wind."

When the two bars were slammed ominously in place I looked down the ramparts. We really needed a proper fighting platform but the men had a wooden wall behind which they could shelter. If this was an army that was large enough to attack York then they could swat us like flies. All that we could do was to wait and see the danger that would approach.

Benthe and the women brought food and ale to the men and we ate while we watched. I was still chewing when I heard the sound of men. I wiped my mouth and shouted, "Not a stone is to be thrown nor an arrow loosed until I give the command. We stand in silence. I want every man to listen to my words and my commands."

Our Sundays had not been in vain, "Aye, my lord."

We heard the sound of doors being broken as the horde from the north found the first houses. As more light lit the village I saw it reflect from mail. This was an army. There were four men on horses and they were leading a mob. Numbers were hard to ascertain but they were in their hundreds. Our silence had an effect. The faces staring down at them made them quieten. The four riders stopped at the gate and the four men removed their helmets.

"I am Oswiu of Northumbria and we are come to retake the land from the Normans. Join us and York will be our first victory."

I shook my head, "Eisicewalt wants no part in a rebellion that is doomed to failure. We will not halt your progress nor will we join you."

One of the others laughed, "If we chose to we could tear down your flimsy walls and take this ant hill."

I nodded, "Perhaps but then you would lose many of the men you lead. I am a soldier and know that a defended wall will make men bleed."

Oswiu nodded, "He is right. York is our target. Eisicewalt will be here when we are done and we can take this at our leisure." He grinned, "Then we will enjoy the spoils of war."

The army tramped off. I counted the numbers and there were five hundred men. I turned to Father Gregory as the last ones passed, "That is not enough to take York. There must be other armies. We have work to do."

"You heard him, my lord, he will be back."

"I know." I sighed, "What would you have me do? Abandon the people and flee? It will take time to take York, if at all. There will not be five hundred men who march north." I turned and shouted so that all could hear me, "I want ten men to go to the houses and see what mischief they have caused. For the rest, I want stakes cutting and embedding in the ditches. We are almost in a state of siege but I believe that with strong hearts we will prevail."

The gates opened and ten men, armed, I was pleased to see, raced back to their homes. Father Gregory said, "Why did he not attack us when he saw that you were Norman?"

I shook my head, "He did not see a Norman. I spoke in English and he saw neither my helmet nor my shield. My hauberk looked much like his byrnie. They will be curious but it is clear that they come from so far away that they do not know who is lord of the manor. Oswiu is Northumbrian." I saw him take it in and I pointed to the sword he wore, "Could you use that?"

He smiled, "I could swash it about and my arm is strong but if you are asking if I am a swordsman then the answer is no. However, I do not relish being butchered without defending myself. It availed the monks on Lindisfarne little good. Jesus may not wish us to take lives and to turn the other cheek but I still have work to do here and I will do it."

When the men returned they reported that doors had been broken but as most of the things of value had already been removed there was little hurt. I joined my men and we planted stakes in the bottom of the ditch. I had mailed mittens and using my dagger I cut brambles from the hedgerows and used them to cover the stakes. It took time but it made the ditch look shallower and hid the deadly surprise that was there.

At noon we ate. Ethelred's haunch was cooked. Spread amongst the villagers there was little meat in anyone's bowl but there was goodness and we had plenty of bread. Benthe and the women spent all day kneading dough to cook. The smell of cooking bread was as good as a meal and bread would keep us going.

After we had eaten I gathered the men and boys. "This would have been a task for the future but the arrival of our enemies has made the matter urgent. We will build a fighting platform. The road wall and the south wall are the most urgent. I saw from their faces that the concept was unknown to them and so I explained and demonstrated. "The mound in which the palisade is embedded is not flat. We need it to be flat and we need it to be higher so that we can hurl stones over the palisade. We need a timber walkway. The timber is over there." I pointed. "We need to make a firm walkway that will support," I smiled and waved a hand down my hauberk, "a knight wearing mail. The test will be if I can walk safely down it."

By the evening the road wall and south wall had a fighting platform. More soil would be needed to pack beneath but it was a solid enough platform. I arranged three watches. I was the captain of one, Ethelred a second and Lars the third. Aethelstan was with Ethelred and Alfred with me. Drogo and Gandálfr were with Lars. I took the hardest watch, the middle one.

As I sat before my fire Benthe came to me with a beaker, "Here, my lord, a little something I brew. It is made from fermented plums and aged. It will keep you warm this night and give you comfort."

"Thank you." I sipped. It was as though I had put a hot coal in my mouth but it soothed as it went down. "That is a powerful drink."

She nodded and I saw a sad smile at the memory it evoked, "It was Eadwine's favourite. I made a jug a year. None has been drunk since he died and so it is stronger." She turned to leave but paused at the door, "Take care, my lord. We need you to keep us safe. You are young but you are wise. Ethelred says that he would follow you to hell and back and that is a compliment. The only man he ever truly respected was Eadwine."

The powerful brew worked and I fell asleep in the chair. It was Aethelstan who woke me for my duty, "The men are on the walls, my lord. All is quiet."

The night was dark and the only sounds we heard were those of animals hunting in the night. We had a peaceful watch. I woke Lars and took off my mail when I went to bed. We had survived the first night. There was a pattern to our lives as we waited. The men toiled to improve the fighting platform and the women made bread and food. The children tended to the animals and we lived so close that it made us one. I would not have wished the threat of death but the effect was to make the manor united.

Chapter 10

Four days later we heard hooves from the south and I called the men to arms. We stood solidly armed facing the road. To my delight, it was Edward and a man at arms I did not recognise.

"Open the gate."

By the time they had entered, I was in the yard. Edward babbled out his news, "The enemy is defeated, my lord. The Sheriff trounced them. He and his knights are chasing them through the countryside."

Father Gregory dropped to his knees, "Thank the lord."

"You are all safe, my lord?"

"We are."

I looked at the man at arms who dismounted and bowed. "I am Bergil, my lord, and I have a message from Master Belisarius."

I opened the short message,

Sir Richard,

This is Bergil who was one of your brother's men. Due to no fault of his own, he cannot stay in York. This is a good man and he will be loyal to you.

Belisarius

It was an intriguing message but I trusted the cleric.

"Welcome Bergil. Edward, until we can make arrangements he will need to share a room with you. Take him to his new chamber."

They left and I turned my attention to the people inside my manor. Their eyes all looked up to me. I held my hands up for silence but there was really no need. "We have good news from York. Those who promised rebellion and destruction are now dispersed."

There were cheers.

I waited for them to subside and then added a word of warning, "Until men from York arrive to tell us that the roads are clear of danger, we will all live within these walls. Better to have discomfort for a few days than men lose their lives."

I was gratified when both Benthe and Ethelred nodded their approval. They were my means of gauging what I did was right.

"While we are all here we will continue to build the fighting platforms and give some thought to two towers."

We all laboured hard. Bergil stripped to the waist and joined us. At noon, while we ate, I spoke with both Edward and my new man at arms. "Was there danger in York?"

It was Bergil who answered and he shook his head, "Oh, they had numbers but no skill. They tried to take the walls and were soundly beaten back. They left many dead in the river and in the ditch. The new castle at Baile Hill was a surprise to them. His lordship chased them hence. They can still cause mischief, Sir Richard, and I believe that you are right to be cautious. When the earl comes here, and he promised he would, then we will know that the danger has passed."

The message was still close to my shield and I nodded at it, "An intriguing message and I am guessing there is more to it."

He looked at Edward, sighed and nodded, "I have served the earl since before Senlac. I did not serve when you lived at Graville, my lord, and knew not you. You know the captain of the men at arms, Raymond?"

"Raymond of Harfleur?" He nodded, "He was a new man at arms when last I served with my brother."

"He is now a captain. The others who were above him were promoted. I thought he was my friend." He looked at the ground and shifted a couple of pebbles with his foot. "There was a woman in York. She served in the inn called The Saddle and her name was Seara. I found her attractive and we enjoyed our time together. Captain Raymond came one night and seeing her began to court her for she is comely. She was flattered by his words for I have few words to sway the hearts of women and she chose him." He was silent for a while, "That might have been bearable but he began to flaunt his success in front of me and my shield brothers. I could not bear it and I struck him. I was taken before

the earl and I told him my story. I had not been sentenced when
Edward here arrived and then I was called upon to fight. When
the earl took his men to chase the rebels I was left behind and it
was Belisarius who told me that he and the earl had discussed the
problem and the solution seemed to lie with you."

He was silent and I filled the silence, "And for my part, I am
right glad to have another blade here but I need to know that
your heart is with me and not languishing in The Saddle."

"When I give my word, my lord, I keep it. I confess that I am
still smitten by Seara but she has made her choice and I can do
nothing about it." He waved a hand, "You have made a good
start here, my lord."

"And with your help, it will be even better." I pointed to
Ethelred, "He is the other warrior in the village. I would have
you be captain of the first watch tonight. Edward and I will take
the second and Ethelred can take the third."

"I will be ready."

I slept easier that night not least because I now had another
warrior and Edward was safe. When Bergil woke me, it was with
the news that all was quiet. Edward, Alfred and I set our sentries;
there were six of them and then the three of us stood on the
gatehouse. It was the strongest part of our defences but I knew
that it would not resist a determined assault. We peered out into
the darkness. I had stood a night watch before but Edward had
not. This would be a learning experience for him.

He suddenly started and touched my arm. He pointed to the
wood to the west of the village. He hissed, "A movement!"

I nodded and whispered, "A hunting owl. You will learn to
identify such things. Now just watch. The watch will pass slowly
but every minute that you stand a watch will make you a better
warrior."

I knew when it would be time to wake Ethelred and I took a
turn around the new fighting platform a short while before I
needed to do so. It was not a wide platform and I had to edge
around some of the sentries. It was as I did so that I caught sight
of a movement that was not an owl. I stopped and studied the
tree which appeared to have moved despite the fact that there
was no breeze. I kept still and the man I had just passed, Aelfgar,
sensed my stillness and emulated me. We were rewarded when I

saw the figure detach himself from behind the tree and move towards the walls. Another followed him.

I hissed, "Warn the others and stand to."

I hurried back to Edward and Alfred. "There are enemies closing. Go and rouse the men but do so quietly."

They hurried off and I donned my helmet and pulled up my ventail. I fastened it to the helmet and then picked up my shield. There was a throwing spear leaning next to the upright that would, in the fulness of time, become a small tower. Despite my admonition and request for silence, there was noise within the hall as men grabbed weapons and hurried to the walls. It was understandable and I am not sure that those wishing us harm heard it. It could not be helped in any case. The noise as my men ascended the ladders must have alerted those outside the walls for, with a sudden roar, men ran towards the walls which seemed to me, flimsier than they had been. I grabbed the throwing spear and held it horizontally. Edward and Alfred were the first to reach me and I saw that Edward had donned his helmet and Alfred his arming cap. Both held spears. We had raised the bridge over the ditch and secured it to the gate. If they wished to break through then they would have a double obstacle. I glanced down the wall and saw that my archers were now in place. The boys on the roof had no targets for it was dark and so we had to wait until the enemy closed to the ditch.

I saw one warrior, he had no mail but wore a helmet and had a short throwing axe, trying to leap across the ditch. He almost made it but the bank close to the palisade was both steep and slippery. He fell back to be impaled upon the stakes. He did not die immediately but moaned in pain. Of course, he was now a bridge across the stake-strewn ditch but it was one less enemy to fight.

I had the balanced spear ready but I waited as the charging figures rushed at the ditch. Most tried to do as the first had done and leapt. The banks were our ally and they fell back. Not all suffered mortal wounds like the first warrior, some had their legs and feet impaled. Some held shields above them as they struggled to extract themselves. Others managed to pull themselves towards the palisade. The survivors were the targets.

"Use the stones first."

Edward and Alfred were with me along with Absalon, a farmer with a strong arm, and they obeyed me. They took the rocks and threw them down on men who were desperately trying to avoid the traps. I saw the warrior called Oswiu appear. He was mailed and held a shield and an axe. He began to shout orders. "Use the bodies to cross. There are only a handful of warriors within."

His northern voice rallied them and they began to make a more determined effort. From the numbers that I could see our wall was the one they were attacking. I wondered if I could risk pulling men from the other walls. The gatehouse was relatively secure but the walls could be scaled. The dead and dying, although few in number, were the bridges that the men of Northumbria used. With shields before them, the stones were less effective. Soon they would reach the wall and I could see that the dozen men I had on the road wall would be overwhelmed. There had to be thirty or so men trying to get at us.

Bergil appeared, "My lord, I have brought a couple of men from the north wall. Ethelred can hold it."

"Find a place to defend."

"Aye, my lord."

The light from the new sun was beginning to rise behind us. It would be some time before it allowed the slingers to be able to use their slings and the men on the road wall would be hidden in the shadows, but the sun gave us hope. Oswiu must have seen some of us silhouetted against the light for he shouted, "On the gatehouse! Send arrows."

As he did I saw my chance and I hurled the throwing spear. His reactions were slow and he failed to bring his shield around quickly enough. The spear did not kill him but drove into his thigh and he fell back. Three of his men stood around him with shields and the men on the walls cheered. It was a small victory but three good Northumbrian warriors were not attacking the wall while they tended to their leader.

Arrows slammed into the palisade and I pulled my shield around, Edward and Alfred held their shields before them. The stones we had gathered were now gone and both of them did as I did and drew their swords.

I saw a hand on the wall to my left. It had grasped the top of the wall and was pulling the warrior over. In two strides I was there and as his head appeared I hacked through his hand. He fell screaming to the bottom of the ditch.

Oswiu's voice told me that the enemy leader was still alive. He shouted, "Back to the houses and regroup." As the Northumbrians fell back there was a cheer along my walls. My people thought we had won but this was just a respite. It was, however, a time we could use.

"Bergil; go around the walls and find out if we are surrounded. If not then reinforce this wall."

"Aye, my lord. You have a good eye."

"Alfred, go and bring ale for the men. Edward, walk this wall and raise their spirits."

I saw in the growing dawn that there were just six bodies in the ditch. Others, like the one whose fingers I had taken had fled. I wondered if they had brought healers with them. I looked down the fighting platform and could not see any losses. The Northumbrians were in the houses on the other side of the road and I knew that they would be making ladders or improvising items that could be used in an escalade. I peered to the east. The sky was lighter but it would not be a sunny day. The sun would not blind their archers. The night had hidden us but now my men would have to show themselves and would be targets.

Alfred was the first to return and I held out my coistrel for him to fill. He peered over the side of the gatehouse. The dead were lying at unnatural angles. "Your first dead men, Alfred?"

He nodded.

"They are the enemy and would be alive had they not attacked us. Remember that."

A trickle of men appeared, and I pointed my sword to show them where they were to stand. Bergil had not stripped the walls, but the extra six men might make the difference. When Alfred returned with the empty jug he said, "My mother asked if you wanted food to be cooked."

I felt the air. The slight breeze came from the east, "Aye, and tell her to bake bread."

He frowned, "Bake bread, my lord?"

"The ones attacking us have no hot food and the smell of bread will madden them. They failed to take York and fled. They will be starving. It is a small thing but you use everything that you can." He nodded and ran off to the hall. I remembered the taunting of the English by Taillefer. That had worked too but at the cost of my friend's life. I was risking all by taunting my enemy with the smell of baking bread.

Edward stood next to me. "The men are in good heart. Your spear throw worked, my lord."

"I took a chance but I am not as accurate as I should be."

Bergil stood next to me on the other side and took off his helmet, as I had done. The slight breeze was cooling. I slipped the coif down and took off the arming cap to scratch at my itchy head. Bergil still had ale in his coistrel and he drank it. "They outnumber us and they have more warriors than we do."

"Believe me, Bergil, the men on the walls are ten times the warriors they were when I first arrived."

"I was not criticising, my lord, but trying to work out what they will do next." He pointed. The light was glinting off mail, "They will use mailed men protected by shields to get close to the wall. They know that the ditch is filled with traps and will be planning how to avoid injury. The stones from the boys will annoy them only and our arrows will be too few and too ineffective to pierce mail. They will try to take the gate. If you are slain then their victory will be closer."

"What I cannot understand, Bergil, is what they are doing here."

"Saving face. It is a long way north to Durham and Bebbanburg. They lost at York but they will want to have something to take back to show that this attack was not in vain. There is little between here and the river. The earl will be harrying many bands such as this one. The man you hit with the spear may well be seeking to increase his power. The sacking of Eisicewalt may not be like the fall of Rome but it will be a victory."

"Then we shall have to deny them." I desperately wanted to make water but I knew that the moment I left the gate then the enemy would attack. Sure enough, Edward pointed at the movement from the houses opposite and I saw men appear. They had a wedge of mailed men with shields and, behind them the ones without mail carrying ladders and doors taken from the houses. They had improvised bridges.

I cupped my hands, "They come. Slingers, when you have a target you think you can hit then send your stones. Archers, do not waste arrows on the men with mail. Seek flesh."

I donned my arming cap and coif. I slipped on my helmet and fastened it. Then I tied my ventail. I drew a sword and held my shield before me. There were five of us on the gatehouse and the light I saw glinting from the axes told me that they were going to bridge the ditch and destroy the gates. We five were their target. The first stones rattled off helmets. They were not wasted for a stone hitting a helmet could disorientate a warrior and was a most disconcerting experience. Anything that sapped the resolve of our enemies was to be applauded. We did not stop the wedge. An arrow flew from my left and struck a man at the rear. It hit his leg and as he dropped a cheer went up. The man broke off the arrow and tucked in behind the others. These were determined men. Oswiu did not join his warriors. I saw him and two of his oathsworn by the houses. A heavily bandaged leg showed his wound.

When they neared the ditch, the wedge spread and shields were raised to protect the men without mail who carried the doors taken from our houses and were throwing them over the ditch. They put them next to the gates. One of the men was felled by a stone but we did not see the result as the shields closed up. The man at the fore of the wedge had a Danish helmet with a face mask. He raised his axe and shouted, "Forward!" Like my men these had practised moving in a wedge for they kept together even over the shifting, improvised bridges. Stones and arrows were thrown but the shields made a protective cover over the axemen. They had two elements to destroy but without boiling water or fire, we could not harm them.

I turned to Alfred, "I want every man from the east wall and half from the north and south wall. I need your brother as well as Ethelred, Lars, Drogo and Gandálfr. Bring them here."

Bergil asked, "What do you plan, my lord?"

"They will break through, and we can do nothing about it, but we too have practised the wedge. When they charge into the yard they will sense victory and order will go. I intend to meet them with our own wedge."

He nodded, "Without fire or boiling water we can do little else."

"I will wait until the others arrive and we will swap men over. I need Edward, you, Ethelred and Aethelstan at the fore for we have the best mail and weapons. Their best warriors are at the front and if we can kill them then we stand a chance."

As men arrived we swapped over. Bergil, Edward and Alfred were the first to descend. I waved Ethelred and Aethelstan to stand at the gate. I let Ethelred and Bergil organise them. I would be at the fore. Draco joined me at the gate. He had a helmet and a shield. His father had Danish blood and he had inherited good weapons. I said, "You need to make them think that you are me. Keep in the shadows and shout orders. Use Edward's name and others. We shall ignore you."

The young warrior grinned, "It will be an honour, my lord."

Ethelred and Bergil stood next to one another. Lars, Drogo and Gandálfr formed up behind them and Alfred and Aethelstan behind them. It was a small wedge but we were the best that I had. We each had a spear and we stood tightly together. Already I could see light appearing through the gates. We would have to make new gates and a new bridge but they were blunting axes as they tried to hack through the wood. It was a small thing but I would take any kind of hope that saw my manor survive.

"When they come through, I will shout, 'now' and we all move off on our sword legs. We push them into the ditch. There are still traps without bodies and our men on the walls may well have a better chance to use stones and arrows if we can disorder their wedge. Alfred and Aethelstan, you need to push into the backs of the three before you. We go no further than the gate. We become a human barrier."

I heard Draco exhorting everyone but me to do great deeds. He was playing his part well. The slingers and archers were also enjoying success for I heard cheers whenever one struck an opponent. I watched as the axe hacked into the top bar on the gate and knew that it would be a matter of time before the second one was broken. Then the gates would burst asunder and I had to time the attack to perfection. I had never done this before and I wondered if I was ready. It was as doubts assailed my mind that I heard my grandfather's voice in my head, '*You are ready.*' I knew not whence it came but it stiffened my resolve. The second bar broke and the gates were pushed open. The four Northumbrian warriors had no shields up but held axes in their hands. Shields were held aloft by others.

"Now!" I stepped forward and was lunging with my spear even as the shields were lowered. Stones cascaded from the walls and as I speared a Northumbrian axeman I saw two men fall into the ditch. Ethelred and Bergil were warriors. Despite the byrnies worn by the axemen, the sharpened spears sliced through mail rings and into flesh. I pulled back my arm and rammed my spear into the face of the man who was still holding his shield aloft. My shield punched at the man next to him as Bergil's spear gutted him. We were at the gate and I shouted, "Hold!"

The bows and slings now had targets and men fell. Two Northumbrians, both wearing byrnies, ran at me. A sword sliced through my spear and I rammed the stump at him. Dropping the useless weapon I drew a sword as a second sword scored a line along my hauberk. Ethelred's spear was ready and he struck the man so hard that the spear emerged from his back. My sword came down to hack into the neck of the other Northumbrian. The survivors retreated a little but presented a solid wall of shields. My wedge was too small to take on such an enemy and if we fell back then the gate would be lost.

It was then I heard the horn. I was the only one who recognised it. It was the horn used by the lord of Graville. It was my brother. I saw Northumbrians looking over their shoulders at the sound of the horn and the drumming of the hooves. The Sherriff of Yorkshire had just forty men with him but they were all mailed as well as mounted on the finest of horses and they crashed into the disordered line of Northumbrians who saw victory snatched away from them in a heartbeat. The attack disintegrated. We had slain their best warriors and Oswiu and those that could, went to their horses. I doubted that they would escape as my brother's men were mounted on the best of horses. Chasing down fleeing men was a sport and not war.

Eisicewalt had been saved. We had lost our gates but we had survived. We cheered. The attack broke the enemy who simply fled. Most did not manage to escape. The slingers and archers on my walls took their toll and my brother's men had their vengeance for the attack on York.

As my brother and his horsemen chased the routed rebels I shouted my orders, "Clear the dead from the ditch and salvage whatever you can from them." This was an opportunity not to be missed. There were byrnies, axes, spears and swords. We could use all of them and the next time danger threatened then we would have the means to repulse the enemy more effectively.

I saw that when the horsemen returned, after half an hour, my nephews Robert and Gilbert now carried my brother's banner and horn. I was assisting my men to hurl the bodies, stripped of anything we could use onto a pile. The pyre was at an unused corner of the field opposite my gates.

We stopped when my brother reined in, he dismounted and held his arm out for me. "Richard, your timely warning meant that our enemies had a warm welcome. I thank you."

"And is the threat gone, my lord? Can my people return to their homes?"

"They can. We arrived this morning for we had camped just to the northwest having slaughtered one band. These are the last." He turned, "Captain Raymond, take the heads from the leaders and have them stuck on the ramparts as a warning."

I gestured towards the hall, "Would you care for food and ale?"

He shook his head, "We will return to York. Although we sent the enemy hence easily enough they still managed to damage the walls. This attack has shown me the dangers. I am confident that we can hold out for a year if we are attacked again. I shall send that message to the king." He put his arm around my shoulder and led me to a quiet corner, "Bergil is a good man, Richard. I was loath to lose him but you know that there can be no dissension in a body of oathsworn."

"I am grateful, my lord, for we have few enough warriors as it is. The weapons from the dead will make us stronger next time."

"Good. I know that you are isolated here and when the king made his gift, I feared for you. You have shown both maturity and skill. When the king has dealt with Eadric in the west and the new threat, Hereward, in the east, then he will cast his eye here and finish the job that Bishop Odo started but did not finish." He had returned to his horse and he mounted. He took off his helmet so that his face could be seen and shouted, "Men of Eisicewalt you have shown that you are truly warriors and I thank you. My brother here has shown that he too can lead and I see this as the union between the men of England and of Normandy. Farewell."

The column of men clattered out. The heads of the leaders were grisly reminders of the battle. I decided I would leave them for just two days and remove them. My people all looked to me as I turned, "Eisicewalt has shown what it can do and, like the Sherriff, I am proud. You may all return to your homes. I know that much will need to be repaired. If I can help, then please ask. When time allows we will repair the damage to the walls." I waved a hand towards the pile of bodies. "When the dead are burned there will be a blackened piece of earth. Remember that we were innocent in all of this. These Northumbrians chose to attack us and none should feel any guilt for their deaths. We now have a chapel and, over the next months Father Gregory shall have his church. When it is built, we will hold a service to celebrate this victory."

Everyone cheered. As I headed into my yard, I saw that Bergil, Ethelred, Father Gregory and Edward were standing together. As I approached, they bowed. Bergil said, "The Sherriff was right, my lord, you are a leader, but we all know that we were lucky. Had they attacked every wall then we might have been in trouble."

"I know but I also saw in every man on our walls, determination. We now have mail, helmets, swords, spears and axes. Bergil, your task is to put them in the armoury so that we can sort them. Ethelred, I would have you and Edward put faggots near the dead and burn them. The wind is still from the east and will take the stink away from the manor."

"My lord, I would go with them. I will say words over them. They were ill-led and misguided but someone should speak at their passing."

"You have a good heart, Father Gregory, of course. I shall go within and disrobe."

As I passed the men and their families returning to their homes, I was warmly greeted. I was the lord of the manor and none would attempt to embrace me but I saw that they wanted to. They thought of me as one of them. The smiles on their faces and the warmth of their words touched me more than anything. I would not have wished for the attack but the result had made Eisicewalt and its people stronger.

The hall had been emptied. Benthe, Birgitte and the two serving girls were making it ordered once more. I smiled, "Benthe, I saw little of you in the battle but I know that you held the people together, I thank you."

"My lord I saw you, more than once, alone on the gatehouse. You showed no fear and you inspired everyone. It is we who thank you. Would you have food?"

"I will change from this martial mail and then I will be ready." I smiled, "I could eat a horse… with the skin on."

Chapter 11

The months leading up to Christmas would always be busy ones, but the repairs to the damaged homes meant that there were not enough hours in the day. There was urgency amongst all the people for they had seen how close we had come to disaster. Father Gregory and I decided that we would delay the building of the church until the next summer. There was not enough time to build it in the shortened days of winter. While my farm labourers harvested and planted and Ethelred watched out for game, the five of us worked to repair the gates. We were lucky that the Northumbrians had not tried to destroy the hinges. They still functioned and we soon repaired the actual gates. Where we had to begin anew was with the two barring poles and the bridge. It was Edward who conceived the idea of two metal eyelets on the bridge and two more on the gatehouse. It would allow us to pull up and lower the bridge from above. We also used some of the damaged metal we had recovered from the dead to stud the underside of the bridge. Bergil pointed out that the metal would blunt axes. The work helped the five of us to become as one. Bergil still brooded about the way he had been treated in York but saw, thanks I think to Father Gregory's council, that he now had a better life and a chance of position. He still pined for Seara but knew that she was beyond him. He threw himself into making the three young warriors into men. Edward was almost a man but Bergil gave him things I could not for I was the lord of the manor. They grew close and Aethelstan and Alfred began to look upon the new warrior as some sort of favourite uncle. It also helped that Ethelred and Bergil bonded from the start. It was as though they were brothers separated at birth. When Ethelred visited to drop off birds or the game he had hunted, the two of them would chatter like magpies. It was good for them both.

I also found time to ride to Malton. The attacks had delayed my acquisition of sheep. I rode with Edward, my pueros and Lars to the farmer I was told had spare sheep. Malton was the smaller manor but neither it nor its neighbour, Norton, had a lord of the manor. Ethelbert was a good farmer and had a large flock. He and the villages had not been touched by the attacks and he happily sold me a tup and twenty young sheep. They were a hardier variety than the ones I had already and would improve my flock. He was happy not to have to have such a large flock over winter and my gold was more than welcome. It took time for us to drive them home and we did not reach there until dark and they were penned.

This would be my first Christmas in the hall and both Benthe and Father Gregory were determined that it would be a celebration that would live long in the memory. They decided that it would be a fitting reward for me. It coincided with Ethelred's news that the old boar, he called him Caesar, had been hurt by a younger boar in a fight for supremacy over the herd. Ethelred told me that the old boar would not last the winter. "He does not deserve to starve to death and die alone. We will honour him by hunting him. By Christmas, his flesh will have tenderised. We would dine well."

I was happy to hunt. I left Lars and the others to finish collecting the last of the crops from the fields and use the bullocks to plough the furrows for the winter barley and oats, and the six of us prepared to hunt. This time we all had boar spears. Although the old boar was injured he could still move quickly enough and had tusks that could tear the guts from a man. I remembered the hunt in Graville with the Earl of Mercia and his sons. The hunting of the stag and the deer had been good preparation for the three young ones and with Bergil's arm and eye we were better prepared. We came upon the young boar and the herd first. We gave them a wide berth.

Ethelred said, "Caesar still likes to graze close to the sows." He chuckled, "He has the optimism of an old man. He will not be far."

We three older ones were at the fore with the three youngsters backing us up. I was on the right and Bergil was on the left. Ethelred, the hunter, was the tip of our arrow. I held the boar spear in two hands. Ethelred had described the size of the beast and the three of us were under no illusions. It would take a combination of all of us to take him down.

It was Caesar who initiated the attack. These were his woods and had been his domain. We were the intruders and he launched himself at Ethelred. He might have been injured but his cunning had kept him hidden until the last moment. Ethelred held his ground and rammed the boar spear into the mouth of the boar. I plunged my spear into the shoulder. Bergil dropped to one knee and drove his spear into the belly of the beast. I am not sure which one killed the boar but it expired at Ethelred's feet.

Ethelred put his hand on the head of the boar, "You had a good death my friend and you left many young, we thank you."

The six of us were as excited as children given their first taste of honey cakes. We rammed the ash pole through its mouth and out of its rear. It took four to lift it. Alfred and I carried the spears as we headed back to the hall. As we walked Ethelred said, "We need to gut and skin it as soon as we are back, my lord. It is so big that I would suggest we split it in two. We will need to make a larder that is secure from rats. It would be a shame to share it with rodents."

"I am in your hands, Ethelred. We shall feast well on the offal tonight. I would have you and Bergil join us."

Benthe had made a fresh batch of ale and she knew how to cook. The offal was so rich that we needed to serve it with both beans and greens. It was a feast and the evening was a merry one. Bergil seemed to have put Seara behind him, at least for the evening. I saw Father Gregory, who always dined with us, watching him as he ate. Father Gregory was a most perceptive man.

Benthe brought in one of our favourite desserts. She had used windfall apples along with the last of the blackberries and topped them with a mixture of honey, oats and rye flour and cooked them in the bread oven. As she spooned it out, she said, "My lord, how long does Bergil have to sleep with the horses?" For the last day or so Bergil had chosen to sleep in the stables. I think he felt he was intruding upon Edward.

Bergil had enjoyed the ale and had a sense of humour, "Why, have the horses complained to you, Mistress Benthe?"

As we laughed, she rolled her eyes, "It is not right that a warrior like Bergil lives in a stable while my sons, barely youths, live in the hall."

The two youths lost their smiles. I knew she meant no offence to her sons but they took it that way.

Bergil shook his head, "When the spring comes we shall build the church. With his lordship's permission, we will build a small warrior hall at the same time. There will come a time when Sir Richard takes a bride and then Edward, as well as Aethelstan and Alfred will need new chambers. Does that satisfy?"

Benthe looked at me, "Do you plan on taking a bride, my lord?"

Her bold question took me by surprise and I evaded it, "We will do as Bergil says and build a small hall. There is another gap we can fill and make our hall more secure."

Benthe gave me a look that told me she had not been satisfied with my answer.

We also had a couple of old animals to slaughter. The sheep I had bought from Malton meant we could slaughter two old ewes and preserve their meat. Along with the venison we had kept from the first hunt we now had enough meat to keep us going until Christmas. After Christmas, we would eat poorer fare. As October drew to a close we gathered all the leaves and the bones we had used to make the soups we had enjoyed and we made a bone fire. The ash, added to the remains of the dead Northumbrians, would be spread on the fields. Gradually, the soil would become more fertile. Lars and my other two labourers still trained each day with us, but they were farmers and their hearts were not in warrior work. The attack had made them aware that they needed to be able to fight but also that their work on the manor was equally important. I was lucky in the men I led.

Bergil no longer ate with us. That was his choice. He told us that he didn't like to impose. Father Gregory also chose to eat with Lars and our workers. They got on. It was during the day when I got the chance to speak to my captain of arms. That was almost a joke as he only had two youths to command but I knew that the future might bring more men.

"We need a weaponsmith, my lord."

I nodded. My hauberk still needed to be repaired and we had old weapons that could be reused. Having horses also meant that we needed a blacksmith or farrier more. "We will need to keep an eye open for one but they are skilled trades. I am not sure that there is a smith closer than York."

He nodded, glumly, "And why would a smith choose to leave York where there would be plenty of trade to come here where there would not be as much profit."

"You lived in York. How many smiths were there?"

"The earl had a weaponsmith, Baldwin. He lived in the castle. There was a Dane, Bacsegh who tended to deal with those of Viking blood who lived in York and then there was Uhtred the Saxon. He made good weapons, but he also was a farrier and could turn his hand to making farm implements; he and his sons had the best forge."

"Then, when next I visit with my brother I will approach the three of them and see if I can persuade any to come here."

Bergil looked doubtful, "Have you gold, my lord?"

"I do but it is in Caen." I had thought of returning to Caen to pick it up but, at best, it would mean a three-month absence from Eisicewalt and that I could not afford, not until the land was safe for me to leave. I was not poor but neither could I afford to throw my money around. The weapons we had taken were a case in point. We divided the weapons and mail into those that could be used and those that needed repair. There was more that needed to be repaired than we could use. We distributed the usable war gear on the second Sunday after the fight. I ensured that Aethelstan, Alfred and Edward had first choice as well as Ethelred. Bergil was well-equipped and needed nothing. The result was that more than half of our men now had a helmet, a shield, a spear and a sword. Everyone benefitted from the encounter. The slingers were given daggers. To the boys, they were possessions prized beyond money.

By the time November ended, the weather had become depressingly wet and cold but, on the more positive side, the houses had all been repaired and even improved. Ethelred no longer had a home with a leaky roof. The other interesting fact was that more than half of the women in the village were expecting babies. Perhaps it was the close encounter with death, I know not, but it meant our manor would grow.

As Christmas drew closer, I had half of Caesar distributed to the rest of the manor and we had half for us. On the feast of Christmas all of those who worked on my land, including the two servant girls, dined with us. Father Gregory held an open-air service that was bracing, to say the least, on the folk land and then we returned to my hall where the fires were banked up and vegetables put on to cook. The half a boar had been jointed and had been left to cook while we thanked God for his bounty.

We feasted well and Benthe broached a jug of the fermented wine her husband had loved. It seemed a fitting end to the fine feast. I had been there for less than a year and yet we had changed the place beyond recognition as well as having experienced events that had changed all of our lives. As I looked at the two youths, Aethelstan and Alfred, I saw that they no longer looked young. They were filling out their frames and they spoke more like adults than boys. Edward now had the beginnings of a beard and had to shave almost every other day. I had done much to change the boy I had saved from thraldom but Ethelred and Bergil had been equally effective. Even little Birgitte was now more like a young woman. Being around the servants and helping her mother more had made her grow quickly. Father Gregory, in contrast, had never changed. He was as solid and reliable a man as I had ever met. Where Ethelred had shed his drunken habits and cleaned himself up that had been, in part, for Father Gregory. It was as though he had been preparing himself his whole life for the day when he would become the priest in a manor.

As for myself? I could not see a change. There were no polished surfaces to see my reflection but I knew that I was a different man from the one who came north after the campaigns in the south west and I had learned to be a lord of the manor. It would take time for me to discover if I was a good one. The rebellion by the men of Northumbria had been a warning. Would I have the time to become a good one?

The time after Christmas was always hard, even in Fitz Malet, but here in the north, the days were so short that no sooner had the sun risen than it seemed darkness would follow. We worked outside for each of the six short hours we were allowed. I made sure that the horses were exercised, and we watched the borders of our land. This was not the time of year for such an initiative, but I planned on having a patrol to ensure that the land was at peace. When we were indoors, and that was a much longer period, we were not idle. Edward, Aethelstan and Alfred worked

Conquest

with Bergil and he showed them how to make beautiful yet
functional scabbards for their swords. I had inherited mine from
Taillefer and needed none. Instead, I used some rosewood to
carve a chess set. I had taken two good branches and stained one.
I then carved the pieces. The pawns were relatively easy and I
chose to make those first to get my eye in. Then I worked my
way through the more complicated figures, leaving the king and
queen until the end. I made one pair look like my mother and my
grandfather while the other was more like Taillefer and Benthe.
My carving was not especially good but as Taillefer and my
grandfather looked so different I convinced myself that I had
done a good job. My mother had been dead so long and I had
been so little when she had been taken from me that I knew she
was an idealised version. Benthe was the easiest for she was
there before me.

We all worked in the Great Hall which was the warmest and
the best lit. We all worked in companionable silence. The noise
that could be heard was that of murmured conversations. Benthe,
Birgitte and the two servants, now close to being women, sewed.
The cloth I had bought was being transformed with thread to
make a picture that would hang on one wall. Next year, we
would be even warmer. My three labourers toiled outside even
when darkness fell. They were adding wattle and daub to the
home they shared. Lars had been smitten by Agnetha who had
just become a woman. Her uncle, Ned the Tanner, had a
smallholding providing him with food and animals that enabled
him to tan hides. When my men had taken the bullocks to plough
his land for him the two, Agnetha and Lars, had seen in each
other something they found attractive. Lars and the others were
making an extension to the house the labourers shared so that
Lars and Agnetha could be wed and enjoy the privacy of a
husband and wife. Father Gregory saw it as a good sign and
would be his first marriage ceremony.

The days did not seem to be much longer until well after the
turn of the year and February was almost gone but March, whilst
still cold, saw the first green shoots of growth. It was when the
room was finally finished that Father Gregory married them. We
still had a church to build and so we had an open-air wedding.
God smiled on us. The wind came from the south and not the

139

east and the sun shone. There was no rain and for the time of year was as perfect a day as one could have hoped. Everyone in the village trooped back to my hall and I gave a wedding feast. Much of the meat was the last of the venison and wild boar we had salted in the autumn but it was still tasty. The generosity of my bounty was appreciated. As I sat, in the shelter of the hall, men who were old enough to be my father came to talk to me about the future. Bergil regarded himself as something of a bodyguard and although I felt no threat, he hovered close by. The senior men of the village spoke to me of their hopes and fears for the future. I realised that until I came they had faced an uncertain future. I knew that they had reason to be fearful. In other parts of the land, much further south, whole villages had been evicted by Norman lords who turned the farmland into hunting land.

During lulls in the conversation, I smiled as I saw young girls from the village flirting with Edward, Aethelstan and Alfred. They were the suitors that the girls sought. The three did not seem to know how to handle the attention. I realised that I would not have been comfortable either.

Lars and Agnetha retired early and the village waited until the bloodied sheet was thrown out. There was a cheer and they all went home.

As I entered my hall with Benthe, Bergil and Father Gregory, Benthe smiled and said, "Now the village can begin to grow, my lord. Lars and Agnetha would never have been together but for your coming."

I shook my head, "They would have found each other."

Bergil said, "No, my lord, Benthe is correct. It was the bullocks you bought that brought them together."

We closed the door behind us and barred it. Father Gregory said, "It is like a stone being thrown into a pond. The ripples touch places you cannot possibly know when you throw the stone."

Benthe said, "A fishpond, now there is an idea. We could have fish every Friday."

I laughed and shook my head, "We have a manor to finish and a church to build. We have work enough."

She smiled, "I look to the future, my lord and it is bright."

Chapter 12

It was in summer that messengers arrived with news of revolt. The new castle in the West Country, Montacute, was besieged and Devon and Dorset, not to mention Cornwall had rebelled. Close to the Welsh border Eadric had besieged Shrewsbury and in the land of the East Angles a new leader, Hereward the Wake, was attacking and besieging the castles around Eye. They were too far from us to cause too much concern but I knew that the king would have his work cut out putting down three such revolts. We in the north would have to fend for ourselves.

We had begun the church and made the foundations when the Danes came. The first we heard was a rider sent by my brother. He warned me that the Danes were raiding the east coast. It was late summer and men were in the fields gathering in crops. It made for an easy time for the Danes. King Sweyn of Denmark was the grandson of King Canute who had been king of England. He saw his chance to reclaim his homeland. The word was that he had sent his brother Osbeorn and his sons, Prince Harold and Prince Cnut. The figure of three hundred ships was mentioned. I knew that could mean anything from fifteen hundred to three thousand men. That was far more than my half-brother had to defend York.

"The earl says that he does not think you will be in danger, Sir Richard, for you live far from the coast, but there may be Englishmen who seek to take advantage of the situation. We are prepared in case the Danes do come to York. They will bleed on the walls."

When the overconfident rider had left, I summoned Ethelred and Bergil to my hall. I also asked Ned the Tanner. Unlike the other senior men in the village, Ned had a business. He travelled around the local farms to buy hides and then tanned them. He was able to make a profit from the leather goods he made. Indeed, I had bought some leather jacks for my labourers. It was not as good as mail but better than nothing. It meant he knew the farmers who lived close to my land. With Edward, Aethelstan and Alfred listening, I explained my plans.

"The earl is confident but the Danes have many warriors. When the Norse came they had a great victory at Gate Fulford." Ethelred nodded grimly. "The earl says that, at the moment, they are raiding the east coast but the last time they came they sailed up the Humber and then the Ouse. That brings them to our doorstep."

Ned asked, "My lord, you are not asking the men to gather inside your walls as we did the last time are you? We all have fields to tend and lives to lead."

I shook my head, "No, but I want my hall's defences to be improved. I want the two towers in the gate finished. I want the ditches deepened. I ask for an hour a day from each household." Ned, as spokesman, agreed. "When enemies come, and it could be Danes or it could be Englishmen, then I want everyone within my walls. The difference shall be that Bergil, Edward, Aethelstan, Alfred and I will ride forth each day to look for the enemy. Ethelred, and the men of the village will have to do without our help."

Ethelred gave a wry smile, "My lord, you will have the more dangerous task."

"I suppose. I want every man to work in his fields armed and with a helmet and shield close to hand. Those who cannot labour can watch. I fear an attack from the south and that is where I shall concentrate our rides, but the north is also a danger. Ethelred, your house is the last bastion."

"I will keep a good watch."

We started the next day. The two youths could now ride and they rode the hackneys. Bergil had his own horse and I rode Geoffrey. Louis was too old for war and he grazed in the fields. This was not the work of a horse like Parsifal. We did not take lances but spears and we rode mailed and helmed. That first day we rode as far as Shipton. It was relatively close to York and had no lord. My half-brother was the one who collected the taxes and the fees. We stopped at the water trough and I spoke with the headman, Erik. He was of Danish descent as was shown by his blond hair and plaited beard.

"Have you seen any enemies?" I did not say Dane for fear of offence.

He knew what I meant and said, "No, my lord, but if Danes come then they will come by ship and the first that we shall know will be when they are amongst us."

"And are you prepared?"

He shrugged, "We have neither wall nor tower. We shall flee to York. It is but six miles from here and if an enemy comes we know how to run." He looked me in the eyes, "We shall pray for you. While York has walls of stone you have willow and ash."

"And men behind the palisade who are willing to fight."

"Aye, my lord, I fear that we have grown soft but we are loyal to York and the earl seems like a kindly lord. We shall prevail."

As we rode north, I was not so sure. The Danes might move far quicker than they expected. This time, when we neared my hall I looked at the land the way the Danes might. The trees were an ally for there were no farms north of Shipton and the road cut its way through the forest. In places, the trees arched over the road. It was when we were half a mile from the village that we passed the first farm. Forlan was also of Danish descent. His father had been at Gate Fulford and while he had not died in the battle he had succumbed to his wounds. Forlan was relatively young with a young wife and a son. He had a strip of land he tilled and he had two cows which he milked. They exchanged the milk with other villagers. He also had a small orchard.

We reined in and he came from the field where he had been planting beans. He did not grow just one crop but his mixed crops gave him a variety of vegetables. Like the other villagers, he trapped small animals and birds to give him some meat in his diet. He came over. "Eliza is indoors feeding the bairn, my lord."

I was pleased to see his spear, sword, shield and helmet were close to hand. He had his father's weapons. "You know that if the enemy comes from the south, and that is more than likely, then yours will be the first farm they see."

"I keep a good watch and at the first sign we will join you at the hall."

"Do not tarry. I need warriors like you on my walls."

"Fear not, my family will be there."

I liked his confidence but knew the danger in which he lay. We returned to my manor and after seeing to my horses, we joined Ethelred and the men giving their hour a day of labour.

The two small towers were almost complete. They added just four feet to the height of the gate and were only big enough for one man but we now had two archers who could use the elevation and the wooden protection to send arrows down at an enemy. The ditches were deeper and wider. The exception was by the gate itself. The width of that ditch was determined by the height of the gates. Since the attack of the Northumbrians, we had also levelled off the uneven palisade. It made the defence easier and now that almost every man had a shield of some description we were no longer in as much danger from missiles. We had learned our lesson from the use of stones in the last battle and we now had small piles close to the palisade. We had dug more out from the enlarged ditch and we now knew which size was the most effective. Bergil had pointed out that the slingers were not particularly effective on the roof of the hall, not least because of its precarious nature. They would be spread along the walls.

That evening, as we ate, I discussed with Bergil, Ethelred and Father Gregory the progress and what else we could do. "In a perfect world, we would have boiling water, my lord, but I do not see that as a realistic choice."

"I agree, Bergil, and if we had a weaponsmith then we could use darts. Let us look at our strengths first."

Ethelred finished chewing and he said, "We could use fewer men on the south, north and east walls."

"That is a risk."

"What if we used women to make it look as though the walls were defended? All we need are numbers. If they attack where we are weak then they can summon help."

"We need a horn."

Ethelred smacked his forehead, "I am a fool. Excuse me, my lord." He rose and fled the hall.

Bergil gave me a bemused smile, "Strange."

Father Gregory had a huge smile on his face, "Whatever the reason it is not because he is a fool, my lord. I think he has spied a solution and berates himself for not thinking of it sooner."

When he returned we saw the reason for his flight. He had with him a bull's horn. "I took this at Gate Fulford. The Viking

Conquest

who was blowing it did not see my blade as I took his arm and then his head. I had it as a trophy. In my dark days, I forgot it."

"Then we can use this. Is it easy to use?"

"The skill can be taught."

I turned to Aethelstan and Alfred, "Then whichever of you learns to use it first becomes the blower of the horn."

The offer was enough and two days later it was Alfred who managed the first strangled notes. His skills improved dramatically after that.

It was a week later that we heard the dire news we had been dreading. York was under siege. My brother had promised the king that he could hold out for a year. I did not see that happening. Even fifteen hundred Danes might be too much for my brother and his small garrison to contain. We stopped work on the church and I had my men gather in all the crops. For safekeeping, we stored them in new granaries. I had ordered them built when we heard of the Danish raids and my decision now seemed prescient.

"Tomorrow, we ride to Shipton. Perhaps I can persuade the people there to join us."

Ethelred shook his head, "Would the men of Eisicewalt leave for Shipton if the threat came from the north?"

I knew the answer but I decided to ride anyway.

When we reached the village we saw that they had erected barricades. Erik stopped work and pointed to a handful of men and their families busy cutting saplings to make a barrier. "We were too late to get to York before it was surrounded. We have our first refugees from York, my lord. They told us that the Danes came up by river and split the defence of the city between the two castles. They are causing great mischief and slaughtering any that they find." He shook his head, "They came so quickly that we had no time to get to the safety of their walls but now that refugees are arriving it seems that York is not as safe as we thought it might be."

My brother's bold claim was now revealed as an empty boast. He might have been able to defend the walls but without a chain across the river then the Danes could come and go as they pleased.

"If you wish you can bring your people north."

He shook his head, "King William will either send men or come north. The longer York holds out the better the chance we have of survival. It is a kind offer." He paused, "If we fall then I beg you to help any survivors."

"You know that I shall."

As we rode north, I said to the others, "My fear is based on the Northumbrians. The Danes, if they take York, will have good land to raid south of here but the Northumbrians can cross the Tees and incite those who live north of us to plunder our land. Northumbria could simply take Yorkshire."

"Then tomorrow, my lord, we should ride north."

There were few farms north of us until Tresche, a hamlet of just ten houses. It was a long ride but we visited there.

As we rode Edward said, "My father and uncle did not like the men of Tresche. They are all of Danish descent and are treacherous. At the Battle of Gate Fulford, they joined the Norse."

Two brothers, Orm and Thor, were the headmen and I did not like them from the first. Perhaps my judgement had been coloured by Edward's words of warning. However, their eyes told me that they cared not for me. I told them of the arrival of the Danes and they shrugged.

Orm said, "It matters not to us. We are of Viking blood and have always lived here. When the Danes ruled York we were treated well. They did not take the folk land. We will learn to live with them again."

I had done all that I could but, as we headed south Bergil said, "Well we know one thing, my lord."

"And what is that?"

"If the Northumbrians come then Orm and Thor will happily throw in with them, and they will be at the fore of any attack."

He was right. We had warned the farms closer to Eisicewalt and done all we could for them. I had invited them into the shelter of Eisicewalt. If none availed themselves then it would tell me they were opposed to King William. As the village hove into view our isolation became all too clear. We had Danish enemies to the south and belligerent Englishmen to the north. We spent the next day working on our walls.

I knew that in the time since I had visited Shipton, much could have happened. I left Ethelred to organise our men and the defence of our village and the five of us rode south. We were barely five miles down the road when the spiral of smoke warned me that there was danger ahead. I fastened my ventail and commanded the three young warriors to pull up their shields. Bergil had already fastened his ventail and his long shield was close to his body.

"You three ride behind Bergil. Listen for my command and watch for danger."

The trees that had grown unchecked since the Romans had first built the road made it tunnel-like in places and that created shadows where it was hard to see what lay ahead. The sound of combat suddenly erupted. The suddenness of the noise told me it had just started. Lowering my spear I spurred Geoffrey. As we turned a corner I saw a wagon stopped in the road. Two Danes held the traces and the horses while a huge man stood on the top and swung a two handed hammer in a wide circle. There was also a man wielding a spear. A woman, two youths and a girl brandished spears at the Danes who were trying to ascend the wagon. The swinging hammer was slowing them down but the man would tire and then they would all fall. I did not shout a command for it was clear what we needed to do.

We were just forty paces from them and Geoffrey was moving well so I spurred him again. I did not go for the Danes holding the horses. I could leave them for Edward and my pueros. My arrival caught them by surprise. Instead of attacking the men who held the horses, I rode to the right of the wagon and speared the man attempting to climb up the side. I pulled back and his body fell. The Dane next to him turned, snarling, with spear and shield ready to fight but I was a Norman horseman with all the advantages of height and mail. My spear rammed into his face breaking his nose before spearing his skull. I heard the man on the other side of the wagon scream as Bergil struck and killed him. I wheeled Geoffrey towards the rear of the wagon. It was there where the bulk of the Danes, eight of them, were trying to get at the woman and what I took to be her children. Bergil and I arrived simultaneously, and that tiny moment of distraction was enough for two to die in two stabs with our spears. The woman brought a spear down on the head of a third Dane who sank to his knees. I heard hooves and knew that Edward, Aethelstan and Alfred had finished off the Danes at the front of the wagon. As Bergil slew another Dane the last four turned and ran.

"After them. We need them dead."

We took after them. It was all too easy to chase down the four men. They could have taken to the woods where they might have evaded us but the road led them, I assumed, to the rest of the war band. The four were skewered. I heard a cry from the wagon and knew that the Dane who had been knocked to his knees had died.

"Edward, you and Aethelstan take the weapons from the dead and then hide the bodies amongst the trees."

"Aye, my lord."

Bergil pointed to the wagon, "That is Uhtred the Saxon, my lord, and I know the man too but I cannot recall his name."

When we reached the wagon, I saw that the smith had ended the life of the injured Dane with one mighty blow from his hammer.

He saw my spurs and said, "Thank you, my lord. Are you Sir Richard Fitz Malet?"

"I am."

"Then it is your home that we seek. This is my family and a fellow refugee, Egbert. We fled the disaster of the Danes."

I dreaded his words for his flight did not suggest a victory in York. "We will talk later. My village is just four miles or so up the road. Help us to take the weapons from the dead and then hide the bodies."

It did not take long and with Edward and Aethelstan leading the wagon back to our manor, Bergil, Alfred and I rode south down the road to ensure that there was no immediate threat. We reached Shipton without meeting anyone and saw then that the village had been taken. We hid in the trees and saw the excesses of men who had won a victory and were now enjoying the spoils. I had seen enough and we headed back up the road.

Bergil said, "It does not bode well that Uhtred fled."

I had put those dark thoughts from my mind but now Bergil made them resurface, "And with Shipton taken then we are, once more, in a state of siege. They will miss the Danes we slew but I hope we have bought a day or two. They will seek their comrades and only when they find their corpses will they work out who did it."

We caught up with the wagon close to the farm of Forlan. I reined in, "The Danes have taken Shipton. It is time, Forlan."

"Aye, my lord, we shall follow."

We told the other farmers the same. As the wagon pulled into my yard, I sent Edward and the pueros to tell the rest of the danger. Over the next night and day, they would enter the manor. This time they would bring all that they had. The attack of the Northumbrians had warned them what to expect.

I unsaddled Geoffrey and by the time I had emerged, Benthe and my labourers had come to help the refugees. Bergil shouted, "There is room in the stables for the horses, Uhtred, but we could use the wagon as an extra barricade behind the gate." Bergil and I had planned on using our own wagon as an extra fighting platform but Uhtred's was much bigger. The huge smith nodded when I suggested it to him. It was not that he was particularly tall, I was taller but his chest seemed as broad as two men.

He shouted, "I have brought my anvil and tools. I was not going to let the Danes have those."

"For the moment they can be stored in the stables. We have more urgent and pressing matters."

I looked at Benthe who seemed to understand the unspoken question. She, in turn, looked at Father Gregory, "I know it is an imposition but could you let this family have your small dwelling? The villagers know each other and ..."

He smiled, "I shall sleep in the chapel. I think that in the testing times to come, I want to be as close to God as I can be."

Edward and the pueros returned, "Most will come in the morning, my lord." He gave me an apologetic shrug, "I said that they had the time."

He was right, of course, and I nodded my approval. "Forlan and the ones from the south will be coming. We have much to do."

It was as though a whirlwind had suddenly swept into my manor. I went inside to shed my mail and, if truth be told, to clear my thoughts. We still did not know the full story of the disaster but the presence of the Saxon told its own tale. What had happened to my brother, my family? I had not been close to them but they were family. I hoped that Robert was safe in Shepton but as the west was in chaos and disorder who knew? I might be the only Malet left by the end of the year. Once dressed I went to help. There was much to do. Forlan and the others had stayed with us before. The two barns were familiar to them. They put their animals with mine and then went to the barn to claim their piece of it. Until the danger had passed they would have to live cheek by jowl. The siege, and I knew there would be one, would surely test the harmony of Eisicewalt. Benthe, Birgitte and the servants had disappeared when I came out of the barn. They would be making the meal that was for eight into one for almost double. There would be more bread than anything but it would be food and it would be hot.

It was dark by the time that the gates were barred and, while we ate, Lars and his men watched from the gatehouse. The table was crowded and we had improvised seats for Uhtred's family. Father Gregory looked at me and I nodded. He said Grace. "Dear Lord, we live in hard times but we thank you for this family that was saved this day. We pray for the souls of those in Shipton and thank you that, thus far, we have been spared. Watch over us for we are good people. We thank you for the bounty of his lordship's table. Amen."

We ate, at first, in silence and the first to speak was Nanna, Uhtred's wife, "This is good bread, Mistress Benthe."

Her words broke the ice and as the two women discussed the recipe and the best way to make bread, I turned to the giant next to me, "Tell me all, Uhtred. All around this table know our parlous condition. Do not spare me the details. I fear I might be the only Norman presence north of the Humber."

He nodded, "That you are, my lord. York has fallen." His words made all other conversations cease. "Your brother did his best but first one castle fell and then Baile Hill was besieged. It was then that I decided to flee. The earl had taken all the warriors within the castle and there was no room for the likes of me. Those with Danish blood welcomed the invaders, God curse them, and there were others who chose to display signs of friendship. I had my family to think of and we slipped out of the northern gate. The Danes were too busy trying to take the walls.

We were a mile north of the city when Egbert here joined us."
He pointed to a man I had taken to be a relative. He had been the
one on the wagon wielding a spear.

He took up the story. "I am, sorry, I was overseer of the
cellars in Baile Hill. The earl and his men fought bravely but
eventually, the keep was taken." He looked at Bergil, "All your
comrades were butchered. I only escaped by feigning death."

I watched Bergil's face. He tried to hide his emotions but he
could not. I knew what he was thinking. Had he not had a falling
out then he would be dead too but, at the same time, he had lost
shield brothers. I put my hand on his and squeezed.

I asked the question I was not sure I wanted an answer to,
"And my family?"

"They were taken. I was hiding when they were fetched from
the donjon. Osbeorn himself took them. The earl and his sons
had bloodied surcoats but they appeared unharmed. I slipped,
unseen, from the castle when the Danes took to despoiling the
bodies of the dead." Once more he looked at Bergil, "Captain
Raymond's head was impaled on the gatehouse."

The name of his rival made Bergil start, "His wife, Seara?"

"I know not, my friend. I had to evade Danish soldiers. I did
not head south for I knew that was where their ships lay and I
went, instead, north. I ran. When I caught up with Uhtred here I
almost wept that I was not alone."

Uhtred took up the tale. "We reached Shipton and I told the
headman, Erik, of the disaster. I did not think their barricades
would hold back an army and he said they would not leave. He
told me of Eisicewalt and we left before dawn. We heard the
sound of combat and I urged my horses on but they are old and
the Danes you saw caught up with us. Had you not arrived, my
lord, then while Egbert and I might have taken some with us we
would be dead and my family..." he put his hand to his mouth,
unable to continue.

"I would say that you are safe now, Uhtred, but I will not tell
a lie. We are in danger but, unlike Shipton, we are prepared. We
now have more warriors for our walls and we have endured an
attack once before."

Everyone nodded but the brooding silence told me that they were thinking the worst. It was Father Gregory who broke the silence. "King William? Will he come?"

"That is a most pertinent question. The rest of the land is in disorder but the loss of York, its garrison, not to mention the earl will spur him. It is a long way for him to come. He will head north but York cannot expect him for at least two weeks, perhaps longer. We have to hold out that long."

Father Gregory nodded, "Then, with God's help, we shall."

Chapter 13

There was a sombre mood until we retired. Father Gregory's words had helped but we all feared the worst. I rose early and that was partly because the influx of villagers into my walls began early. Ethelred had volunteered to stand the night watch and it was he who had opened the gates.

As I was eating my breakfast Bergil entered, "My lord, I thought to take another patrol south today?"

"Is there a good reason behind the request?"

"Egbert's story told me that there might have been others who escaped. We owe it to them to provide help if we can and another reason is so that we can see if the enemy have moved north of Shipton."

I nodded, "They are sound reasons. Edward, saddle Parsifal and tell Aethelstan and Alfred that we ride abroad this day."

Already Ethelred was organising the men from the village and I saw that Uhtred had set up his anvil and was making a forge. He had not asked permission to make a workshop but I was happy for him to do so. I saw that he was using the open area close to the bread ovens and that made sense as it minimised the fire risk to the hall. When we left the hall and headed south, we were alert from the moment the horses' hooves clattered onto the stones. It would be Bergil and I who had the skills to see signs of the enemy but the other three could learn. We did not ride hard for that would have made a noise and we did not need to go close to Shipton. My plan was to search the four miles south of the hall. There were open areas and if there were survivors who had headed north they might have sought them out. However, such places would be equally attractive to Danes.

I had misjudged my pueros for it was Aethelstan who spotted the tracks that led from the road and into the trees. He had sharp eyes and both Bergil and I had missed them, "Lord."

I reined in my horse and looked to where he pointed. There had been a shower in the night and the ground there was wet. There were footprints and the branches of the bush that grew close to the tree had been broken. Someone had left the road.

I dismounted, "I will not risk the horses in the woods. Edward, stay here with Aethelstan and Alfred. Guard the horses."

"Should we not come with you?"

I said, mildly, "Guard the horses." The truth was that the three of them, improved though they were, had neither the skills nor the reactions that would be needed. I left my shield on my horse and waved Bergil forward. The tracks were easy to follow and I was annoyed with myself for having missed them. It became clear that we were following the track of a number of people. There was a path and they had found it but branches at the side of the path had broken leaves. Someone had hurried through the trees.

I stopped when I smelled woodsmoke. There was a fire. In stopping I was able to hear the noises in the trees and I heard voices. They were Danish voices. Bergil heard them too. I silently slid my two swords from their scabbards and headed in the direction of the voices. They were trying to speak quietly. I halted when I saw the backs of the six Danes. They wore no mail but had helmets, spears, swords and axes. They were in a half circle and pointing into the trees. The sun had risen higher while we were in the trees and I saw the spiral of smoke that rose from the camp ahead. The Danes were stalking those in the camp and that made the people there our friends. We were outnumbered but we had the element of surprise on our side and, besides, we were both mailed. Their most dangerous weapons were their axes which could break limbs. I knew that Bergil would know that too and I selected the Dane I would slay first; he would be an axeman.

I headed to the right and Bergil, naturally, to the left. Perhaps one of the Danes sensed the movement, whatever the reason the one closest to Bergil half turned and Bergil did not hesitate. His sword hacked across the Danish throat. The man did not scream but his gurgle of death alerted the others and they turned. I had already chosen the first to die and my right-hand sword sliced down on the man with the axe. A spearman lunged at me but I deflected the spear with my left-hand sword and sliced through his arm with my other. The Danish sword that came at me reached my mail but my reaction meant I pulled down my left-hand sword so that the Danish blade merely scored a line down my mail. My right hand darted like an arrow into the man's throat. The spearman tried to raise his sword with his one arm but he was losing too much blood and he collapsed in a heap. Bergil had two men to fight and I slid my sword into the back of one as Bergil took advantage of my distraction to end the life of the other.

We looked around and saw that the Danes were all dead or dying. We kicked the weapons away from the hands of the dying and then headed towards the fire. There were people cowering.

Sheathing my swords, I said, "Fear not, I am Sir Richard Fitz Malet and this is Bergil…"

I got no further for a young woman detached herself from the cowering group and hurled herself at Bergil, "Bergil!"

"Seara!"

Fate had intervened. There was one old man, two youths and another young woman. The old man said, "Thank you for your timely rescue. We managed to make it from York unseen until we reached Shipton and then we must have been spied. We left the road as soon as we could and hid in the trees."

I shook my head, "And you lit a fire that drew the Danes like moths." I smiled to take away the criticism. "Never mind, all is well. Come, bring your belongings." As they did, I said, quietly, "Bergil, the weapons."

He nodded but his face showed such joy that one might have thought he had enjoyed a vision of Christ.

Laden with the arms taken from the dead Danes we headed back along the path. Edward and the pueros had heard the skirmish and had weapons drawn. "Dismount. We let these ride. It will make for a swifter journey. Load the weapons on the horses."

Our collection was growing; apart from the two axes we had four swords a spear and four seaxes. Of course, we had more mouths to feed but that was a minor consideration. The two youths sat on one horse and that allowed us to load the weapons on the other animal. It was quicker letting the refugees ride but when we saw Forlan's farm I breathed a sigh of relief. Bergil and Seara had spoken the whole way north but I had not questioned the others, there would be time for that. Work ceased as we rode in. Benthe was becoming used to this and she directed the newcomers to the few empty places in the barns. We were crowded and I was keenly aware of the risk of disease spreading through the villagers. That was why we had most of the people spend their days outside. The fresh air was an ally and they were all put to work. I allowed Bergil and Seara some time to speak together. He deserved it and I went to speak to Ethelred and Uhtred. They were still building a workshop.

The piece of land they had chosen was not used and I did not mind a temporary workshop but once the danger was gone then I would have it removed. It was too soon to speak of the future. None of us knew if we even had a future. York had fallen, what chance did we stand?

Ethelred looked up from his labours, "More lost sheep."

I nodded, "And one of them is Bergil's love, Seara. Strange, eh?"

Uhtred shook his head, "My lord, I believe in Christ and I worship each Sunday but there are things in the world that cannot be explained. I, for one, am quite happy about that." He pointed a huge paw at the weapons, "More dead Danes?"

"Aye, and we have their weapons but they will soon begin to wonder who is killing their warriors."

"You have time. We managed to escape with a wagon because they were too busy sacking, raping, and pillaging. I do not think that King Sweyn was wise to send his sons. Now if he had come himself then we would have a Danish army knocking on our door. I think we have some days and by that time I can begin to make weapons. The poor metal you stored can be reused as darts. Anyone can throw them and they are easy to make. When I have set up the grindstone we will put edges on every weapon we can find. This time the Danes will find that Uhtred the Saxon can do more than make weapons, he can use them."

I nodded, "And all the villagers are within our walls?"

"They are."

"Then we bar the gates and pull up the bridge. Unless Seara has told Bergil anything different I will assume that this handful is the last we shall have to face."

Ethelred said, "Before you do that, my lord, let me go with Edward, Aethelstan and Alfred. Let us take as much bounty from your woods as we can. You have many mouths to feed and hunted game gives not only meat but bones to make stews and soups that can last a long time. We can forage mushrooms and greens too." He gave a sad smile, "Even in my darkest moment of despair I could always feed myself. Let me feed Eisicewalt."

"It is a good idea."

Uhtred said, "And take my sons. They are poor hunters but they have broad backs and can carry wood and animals back. I need them not."

As the hunting party left I sought Bergil and Seara. He had gone to the hall and they were seated by the fireless hearth. They looked up guiltily as I entered and I saw that they were holding hands. "I am sorry to disturb you, but I need information."

Seara nodded, "Of course, my lord, I am grateful that you found us."

"I think that God guided us." They both made the sign of the cross. She closed her eyes and then began the tale, "The earl took all the fighting men into the castles. We took shelter in the churches in the belief that the Danes would respect sanctuary. We were wrong. As soon as the castles fell they stormed the churches and slaughtered the priests. I knew that my Raymond was gone but I would not give myself up quietly." She pulled a seax from beneath the folds of her skirts. There was still dried blood on it. "I let the first Dane take me out of the church. He thought me afraid and was confident. He laid me down and as he pulled down his breeks I gutted him and I ran. I know now that I should have taken his weapons but I just ran." She nodded at the other young woman. "I came across Maud who had a Dane straddling her. He did not see me as I dragged the seax across his throat. The two of us ran to the north gate. The cathedral's doors lay open and the slaughtered priests told their own story. We came upon Walter, Garth and John, just outside the gates. They were hiding having escaped the slaughter of the cathedral. The Danes were too keen to spill their seed to worry about the men who had hidden."

"Then there may be more that escaped?"

She shook her head. "Walter worked by the river. He was a clerk who tallied the goods that were landed. He had no skills we could use and the two youths were just that. Brave enough but they did not have the cunning to give them the best chance of survival. Maud and I knew what the Danes would do and that gave us an incentive. I directed them and they followed me for I had a weapon and they had none. We left the road and hid behind some houses just north of the gate. We found food within the houses and we ate. It was while we were there that a warband came from the gates. We did not move but we heard the sounds of battle where they caught the refugees. We waited until dark and there was silence and then we moved. When we did and passed the site of the battle we found other refugees. All had been killed and their bodies despoiled." She shook her head, "Do not ask me more for my nights will be haunted by the memory."

She was clearly distraught and Bergil stroked her hair as he continued the tale. "She led them north, my lord, until they saw the desolation of Shipton. She spied the Danes there and led her lost lambs around the town." He smiled, "She is a clever one. They were tired and she knew that they needed to rest. Eisicewalt was but a vague hope. They knew not where it was and she feared that, like Shipton, it had fallen. She led them into the trees and they found a camp. It was Walter who insisted on a fire and by then poor Seara was exhausted and could not argue. The rest you know."

I nodded, "One more thing, Seara, and then I shall leave you. My brother, the earl and his family, what do you know of them?"

"I speak a little Danish, my family lived in a street of Danes and when we hid we heard Danes crowing about how they would get a fortune in ransom for the Sherriff and his family."

I was relieved. Their greed would be their undoing. I knew King William. He would not pay a ransom but he would come north. The news of the ransom demand also gave me hope. The Danes would secure their new stronghold while they awaited the arrival of the ransom.

"One more thing, my lord. I know that Bergil told you the tale of how I spurned him and chose another. I am ashamed of that action now. Put it down to the words and promises that Captain Raymond made. Even before the Danes came I regretted my action and I wished I had not done what I did to Bergil. He has forgiven me and I pray that you do too."

I shook my head, "There is nothing to forgive and, to be fair, Mistress Seara, while I know the world of war, the world of women is an unknown domain to me. So long as you and Bergil are happy then I am content."

Bergil beamed, "We are."

"When you are ready there will be work for you. We have much to do."

I went to my chamber and took off my mail. This was a day for working. Father Gregory came to me at noon with food, "My lord, you need to rest."

"If you could ask God to give us more hours each day then I might rest."

He sat next to me and said, "I hear confessions each day. Sometimes the confessions are so trivial that I wonder why they are made. I have come to the conclusion that telling another of your problems often helps. While you eat unburden yourself to me. This is not the confessional but I swear that what you tell me will go no further."

I nodded and sighed, "I think that, in the short term, we shall be safe from the Danes. They will want their ransom but there are many who live close to us that might seek to benefit from our plight." I told him of the men of Tresche. "There will be others and the men of Northumbria will see their chance. The whole country is in rebellion. We are the last Norman bastion. If we are taken then King William will have an even harder task to reclaim his new land."

He smiled, "I can offer no advice for I am no warrior but do you feel better for having explained the problem?"

"What do you mean?"

"You know the problem and you are a warrior. What can you do about it?"

"If I did not have the problem of so many people to defend I would take warriors and attack those who wished us harm."

He stroked his beard, "We have men enough to watch the walls. If you are right then the danger is not from the south, not at the moment anyway, but from the north. Your advantage is that you are mailed and horsed. You can move more quickly than any warband that seeks to harm you. Trust in the people on your walls and take your best men to hurt and discourage those from the north. At the very least a ride to Tresche will tell you if there is a problem."

"You are right, Father Gregory, and it does not sit well with me to squat behind my walls and let the land be ravaged."

When Ethelred and his hunters returned it was with two deer and ten smaller animals and birds. In addition, there were foraged mushrooms and greens. The dried beans could be left until the fresher fare was used. I sat outside with Bergil, Ethelred and Uhtred. Father Gregory was tending to the needs of the new refugees. I explained what the priest had said. "If you, Uhtred, could take charge of my walls then I could take my mounted warriors," I smiled, "and I include you in that Ethelred, to ride north and discover the intentions of the men of Tresche and, perhaps, the Northumbrians."

Bergil said, "It is a risk but one worth taking. There are few of us but a charge of horsemen with spears can dishearten an enemy. They always count one horse as two and even young men like Alfred can appear more fearsome. It is a good plan."

"And this way we keep the manor safe and keep improving the defences."

Ethelred pointed to the walls, "Remember the problems the slippery ditch causes. The rain has helped but if we have the men on sentry duty use the ditch as a latrine then it will add to the problems."

"Good, then we rise before dawn and head north." I turned to Uhtred, "If those toiling could make temporary dwellings then we reduce the risk of disease."

"I will put my mind to it, my lord." He hesitated, "My lord, when this is over…, if this is over, I would like to live here. I like the people and I do not feel that I am an outsider. I have seen a plot of land where I could make a workshop. I might not make as much coin as I would in York but there are other considerations. A man needs a safe life for his family and not a pile of gold."

"We would be honoured to have Uhtred the Saxon and his family in Eisicewalt. You will complete the picture that was begun when I first came."

We left after a hearty breakfast. The two pueros were now mailed. They did not have a mail hauberk, but the leather jacks studded with metal would not impede their movements and would give protection. Helmed and with shields, they no longer looked like boys playing at being warriors. We headed for

160

Tresche but I took detours to see if the farms north of my land and not in my manor were untouched. The first two, just a few miles south of Tresche, were deserted. When we neared the third we slowed for we could hear the sound of the clash of arms. The farm lay off the road and was in a slight hollow. Edmund, who farmed it, had complained the one time I had spoken to him of the flooding that he often endured in wet weather. He had two sons, a wife and a daughter. We rode not down the farm trail but used the small orchard he had planted to try to dry the ground out, as a disguise. We halted just one hundred paces from the farmhouse. We were too late. We heard the dying screams of his wife and then the roar from the men who had attacked.

The farm itself and the outbuildings hid the scene from our eyes but we heard the shouts and cries from the victors and we could all imagine the scene.

One voice sounded above the others, "This is just the start. Those who supported the Normans are now dead or fled. There is nothing to stop us from taking Eisicewalt."

There was a cheer and then a dissenting voice cried out, "They have strengthened their defences. The last time the men of Northumbria came they left their corpses for the crows."

"Earl Waltheof is ravaging the Tees, even as we speak and he has promised that he will bring men as soon as he can. We lose nothing by making a sneak attack." There were murmurings and mumblings. "Let us take what we can from this farm and then make it a pyre and a sign for all those who forget that we are English."

I turned to the others and said, quietly, "Let us disrupt their mischief. Ethelred, you know this farm, is there a way we can approach it without being seen?"

He nodded and pointed to the east, "The land there is lower for there is a beck. We can use the dead ground to make our approach. The farm has a yard but no gate. If we charge while they are destroying the farm they will not have shields raised."

"Then we will follow you. We three will lead and Edward and the pueros can ride behind. My purpose is to kill as many of them as we can and to avoid any hurt to us or our horses." I turned to the three without experience of war. "If your spear is stuck then let it drop. We ride through and then head for Tresche."

Bergil said, "Why, my lord?"

"I recognised Orm's voice. Let us give the men of Tresche a taste of their own medicine. We will sack their homes. If the men are here then the homes will just have women. We drive off the women and fire their homes."

They nodded. It was draconian but these were perilous times.

We followed Ethelred until we reached the beck. We let the horses drink while we hefted shields and couched spears. When we were ready we formed two lines. I was riding Parsifal. He alone would strike fear in the hearts of the men of Tresche.

The noise of the fires they had started, allied to the noise they made as they smashed up the belongings of the dead hid our approach. As we rose from the hollow a scene of horror met us. Edmund and his family lay butchered and despoiled. I took in that there were at least twenty men before us. As Ethelred had said they had no weapons in their hands and the first three men that were speared died quickly. I saw Orm duck behind a wall while four others, braver souls, grabbed weapons and ran at us. The sight of Parsifal's snapping jaws made one man recoil and Bergil had an easy kill. I had the time, thanks to the height of my horse, to use my spear and drive it into another warrior's face. The other two fell and mindful of my own words we headed up the farm trail to the road. I wheeled right and, after glancing behind to see that Edward and the pueros had survived, rode towards Tresche. I reined in my horse so that the others could join me.

"Anyone hurt?"

They shook their heads. Edward said, "I speared a man."

Bergil said, "Your first?"

"It was."

"The next will be easier."

Alfred said, "I struck a man but I know not if I killed him."

Ethelred said, "A wound from a spear means he will not be as effective a fighter in the future."

I worked out that we had slain half of the raiders. Whilst not a complete victory, as I had led three untried horsemen, I was pleased with the outcome.

When we neared Tresche I saw that the villagers were going about their business. Women were preparing food, children were feeding the fowl. We formed a line just one hundred paces from the village and, as I expected, we were seen. The women gathered up their children and drove as many animals north as they could. We galloped in.

"Burn the houses and spill the food on the fires. A hungry man who has to rebuild his home has less opportunity to hurt us."

By the time we left, with a dozen fowl fastened to our cantles, the village was on fire. I was aware that the men we had left might well be on the road and so we left the road a mile south of Tresche and only rejoined it after Edmund's burnt-out farm. By the time we reached my manor, it was getting on to dark. I had not enjoyed either of the things we had just done but knew that they were necessary. We were in a war of survival. I was Norman and the Danes and the rebel English wanted to drive me away. Fate had placed me in this position and I was honour bound to defend the people of my manor even if it turned my stomach to do what I had done.

That night I told Benthe, Father Gregory and the senior men in the village of our actions. "I believe I have bought us time but we know that Waltheof will be bringing an army and as Oswiu was a kinsman, then we can expect little mercy. Let us use the time we have left wisely."

Chapter 14

I sent out four men each day, two to the north and two to the south. Riding sumpters, they acted as sentries just a mile and a half from the manor. They were there to give us early warning for their sumpters would let them reach us quickly if there was danger. Each day we opened the gates and the people tried to gather as much food as they could and tend their fields. I would not risk them returning to their homes but the semblance of normality helped.

Two days after our raid a family was found by my northern sentries. They had come all the way from the Tees. Aelric, Anya and their four children had managed to flee before they could be taken by the men of Northumbria. They were emaciated and hungry but grateful for the welcome that we gave them. As they lived on the banks of the northern river, we knew that the Northumbrians were still a week away. A marauding army does not travel fast. The men of Tresche had been hurt too much for them to be a threat and so we enjoyed the respite.

My only fear, in a prolonged siege, was our water supply. The Haverwite Beck had been diverted at some time in the past and gave us a steady supply of clean water. If the Danes were clever enough they could dam or block the beck. There was little we could do about it until after there was peace, by which time it might not matter as much. However, as a precaution, I had as many barrels and pots filled with water as we could find. I had them placed close to where people ate and slept. If nothing else it gave them shorter journeys for water.

It took a week for the Danes, rather than the Northumbrians, to appear and during that time the defences were added to and Ethelred hunted more food. The sentries on the sumpters galloped in from the south with the news that a warband was coming. I had the horn sounded to recall the northern sentries and to alert those within the manor. We had enjoyed enough time to prepare for this. Those without mail immediately took to their positions on the wall. In my case I donned mail as soon as I rose and, to me, it felt like a second skin. I was on the wall when the northern sentries rode in.

"Close the gates." The gates were closed and I heard the double bars drop. "Raise the bridge." Men hauled on the ropes which passed through the metal rings and the bridge was raised. Its base was now studded with more fragments of metal, beaten there by Uhtred's sons. They were the detritus from his work and would have been otherwise wasted. They would not stop an axe but the metal would both blunt and reduce the efficacy of the blow.

By the time we saw the four Danes on horses appear at the head of the metal snake, my walls were manned. We were not York nor were we a tiny morsel that could bitten, chewed and digested easily. We would stick in the Danish throat and, I hoped, choke them.

They kept more than an arrow's length from the hall and that necessitated them riding through the one derelict farm in my village. It had fallen down more than a generation ago and now sported tares and weeds. It was also boggy and stony ground as men had tried to make paths through it with stones. It was petty but I enjoyed the sight of their horses having to pick their way through it and the shouts as men were scraped and scratched by bramble bushes. They stopped and I watched them form up. It told me much about them. The four riders remained mounted and the Danish warriors behind them formed three ranks. They were making a shield wall and, as the Northumbrians had done, were attacking our strongest point, the gatehouse. I knew then that they had not scouted us out. My sentries had done a good job and given us a good warning. The four leaders conferred. I saw their hand movements as they gestured at the two tiny towers by the gate and the ditch. The Danish shield wall waited in their ranks for almost an hour as the debate raged.

Ethelred and Bergil flanked me and Bergil chuckled, "We have posed them a problem, my lord." Since the rescue of Seara, Bergil had been a changed man. When first he had come he seemed to have a fatalistic view of life and he saw the coistrel as half empty. Now he saw it as half full.

Ethelred said, "I count one hundred and twenty of them, my lord. There are more mailed men than fought us the last time we were attacked."

"They could have ten times that number and they would still have the same problem. They have to breach our wall. Thus far they have not chosen to use the east, south or north walls for their attack and we now have men to man those walls." We also had the advantage that the diverting of the Haverwite Beck had left a boggy area to the long east wall. An attacker would struggle there.

Edward's voice drew my attention back to the Danes, "My lord, they wish to speak."

I saw that two riders had detached themselves and were heading for us. They had taken off their helmets and held up their right hands to show that they had no weapons. I knew that my archers would each have an arrow nocked and would be tracking them. As they neared the ditch, and I realised that they wished to inspect it, I studied them. One was a young man with a plaited beard, moustache and hair. He wore expensive scale armour and I saw that his sword had a richly decorated pommel. The helmet he carried had a fine face mask inlaid with some better metal. In contrast, the other was a warrior. He was older with a beard and hair flecked with grey. I saw that his mail was an old-fashioned but well-made byrnie and his large round shield was well made.

They halted and the young man spoke. He spoke in English. We had Danish speakers but I was glad that he chose English. "I am Harold son of King Sweyn. I am now the Prince of Jorvik." He used the Danish name for York but he was giving himself titles. There was never a prince of Jorvik and I doubted that his uncle, who was the real Danish leader this side of the sea, would have given it to him.

I nodded, "I am Sir Richard Fitz Malet and this is my manor."

He frowned and turned to the Dane next to him. He leaned over and after a few sentences returned his gaze to our walls. "Are you related to Earl William Malet?"

"I am."

"Know that we have him and his family as hostages. This is no longer Norman land but belongs, as it rightfully should, to my father, the King of Denmark and the true King of England. If you open your gates then your people can leave. We wish no harm to those who are English. We come to release them from the burden of Norman masters."

I heard Ethelred snort next to me.

"A generous offer but we will decline. We have some of those who escaped from York and they have told us of Danish hospitality. We shall stay within these walls."

His face had been calm and smiling but now he snarled, "Then we will tear down your pathetic wooden walls and adorn them with the heads of your men."

I nodded and smiled, "That is better, Danish honesty and a rare thing too."

We were speaking in English and my jest made the men on my walls laugh. The princeling did not like it. "I was angry before and now I shall show you the folly of angering me further." He jabbed a finger south, "Your brother and his family will die because of this."

I laughed and saw his face colour, "That is an idle boast for you do not command. Your uncle does and my brother and his family are far more important for they can be ransomed. I see that you cannot speak with a straight tongue." All the while I was aware that the older man was studying me.

I thought the princeling was going to turn his horse but the man next to him restrained him. They spoke again. At first Prince Harold shook his head but the other man pointed to our walls and eventually, the prince nodded agreement to whatever had been put to him.

"This is Eystein the Undefeated, and he is my champion. He said he would fight with you or a champion nominated by you."

Bergil shook his head and said to me, "There is nothing to be gained from this, my lord. It is an empty gesture."

Ethelred added, "Aye, lord. But if you wish I will fight him."

I shook my head, "Do you not see, the carrot is now out of the ground. This Eystein is a clever man. He has been watching me and knows that I am young. He thinks that he can defeat me. However, if I refuse then his men gain heart and my people," I looked down the wall where every expectant face looked towards me, "become despondent. I have to fight."

"But we cannot trust them."

"Of course not, and if I should win there will be a trick up their sleeves. That is where you two come in. Let us hope that God is on our side and that I win. Have this gatehouse packed with our archers and slingers. If they try anything then, God Willing, I will rely on you to save me."

Bergil sighed, "My lord, the gate will be open and if they rush us then the manor will fall."

"The gate will not be open. When I leave, I want the gates closed and the bridge raised."

Edward had been listening and he looked appalled, "But you will be stuck outside. How will you regain the walls?"

I smiled, "You are my squire, Edward, and I know that you will find a way."

Prince Harold shouted, "Are you afraid, Norman?"

"My men think, and I agree with them, that you cannot be trusted."

He adopted a look of outrage that did not fool me for a moment, "I am a Christian and I give my word that win or lose we will honour the outcome. If my champion is slain then we will leave and march away."

Under his breath, Bergil said, "Liar."

I nodded, "Then when you have taken your champion's horse to the other side of the road I will meet him and we will let God decide the outcome." I waited until Eystein had dismounted, taken his shield and donned his helmet and Prince Harold had led his horse away before I descended.

Father Gregory was waiting for me at the foot of the ladder. He made the sign of the cross and splashed some water on my head, "This is Holy Water, brought from Rome. May God be with you, my son."

As the ropes creaked and the bridge was lowered Edward fitted my helmet and fastened my ventail. "I will use your shield, Edward."

"An honour, my lord."

The round shield was better suited to fighting on foot and also had a boss. The men stood ready to lift the bars on the gates. Bergil had Uhtred and ten men ready with shields and spears in case this was a trick. When the gates were opened I saw Eystein waiting for me. He had a hand axe rather than a two handed

Danish one. In his belt was a sword and I saw, from his casual stance, that he anticipated an easy victory. When I had spoken from the gatehouse, I had been bareheaded and he had seen my youth. He thought that I was a callow Norman lord. Taillefer's training would be my secret weapon. I stepped over the bridge and then waited with a drawn sword and hefted shield until I heard the bridge being raised. I wondered if that disappointed Prince Harold.

I spoke no Danish and, clearly, Eystein spoke neither English nor Norman for he suddenly launched himself at me without any taunt or preamble. Behind me loomed the ditch and his wild charge with a swinging axe was intended to make me panic and fall therein. I did not. He was like a wild bull. I watched the swing of his axe and simply pirouetted out of the way. His charge was so fast that he almost toppled into the stake-filled ditch himself. The men on my walls cheered and as the Dane whirled, I saw the anger on his face. His next attack would be more measured. He came at me with the axe, clearly a weapon with which he was comfortable, swinging easily. His shield covered most of his body. What he could not have known was the training given to me by Taillefer where he had fought me using two swords and I had learned to trust my instincts. He punched his shield at me but instead of countering with my sword, I punched back with my shield. Using two swords had made my left arm almost as strong as my right and I saw the shock on his face when my punch was stronger than his. He swung his axe at my head. My swords were good ones but I knew that striking the head would do my blade no good so I blocked the haft of his axe. The axe head stopped just a handspan from my helmet but its progress was arrested and the wood of the axe was caught on my sword. We wrestled until our weapons parted and I saw the clean cut of wood on the haft of the axe. It had been weakened.

"You have him, my lord." Alfred's shout from my walls made my men cheer. It was a small thing but it gave me heart. It also angered the Dane.

He brought the axe head around in a wide swing. The only way I could block it was with my shield and I did so. The head bit into the wood and there was a clear crack. The look of joy on

Eystein's face confirmed that he thought he had made a momentous strike. Once again, his blade struck and he tried to pull away. This time I used the shield offensively. It was weakened and would not take another such blow. I punched at his face. He was holding the axe tightly, he had to, and could not stop the boss of my shield from smashing into his face. He reeled and in reeling, not only released the axe but he fell to the ground. He lay there and I knew I could have struck his leg and hurt him. I did not do so. It was not for a noble reason but for a lesser one. I knew that I could defeat him and I wanted the men watching to see me do it fairly.

He looked in disbelief as I gestured for him to rise and then used the axe to push himself to his feet. It was a mistake for I heard the axe haft creak. The cut I had made with my sword was becoming longer. He saw it too and it made him reckless and decide to end the contest quickly. He took a mighty swing and struck my shield in exactly the same place he had the first time. Edward's shield broke in two but the blow had aggravated the damage to the axe. Even as the Danes all cheered and my people groaned I was drawing my second sword. He came at me knowing that there was no shield to take the blow. It was then he should have used his shield but he was angry and that is never a good way to fight. Taillefer had taught me that. His shield hung to his side as he brought the axe down to strike at my head. Even if the blade did not kill me the weight of the head would. I held up my two swords like a crucifix. I wondered if the so-called Christian prince would see the symbolism in that. I gambled that the strength of my two arms would be greater than his right hand and I blocked the haft and not the blade. The two swords were sharp and they completed the work begun earlier by my single sword. The head fell to the ground and the groans from my walls became cheers. He stepped back and drew his sword. I used a Taillefer trick. I waved the two swords in circles before him, mesmerising him. It drew cheers from my walls. I feinted with my right and as he blocked the blow with his shield my left arm darted and I struck his bare arm, above the battle bangles. The blossoming blood brought another cheer. More importantly, the wound would only get worse and he would weaken. Already he had struck more blows than me and expended more energy. He raised his sword and I saw the pain on his face. He tried to sweep it across my neck. I blocked it with my left-hand sword and then did the unexpected. I pirouetted around and brought my right-hand sword across his back. It was a powerful strike, aided by my swing and not only were mail links cut but as I drew it through his undershirt I saw blood. He must have known the battle was coming to an end and chose to end it quickly. With almost berserker rage he raced at me using the sword and the shield as two weapons. I was forced to move backwards. I blocked each blow but I had to watch my footing for the ditch was looming alarmingly close. It was the wound to his arm that was his undoing. He swung the sword at my left side but it was a weak one and I was able to push up his sword and, using my quicker feet, turned him. He began to lose his balance and as he spread his arms to stop his fall I lunged with my right hand sword and drove it through his throat. He was dead before he hit the stakes.

"My lord!"

I turned and saw the treachery of Harold. He had realised that his champion was losing and sent half of his men at me. I could either stand and fight or run. A fight would result in my death and all the good work I had done would be undone. I took a chance and used the body of the dead Dane as a bridge to cross my own ditch. He had fallen on the stakes and as my weight fell on him the stakes were driven up through his body. I was lucky and avoided one. I used his head as my second step and launched myself at my walls. Above me, I heard the twang of bowstrings and the whirl of slingshots. A spear embedded itself next to my head. I was not close to the gate but the wall adjacent to it. Suddenly, a ladder appeared and Edward shouted, "Climb, my lord!"

Even as I climbed, I felt stones and arrows strike my back. I had a good hauberk and did not feel the sharp pain of penetration. The men on my walls were reaping a harvest of Danes who saw their chance to avenge their champion. As I reached the top eager hands pulled me over and then Alfred used the two ropes they had cleverly tied to the ladder to pull it up. Breathing heavily, I turned. The Danes, foiled by the ladder, were falling back. They had lost ten men in the attack. Allied to the death of their champion I felt that the first day was our victory but I was no fool. We had a long way to go.

Chapter 15

"I am afraid, Edward, that I owe you a shield."

He laughed, "I can get another but a lord like you is harder to come by."

"Thank you for the ladder. That was clever." I turned to Bergil and Ethelred, "We now have the mettle of the man we face. We can expect tricks. Have two-thirds of the men go to be fed and to rest. I want them to take on the night duties. Ethelred, take the first watch and Bergil the second. I will stand here a while."

Aethelstan asked, "Why, my lord?"

"I want them to see me walking along my walls, laughing and joking with my squire and pueros so that they know I am not hurt. Their champion was soundly and fairly beaten and that will suck the heart from them. I want them to see me whole so that they fear to attack."

Edward said, "It might have the opposite effect, my lord, and they may be eager to get at you."

"And that, too, works in our favour."

"How so, my lord?"

"Simple, Alfred, I have beaten their best warrior, no matter who comes for me they will not be as good as Eystein and that will gnaw at their minds and their confidence."

"Are you not afraid, my lord?"

I shook my head, "There is no time for fear in such a situation. Fear is like ice, it freezes. I trusted my ability, and I kept calm. If you three take nothing else from this day take that. Do not lose your temper and fight as though you are fearless." I looked towards the Danes and then said, "Now laugh as though I have told the funniest joke in the world."

They did so and the men close who had heard did the same. When I looked towards the Danes I saw that they had retreated behind the houses opposite my hall. Prince Harold would be plotting.

As the afternoon drew on Birgitte came to the walls. She had changed from the fey young thing I had first met. She was now more confident. "Sir Richard, my mother says I am to fetch you and then she can feed you." She stood at the bottom of the ladder with her hands on her hips looking like a miniature version of her mother.

Alfred said, "You had better obey, my lord. We will shout if they come. You need to be fed."

I nodded. He was right. I gave my shield to Edward and handed my helmet to Alfred. "Walk about as though you are me, Edward. If you wish, don my helmet."

"Yes, my lord."

I descended and was greeted with smiles and cheers. It was not far to my hall but every person I passed seemed to want to touch me as though I was some sort of lucky talisman. When I reached my hall and entered I saw Bergil and Ethelred, finishing off their food. "We told Benthe you would wish to stay on your walls but she was adamant."

"It is no matter. I needed to eat and the Danes are still planning." Benthe entered with a large bowl of stew, some bread, still warm from the oven and Birgitte carried a large beaker of mead.

"Now eat, my lord. If you are going to do such foolish things in the future then you need the strength to do so."

I was grinning when I answered, "Yes Mistress Benthe."

She shook her head, "My husband would have followed you to the gates of hell and beyond, my lord, for you are a true warrior." She retreated back to her domain, the kitchen.

I ate and listened as Bergil and Ethelred spoke. "They will come this night and may well choose to attack all four walls."

Bergil chuckled, "And our men will have rested. We know the land, every fold and hollow, they are tired and do not know the land. They have not scouted and the little look they had in the ditch will have told them nothing. There are stakes in all the ditches. If it was daylight when they attacked then they might have a chance of seeing them but at night…I hope they do attack every wall for we can then thin their numbers."

I broke a piece of bread to dip into the juices, "And if they send for more men? They may have thought we would simply roll over and the men they sent would be enough."

Bergil nodded and held up his beaker. Seara appeared from nowhere and filled it. Bergil gestured to her, "As Seara said to me, they have spread their net thinly. We are one manor but there are others they will be trying to take. Each day that they waste here is a day closer to when the king comes for vengeance."

I returned to the walls but saw nothing of the enemy. It was as though they had disappeared, although I knew they had not. Perhaps they hoped to make us sortie and then they could attack us. I know not. More to keep the men occupied I sent four of them down a ladder to the ditch. I had them move the bodies to the other side of the ditch and remove the weapons and mail. In Eystein's case, it was a grisly operation but Uhtred was confident that when all of this was over he could melt the ruined byrnie and make something useful. My motives for removing the bodies were not in the least altruistic. I wanted more stakes embedding and I needed the body bridges removed. I had found them useful. The last thing we needed was to help our enemies.

Towards dusk, Father Gregory joined me. I saw he had strapped on his sword once more. He would be a warrior priest until this was over. He smiled, "God did indeed smile upon you, my lord. Was the making of a sword cross a deliberate act or a happy happenstance?"

"It is a move I have used before and I did not think to emulate the cross but it had an effect."

"That it did, my lord. It made the Danes who were Christians make the sign of the cross while our people took it as a sign that your hand was directed by God."

I watched with the priest for another hour. We toured the walls and spoke to the men who waited behind the palisade. Waiting is always hard and a nighttime attack was something to be feared. The presence of the priest was reassuring and I was the warrior who had fought and defeated their champion. Between us, we inspired a little more confidence and courage.

Bergil came to send me to bed. I went reluctantly but he was not taking no for an answer. "If they come this night then we shall need you on the walls. You fought hard today and you need to let others do some of the more difficult watching. Edward and your pueros will watch and you can rest."

I did as I was bidden. Benthe had some ale heated with a poker and infused with honey. It induced sleep and I slept.

That night I dreamed but the dream was not of the combat with the Dane but of my grandfather and Taillefer. I found them talking. I did not hear their words but saw their smiles. When I tried to speak to them they disappeared. I wondered what it meant.

Edward shook me awake. Even before he spoke, I heard the clash of arms. "They have come my lord."

He held out my hauberk and I donned it. He strapped on my baldric and handed me my arming cap. Fastening my scabbards I was almost ready. I pulled the coif up and we hurried out of the hall and to the gatehouse.

Edward spoke as we raced to the ramparts, "They came on every side. Bergil is on the south wall, Uhtred the east and Ethelred the north."

That made sense as the gatehouse was the strongest part of the wall. I reached the top and picked up my shield so that I could peer over the palisade. A storm of stones and arrows was being sent blindly at the fighting platform but I saw that every man held a shield and the erratically aimed missiles merely banged against wood. I could see that the Danes had made bridges but as they were attacking all around the perimeter they were thinly spread out. My archers and slingers stood aiming at the white faces they saw. They sent stones and arrows down on the men as they crossed. Some merely hit helmets but some hit unprotected limbs and when the men fell from the bridges they plummeted to the ditch and even more wounds resulted.

Even so, some had made the walls and a ladder was bumped against the palisade. I drew a sword and hurried to the place where they would ascend. Their arrows and stones were all aimed at the place where the ladder lay and I held my shield horizontally. It protected me and allowed me to use my sword beneath it. It is hard climbing a ladder, protecting yourself and being ready to fight. I had experienced it and I knew. The first Dane held his shield above him and was struggling up the ladder. Aethelgar dropped a stone. It cracked on the shield but the shield held. The man came higher.

"Get something to push the ladder to the side when I have dealt with this warrior."

As he neared the top, I knew what he would do. Until he could draw his sword his only weapon was his shield and, as I expected, he punched up with his shield. I met the blow with my shield and swept my sword to hack into his arm and his side. He could not hold on and he tumbled, screaming, to the ditch below. Edward and Alfred had two spears and they were pushing against one side of the ladder. It was hard to move as men were ascending.

"Aethelgar, drop another stone."

This time the stone had further to fall and had a greater effect. It unbalanced the man and as he struggled to hold on the efforts of Edward and Alfred, now aided by Aethelstan, meant that the ladder began to fall. Once begun, its descent could not be arrested and it crashed to the ground. The men fell into the ditch. For our wall that was the end of the attack. It was hard to see well in the dark but I estimated that almost twenty men had been hurt in the attack. Some crawled back to the safety of their camp. A few made it but others did not. More lay dead in the ditch than made it back to Prince Harold.

As the night wore on the sounds of fighting on the other walls gradually lessened. By dawn, it was clear that the attack was over. Before we could celebrate, however, we saw the cruelty of the Danes. They fired the villagers' homes. Despite the desire of every man to race and douse the flames, we dared not. It might be a trap and they could be waiting for us. Homes could be rebuilt. The dead could not be raised.

We waited until one of the sentries on the north wall reported seeing the Danes heading north. I was still not ready to take chances. Bergil, Edward, Aethelstan, Alfred and I mounted our horses and we rode, mailed and armed to inspect the damage. I saw that they had buried their dead before firing the village. From the number of graves, we had killed thirty in addition to the twenty odd whose bodies lay in our ditches. As we headed north through the smoke and crackling fires, I reflected that we might have been able to sortie and fight them, perhaps even defeat them but had we done so then we would have lost men.

"Alfred, go and tell the people it is safe. They can save whatever is not burned."

"Aye, lord."

I knew that there would be little to save. We followed the Danes until I was sure that they had gone. We found a piece of high ground and rested our horses there as we watched what had been a snake of mailed men and was now a worm, still heading north. Aethelstan had good eyes, "Lord, there are only three horses."

"Aye, they must have sent one back to York but where are they headed?"

Bergil spat, "Tresche, my lord, and other places where there is dissent. This is not over yet."

The thought depressed me as we headed back to the burnt-out remains of my village. By the time we reached it, I saw that the remaining Danish dead had been stripped and thrown onto Absalon's former house. It had the biggest fire and while some of the houses had been saved, Absalon would need to rebuild, as would many others. The rest of the fires had been doused.

As I neared the villagers Father Gregory called to them all, "Let us go to our church of the open and thank God for this deliverance."

The stink of burning bodies and buildings did not feel like deliverance but Father Gregory was right. The wounds we had suffered to our bodies would heal and we had timber so that we could rebuild. Father Gregory knew how to speak in such a way as to raise men's spirits and by the time we headed back to my hall, there was a more optimistic mood.

Uhtred nodded to the patch of open ground, unburnt and covered in weeds. "With your permission, Sir Richard, tomorrow my sons and I will begin to build our home there. Father Gregory can have his house back."

"You would still stay here, despite the attacks? It is a small manor and there may not be enough work."

"It is a safe place and a good one. Were it not for you and your people then my family would be dead. There is land there I can farm and as for work, there will be enough."

I knew that Osbeorn and Cnut, in York, might send out another column. I needed information. As we ate that night, I said, "Bergil, tomorrow you shall come with me as well as Edward and Aethelstan. We will ride as close to York as we can. If there is another warband heading here we need to know."

Alfred said, "What about me?"

"While the homes are being rebuilt, we need someone to watch the road from the north. Choose another young warrior who can ride and be sentries to the north. I do not think that Harold will return soon but you will spy him when he does and be able to warn the village."

His honour assuaged, he nodded.

We left early and made good time. Shipton was still a burnt-out charnel house that was a reminder of what might have been the fate of Eisicewalt. Our homes were gone but not the people and Eisicewalt would rise, stronger than ever, I would see to that.

We rode closer to York than I had thought possible. I had expected patrols and sentries but we came upon nothing except for unburied corpses. The gates to the city were open but, at first, we did not enter; I was cautious. I saw neither sentry nor warrior. I saw that the walls were blackened where fires had burned. Seara and Uhtred had told us that my brother had fired the buildings that might provide shelter to his attackers. I saw now that it had spread. Only those buildings and walls made of stone were untouched and the white stone was stained with soot.

"What do we do, my lord?"

Edward's question was a good one. I needed information and thus far I had not found enough. "Fasten your ventail, heft your shield and ride close to Parsifal's rump. At the first sign of danger, we will flee. Aethelstan, ride at the rear."

When we were ready, and with couched spears, we rode through the northern gate. That there were people hiding in the houses was obvious but they were fearful and that was to be understood. Most of those who survived were those who had collaborated with the Danes. When we reached the cathedral we reined in and I dismounted. I handed my spear to Edward and then walked to the doors. Bergil rode his horse behind me, his spear at the ready.

I lowered my ventail and held my helmet. As I neared the doors, my spurs jingling, they suddenly opened and there stood Belisarius. His arm was in a sling but he had a smile on his face. "God be praised, we are saved."

I shook my head, "I have but Bergil, a pueros and my squire. What has happened?"

Just then I heard, "Richard, I thank God that you have survived."

Out of the darkness of the church came my brother, Earl William, his wife and my nephews. I confess that emotion got the better of me. We embraced and I fought to hold back tears.

"What has happened?"

My brother shook his head, "Too much and little of it brings me honour. Come let us go outside and breathe fresh air."

Bergil, despite the sour taste of the parting from my brother, looked as delighted as any. He dismounted as did Edward.

I asked, "The Danes?"

"Osbeorn heard that King William was on his way north. They sailed away last night after plundering and sacking the city."

"And they let you go, my lord?"

He shrugged, "We had complied with every request and when we asked to pray in the cathedral we were allowed. Belisarius had taken refuge there already and so we claimed sanctuary. Archbishop Eadred died soon after they attacked and I think Osbeorn felt guilty about the death of the archbishop. He certainly did not wish to invoke punishment from above by dragging us away and so he left. Had he not then we would have been on a ship to Denmark. And you? How did you fare?"

"We were attacked by Prince Harold. I am surprised, for he sent a rider south. Does he know of his brother's departure?"

"I know not." He looked around at the burned buildings, "I wonder if the king will give me responsibility again. I lost him York after promising I could hold it for a year."

Belisarius said, "Do not berate yourself. There were simply too many and you had too few."

"And now, except for you, Bergil, they are all dead. That might have been your fate."

"I know and I thank my luck and God as well as Master Belisarius. I now have a home and a future wife."

It was Belisarius who made the connection, "Seara? She lives?"

"Aye, as do others like Uhtred the Saxon who found refuge with Sir Richard. The king has much to thank him for."

"As do I," my brother shook his head, "when I think how you were treated...Can you ever forgive us?"

"It is family, my lord, and therefore forgiveness is not needed."

I had wanted to return directly to my home as soon as I had the information that I had discovered. My brother implored me to stay. My couple of men were the only protection for the Sherriff of Yorkshire. We stayed in the cathedral. It was two days later that we heard the clatter of hooves riding from the south gate. We had not taken off our mail and we left the cathedral prepared to fight if we needed to. There was no need. It was a column of one hundred mailed men and I recognised the leader, it was my friend Bruno.

He dismounted. There was joy on our faces but on his was a frown, "You are all that remain? The rest are dead?" Bruno, like me, had known some of the men at arms who had fallen in the sack of York.

My brother nodded, "Richard rode in two days ago. The king is with you?"

Shaking his head he said, "No, I was sent by the earl to assess the situation here. Rumours are all that we have had. The king's brother, Robert, has been left to secure Lindsey and the king has gone to Stafford to regain control of that land. When that is done he will head north. He will feast, he says, in York at Christmas."

It was the start of Autumn and that was some months away. My face fell and I shook my head, "Then I must return to my manor. Prince Harold is still there, causing trouble and I fear he may attack us once more."

My brother said, "Bruno, we are like blind men here. What do you know of the Danish fleet? We know they sailed down the Ouse but..."

"They are on the Humber and they plunder the lands there. It is why the king left a sizeable force at Lindsey."

My brother nodded, "It is close to Lundenwic and also close enough to the Honour of Eye. A clever move."

I was less happy, "That does not help me or my people."

Bruno said, "I can leave half of my men here to begin the rebuilding of the castles and ride with you to your manor. At the very least we can ensure that the people are safe and then we will return here. King William wants a secure York before he exacts his revenge on the men of the north."

We rode the next day. I had wanted to ride immediately but Bruno and his men had ridden hard. As we rode he told me of the rebellion in the rest of the land, "Men rose but these were not the men we fought at Senlac, they are dead or fled abroad. As soon as the king arrived, they submitted. I have not yet drawn my sword or whetted my lance. My men are eager to fight."

"You have come far, my friend, to lead so many men."

"You could have enjoyed the same for the earl thinks well of you." Neither of us wore helmets and he apprised my face, "Yet you are happy, I think."

I nodded, "I have found men who, whilst not warriors, have the hearts of lions. We have drawn swords and slain many enemies." I told him of the sieges and the threat that Harold posed. "He can rouse the men of the north and use Danish lies to ensnare them. Until the Danes are back in Denmark then this land is under threat."

When we passed through Shipton we halted, and Bruno surveyed the carnage. "This is the work of the Danes?"

"They slaughtered, pillaged and raped."

"Then let us see if my men can enjoy some of the combat you and yours have."

Once we had passed Shipton we fastened ventails and donned helmets. It had been some days since I had left and I knew not what to expect. Even with helmets and arming caps, we heard the noise and clatter of combat.

We reined in and Bruno said, "This is your land you know it better than we. I put my men at your command."

I pointed to the west, "We can ride around the village. If they have sentries and barricades they will be on the road. The Danes destroyed much of the village and we can charge across the open tilled fields. We shall be the hammer and the walls of Eisicewalt, the anvil."

He called to his men, "Let us follow Sir Richard."

We rode in a column of fours with Bruno, Bergil, Edward and myself at the fore. The going was only slightly slower than on the road. The clash and din grew as we rode. The land fell away a little to the west and I wheeled Parsifal and waved my spear to form line. There were too few of us for two lines and we would use the mailed weight of Norman horsemen to break the hearts as well as the bodies of the Danes and the rebels.

Once we were aligned I pointed my spear and we rode through the burnt field and up the slight rise. At the top of the ridge, I saw the walls of my manor were being assaulted and I spurred Parsifal. The attention of all the attackers was on the walls. There were many more than had attacked us the last time. Even as I lowered my lance, I was able to see that few of the enemy wore mail. These were English farmers who sought to take advantage of the chaos of the times. Bruno had kept pace with me although Bergil, Edward and Aethelstan, riding lesser mounts had fallen back. The first men we speared died without even knowing that they were being attacked. It was the cheers from my walls that made both Dane and rebel turn. What they saw was not a small conroi of men at arms but a wall of steel. It froze them and in that freezing their fate was sealed. I showed no mercy as I plunged my spear into body after body. The first two faced me but then the others turned to try to flee north. It was in vain for our wall of men simply scythed them down. We wheeled and headed north, up the road after them. The speedier three or four managed to get half a mile from the manor before they were slain.

Bruno assigned three men to ride further north and ensure that there were no camps there and we headed back to the village. When we arrived the gates were flung open and men were already ending the lives of the wounded rebels. Uhtred waved me over. A Dane with a gashed stomach was lying on the ground, trying to stuff his entrails back into his body.

My smith said, "I was going to let him have a slow death, my lord, but I thought you might wish to speak to him."

I dismounted and handed my reins to Edward and my helmet to Aethelstan. I knelt next to the dying Dane, "Harold, where is he? I have not seen his body nor his fine helmet."

The man spat and gave me a sad smile, "He and his oathsworn said that they would ride to York and bring more men. He left us for we know that the fleet has sailed." He closed his eyes and winced in pain, "What you see here are the last Danes to threaten the Norman world." He opened his eyes, "Give me a warrior's death, my lord."

I nodded to Uhtred who slit his throat. I rose.

Bruno said, "Then on the morrow, we will ride back to York." He waved a hand at my walls, "Not a castle but sturdy enough. Your grandfather would be proud."

"I am not sure. There are many dead Englishmen here."

"I knew your grandfather and he had honour. These men, the rebels who will not stand and fight for their land are not of the same blood as your grandfather. He would be proud."

Chapter 16

After Bruno and his men had left we began, once again, to clear the dead and repair the damage. As we did everyone told me how Ethelred and Uhtred had kept a good watch and when Alfred brought the news of the warband the manor was ready to fight. The enemy had arrived that very morning and had we delayed my return from York any longer then things might have gone badly for us.

When the enemy dead were burned and Father Gregory had buried our handful of dead I gathered the families on the folk land, "The king is coming and with the Danes fled we can, before winter comes, build homes and our church but it will take everyone to do this. We fought an enemy and defeated him. Now we must fight equally hard to rebuild what he attempted to wreck."

People set to with a will. I worked with them and, over the next fortnight, the village rose like a phoenix from the ashes. This time the village had been savaged as though by a wild beast and this was a chance to bring some order to what had been a chaotic jumble of buildings. With Father Gregory's assistance, I reorganised the land so that the buildings and the fields worked more efficiently. I ensured that the land farmers tilled lay close to their homes. We made smaller streets and roads to make it easier to move around the village. In my manor I had Lars and my men prepare a fishpond. Whilst not apparently urgent, I had decided that a judiciously placed pond would not only provide fish for food but give us an impenetrable barrier if we were attacked again. That was their labour.

At the end of the first week, we had finished Bergil's home which lay within my walls. It was small but it suited them both. That Sunday Father Gregory married Bergil and Seara. The symbolic marriage was a sign of hope for the village and everyone worked much harder the following week. The new buildings took shape far quicker than we might have expected.

It was at the end of that week when King William rode in at the head of an army. It was early in the morning and I knew he would not stay for long. He must have left York early and that suggested urgency. We had replaced the water trough which had been used as a makeshift ram by the rebels and the king's squire watered his horse while the king greeted me. I dropped to one knee and he raised me up.

"None of that, Richard Fitz Malet, in the darkness of the loss of York one light shone like a beacon and that was you. Others might have fled in the face of such danger but you are made of sterner stuff." He leaned in, "And I need you again. Bring your squire and ride with me while we douse the last embers of rebellion." He pointed north, "It is time that they learned who is the king here."

I did not want to go but this was a command and at least Bergil and my pueros would be on hand to protect my manor.

"Of course, my lord. It will take a little while."

He nodded, "You know this land. Catch us up. We will rest this night at that nest of snakes, Tresche." I had told Belisarius and my brother of the danger there and of our actions.

Most of the army did not get the chance to water their animals. The king was keen to put his iron hand around the land and left after a short time.

Bergil, Ethelred and Uhtred came over to speak to me once the soldiers had left. They looked expectantly at me. I smiled and shrugged, "The king scours the land and he wants Edward and me with him. I leave Eisicewalt in your charge. I will return...," I waved a vague hand, "when the king is done with me."

Ethelred stood a little taller as he said, "We will have all finished when you return, my lord."

Aethelstan and Alfred were clearly upset at not being with me. They waited with Edward and me as we prepared. "Can we not come with you?"

"As much as I might want that, the manor needs your swords. The king asked for Edward and for me. I will leave you two to be here, along with Bergil, the guardians of my home. You two will be the vigilant eyes and sharp swords that keep my home safe."

They nodded. I took Parsifal and Geoffrey as well as a sumpter laden with our mail and weapons. As we passed the toiling villagers they halted and waved a farewell. It was then I knew that this was my home and not Fitz Malet. As soon as I was able I would return to Caen and collect my chest of gold. I needed to speak to Carl and my people there and tell them of my decision. The cries of encouragement from my new village were the deciding factor.

We reached Tresche in time to witness the burning of the houses. They had not been totally rebuilt from our raid. It was a foretaste of what was to come. It has been said that King William slaughtered everyone that he found in the north and that it was devastated because of him. That was both a lie and physically impossible. What he did do was to ensure that the North could never again rise against him. We burned the larger settlements and took every animal that we could find. Most people fled when they saw us coming and, in actual fact, we slew fewer of them than our detractors said. We had no battles to fight. As Bruno had said, they feared to face us. Senlac Hill had spilt the blood of their finest and the ones that remained feared us. We reached the Tees at the old Roman Fort of Persebrig having destroyed every village north of mine. After burning the houses he left a small garrison to hold the bridge and then headed east to the coast. As we progressed, he sent conrois of men to ravage and harry the smaller settlements and hamlets. Thornaby had been a prosperous Danish stronghold and there we had our first resistance. Men manned the walls. Their defence lasted but an hour and there he slaughtered every man and enslaved the women and children. They were sent under guard to York. It was a message for the rest of the land. If they fled they might survive. If they fought then they would die. When we reached Marske, on the coast, the king halted. While places like Malton and Norton were raided, he prayed at the church of St Germain before we headed back to Persebrig. We continued west until there were no more settlements to raid. It was only then, at the end of November, that he halted and headed back to York. He had said he would celebrate the feast in York and so he would.

The devastation of the north, certainly south of the River Tees, had a dramatic effect as crops died in the ground while people sheltered from the wrath of the king. With no animals to sustain them, even as we rode south people were dying of starvation. Those that were able, fled further north. It delayed the inevitable. The king intended, once Christmas was over and his men were well rested, to travel north to Durham and then the borders with Scotland. He had the bit between his teeth. We knew that the time just after Christmas was not one to travel.

I had not taken part in any of the chevauchée. Once more I had been with the king's bodyguard and the men I knew well. As we passed through the desolation of the Vale of York I said, "I beg leave, King William, to return to Graville while you feast. I would use this time to put my affairs in Normandy in order."

"You are leaving Normandy?"

I nodded, "The grange was a kind gift but I have rarely been there these last years and I feel that Eisicewalt is my home. I feel an affinity with the people. The grange at Fitz Malet will still be mine but the lord of the manor will be the heirs of my brother. I will bring my treasure to England and make Eisicewalt stronger."

"It is good that you think as you do. Half English and half Norman mean that you are torn. You have made your choice?"

"I have."

"Then all is well."

"I shall not have time to visit York, my lord, would you tell the earl?"

"I will."

I hesitated and then blurted out, "And my brother, what of him?"

He was a sharp man and his eyes bored into me as though reading my mind, "Do you mean will he be punished for the loss of York?" I nodded. "No, for it was beyond his control. Once the Danes decided to come by ship he had little chance of holding out. York needs river defences too. I cannot leave him as Sherriff of York for obvious reasons but Norfolk and Suffolk need a Sherriff and as he has the Honour of Eye it is a good appointment. It is a fitting reward for one whose family has served me so well. I do not forget such loyalty and I punish ingratitude as harshly."

I was pleased. I had seen, in York's cathedral, the shell of a man who had lost his command and his city; a man who had endured captivity and feared for his life. A quiet life in Suffolk would suffice. We parted from the king and the army at my village and I was greeted like a conquering hero. I did not feel like one. I had done little that had been honourable. We had a share of the animals we had taken and I left it to Ethelred to see to their distribution amongst my people. He knew them better than any.

That night I told them all of my plans. Benthe was appalled, "What about Christmas? Will you spend it on the road?"

I smiled, "Probably, but as I will be needed come the spring for the campaign in Durham and Northumbria, then needs must. I have gold in Caen and it will be needed to make this village and its people strong."

Bergil had said nothing and I put him out of his misery, "Bergil, I would have you stay here and watch over my lands. I will just need Edward and my pueros." I knew that he would have offered to come but he was recently married and leaving Seara was an unfair choice for him to have to make. I smiled at them all. Alfred and Aethelstan had just looked as though I had given them the best present ever and I wanted the others to feel as good about my departure. "If there is anything that you need from Normandy then let me know. This will be my last visit for I intend to make my home here in Eisicewalt."

That brightened their countenances although they had no requests to make. I decided to take Louis. Louis was my Norman horse and I would leave him in Normandy. He could spend his last years grazing on the grass of his youth. We took the hackneys and the sumpters. I intended to buy another warhorse in Normandy. Alain, the horse master, had always liked me and I knew he would recommend a good horse.

Well-wrapped against the cold and with beaver skin hats on our heads we rode south. The days would be increasingly short and I intended to ride in the dark too. The advantage was that we rode down a Roman Road and the main towns were now safely in Norman hands. I knew all the castellans, I had been King William's bodyguard, and we would be able to sleep safely. The danger would come on the exposed parts of the roads close to forests, but the recent rebellion meant that Sherriffs and castellans had been ordered to keep the roads safe. I was confident that we would be safe, at least until the New Year.

It took a week to reach Dover and we celebrated with a good meal and a better inn there. We had to wait two days until there was a cog sailing to Calais. I had wanted to get one to Harfleur or Rouen but at that time of year, few captains risked the channel. Once we landed, after a much shorter voyage than the last time, we headed south. This time we were not in Normandy but first Flanders and then France. Here, whilst not an enemy, I could not expect the generous treatment we had enjoyed in England. We made the one-hundred-and-fifty-mile journey in just over four days. Poor Louis was almost out on his feet but he seemed eager to be home and when we clattered into the cobbled yard at my grange he whinnied as though he was home. Heloise burst into tears when she saw me and I was touched. My pueros did not speak Norman well enough to understand all the words that gushed from everyone but they recognised the love that was there. It would be hard to leave Fitz Malet for the last time.

Heloise wanted to evict her whole family from my humble hall but I refused her permission. "We will sleep in the barn. I have been here rarely and I shall not miss my bed. Besides, we are here for a week only and then must return to the side of the king. I have to go to Caen to put my affairs in order. Our work in England is not done."

Carl looked crestfallen, "We thought that you had returned for good, my lord."

I shook my head. We were seated in the hall I used for dining. The children were abed and the food had been finished, "I am here to say farewell, Carl and Heloise. My brother will not be returning and I need to speak to his steward to ensure that this grange is run by you as my bailiff and that this will be your home in perpetuity."

"You are giving us the grange, my lord?"

"Better than that I am letting you live here. If I gave it to you then you could be called upon by the Seigneur to fight for forty days. Any demands for service will still come to me. You shall not have to go to war for anyone again. I will not need an income from the grange and I trust you to both invest and use any profits for those who live on Fitz Malet. This is to thank you for the service you have done me."

They could not understand my decision and we talked late into the night as I explained my plans. For my part, it was an easy one to make. The grange had been a token gesture to assuage the guilt of the Malet family for my grandfather's death.

I understood it but I did not need it. I had earned my new manor on the bloody field of Senlac.

We rose the next day and I went to my other two men to explain my decision. Like Carl and Heloise, they were mystified. I needed to ride to Caen but first I had to speak to my brother's steward and visit the resting place of my mother and grandfather. The steward was understanding. My brother had written to say that he would probably remain in England. The letter had been sent before the fall of York and I wondered if he had changed his mind since then. Leaving my three men with the steward to enjoy cider, cheese and good bread, I went alone to visit the two small graves. The cross on my grandfather's grave had been made of wood and had fallen but I knew where they were and I stood above them, gathering my thoughts. It had been some years but grief has a way of catching up with you. I wept and I was glad that I was alone. I was no longer Sir Richard of Eisicewalt, I was the little boy who had lost his mother too young and who had watched his grandfather slip away, his heart torn out with his eyes.

"I am here to say goodbye. I know it is just your bodies that lie here and your souls are with God. One day I shall join you. I will have stone markers made to show the world where you lie for your little boy has become both rich and a man of importance. I hope that you are proud of me. I now live in England and I know that would please you, Grandfather, but it is not in the land you knew, Mercia. It is in England however I am surrounded by men like you. I cannot see me having a peaceful life but I hope for one that will be useful." I knelt and kissed the ground. "Farewell."

I did not walk directly back to the hall but headed instead, for the farm that was Alain's. Alain was my brother's horse master. He had been a friend of my grandfather and would now be old. Indeed, I feared that he might no longer be on this earth. When I reached the farm, just a short walk from the graves, I saw him leaning on the wooden pen as one of his men schooled a young horse. He had aged. His white hair was thinned and he looked to have shrunk. His eyes were rheumy and I was ten paces from him before he saw me.

He peered myopically at me and then his face lit into a smile, "Richard! It is you!"

"It is, Alain, and I have come home to settle affairs. I am now the lord of a manor in England."

He shook his head and he reached his arm up to put it around my back, "Come within and we shall enjoy a beaker of cider and you can regale me with your tale."

It took until noon for the story to end and we had consumed a good half a flagon of cider. He shook his head, "Your journey has been a wonderful one and the steel of your grandfather shows through. I am sad that this is the last time that I shall see you but I can see that you are destined for greater matters than this little piece of Normandy."

"And I came to see you, not only to say goodbye but to make a request. I need a new warhorse. Louis is getting old and I have brought him back. I thought to give him a quiet end to his life away from the clash and clamour of arms."

"He is welcome here. He is a good horse and I believe that animals talk to each other. I know not how they do it but there are many things about this world that I do not understand. He can talk to my young horses and tell them the life that they can expect. As for the warhorse…," he smiled, "I have one. He was intended for his lordship but I can train another. We have not given him his war name but we call him Scout. He is a clever horse and senses trouble before it comes."

"I like the name but it is a princely gift and I must pay you."

"It is a gift for your grandfather was my friend and besides, with due respect to the Seigneur, I would rather Scout went to a warrior."

I nodded for I knew what he meant, "Can I see him?"

"Of course."

I fell in love with the animal as soon as I saw him. His tail and mane were golden, almost blond while his coat was a coppery red. When I looked into his deep brown eyes that seemed almost translucent, I knew he was for me and I put my forehead next to his. I could feel the acceptance and when I stepped back he whinnied and nodded his head.

Alain clapped his hand, "This is meant to be. We will groom him and I will keep him here until you leave for I like the horse too. He will be the last war horse I train. My sons can school the one for the Seigneur."

I headed back to the hall a little bemused. Fate had sent me Scout and I knew that as much as I loved Parsifal, he was not my horse. He was Taillefer's and I was just his carer. Scout would be different. Scout would be the new Louis.

I was so distracted that I did not notice the two men of arms appear from the shadows close to the hall. They startled me and my hand went to my sword.

One held up his hand, "You are not in danger, Dick, sorry, Sir Richard."

I suddenly recognised them. I had not seen them since I had been a pueros. "Albert, Jean!" I grasped their arms and clasped them. The two had been pueros with Bruno, Odo and me. I had not seen them for many years. They had not come with us when we had gone with the Duke and Earl Harold to fight the Bretons and their faces had disappeared from my memory.

"It is good to see you two. Men at arms, eh?"

Jean was the older of the two and he shook his head, sadly, "Aye, men at arms who are left at home while the rest follow his lordship to fight in England."

I said, quietly, "Captain Raymond and the others all died in York."

Albert said, "Aye, we heard but they died in battle. We are warriors but our skills are never used. We are not needed here. We are like a pair of village constables. We beg you to ask the steward to let us return with you to England. The Seigneur will need warriors. You are now a knight and your words will carry weight. We need the chance to be of service and not end our lives as two old drunks who stand by a door to make sure the cat does not steal the cream."

I understood their plight and I nodded, "I will speak with the steward but I am not sure if my words will carry weight."

Surprisingly they did. The steward had heard rumours of the disaster of York and the slaughter of the men at arms. I had been the harbinger of the confirmation. He was happy to allow the two of them to return with me as he knew the Seigneur would need such men. I felt better too as I was able to help two old comrades and it would make our lives safer. It was too late to travel to

Caen and so Edward and I, along with our pueros, returned to dine with Carl and Heloise. As we ate I asked them to have stones made for the two graves. "I will have gold when I return from Caen. I hope to be away for just one night. Caen holds little but gold for me, here is a much more precious commodity, friendship."

It was a wet, cold and miserable journey south to Caen. We were well wrapped in cloaks but even so, the wind found its way through. This time we had no need for the market and we rode straight to the castle. Like Edward before, Aethelstan and Alfred were over-awed by the donjon. I smiled, "One day King William will have an even more impressive home in England." When we had travelled south the king had told me how he had ordered white stone for his new donjon on the river in Lundenwic. He had shortened the name to Lunden and I thought it sounded better.

Arrius was older but glad to see me. He welcomed the three young Englishmen politely, "We are forgotten now, Sir Richard. Servants seek tasks to keep them occupied. The cook will be pleased to have four guests."

I translated for Aethelstan and Alfred. Edward understood far more than he could speak. Alfred's eyes widened, "Guests?"

I laughed, "Aye, Alfred, we are honoured here."

"You come for your treasure, my lord?"

"I do."

I will have it prepared and be ready for when you leave. You leave on the morrow?"

"Yes, I am needed by the duke."

"Then I will, with your permission, dine with you this night. If this is to be a last farewell then I would make it a good one."

I had not realised that the visit to Normandy would be so traumatic. I did not know I had touched the lives of so many people.

England was so far from Normandy that news, especially at this time of year, travelled slowly. Had I not come I doubt that they would have heard of the disaster of York until the spring. The tales of the conquest lasted until the creamy desserts had been finished. I do not think that Aethelstan and Alfred had ever dined as richly.

It was as we sipped the strong sweet dessert cider that Arrius became serious. "You know, my lord, that you have enemies?"

I shook my head, "I thought that when I slew Sir Durand and his squire that all my enemies lay beneath the ground or were new ones awaiting me in England."

"Would that were true." He played with the napkin on the table. I could see that he was deciding how to tell me something.

I said to the other three, "It is late, if you have finished then retire. We will leave in the morning as soon as the gates to the city are open."

The strong drink had made them sleepy and they nodded, leaving Arrius to speak as openly as he could. The other servants had retired already.

"You remember a knight called Sir Roger de Corcella?"

I had to think back but I nodded, "Aye, I went with him to Exeter in the early days after Senlac."

He smiled, "You might have forgotten that it was your words that made King William give the manor of Shepton to your brother Robert and not to him. It made him and his son, Turstin, bitter men. Their former manor lies close to Ouistreham, but it is a small and mean one. It does not yield much coin."

I could see why they might be upset. Shepton was a fine manor and had brought Robert riches.

"They might have lived with that had you not been given the manor of what is it now? Eisicewalt?" I nodded. "Sir Roger died ignominiously. He fell from his horse and the leg became infected. He died and it made his son bitter. Turstin was not a knight and he returned to the manor with a handful of men. He came here when King William returned and made all sorts of demands. He said that you owed him Weregeld." He shook his head, "Such a strange phrase and I have not heard it for many years. It relates to payment to a family for death in battle and was a Norse tradition. King William laughed and that, I think, saved the young man's life for he had angered the king. He was thrown from the castle and stripped of his lands. As he left he cursed the king and he cursed you. It was fortunate that he had a horse and was able to flee before men could be mounted to punish him."

"What happened to him?" I did not feel guilty for I had done nothing of which I was ashamed but part of me knew that my actions had partly led to the place he had found himself.

Arrius shrugged, "I think he and some of those who followed him became bandits. The manor was burnt and many said it was Turstin de Corcella who was responsible. There have been attacks on the road and merchants have been robbed. With most of the local lords in England, the land is not as safe as it once was. I say this as a warning."

"But he does not know I am here. I gave no warning of my arrival. I am leaving in the morning so what can he do?"

He shrugged, "I am an old man and I like you, Richard. You have never let titles and riches go to your head. I just have a feeling that Turstin will have friends in Caen and your arrival will have been noted. Ride fast and ride hard tomorrow and keep a good watch. I will send half a dozen men with you to escort you to the river. It is the least I can do."

"I think you exaggerate the danger."

He gave me a sad smile, "For your sake, I hope I do."

Had it not been for the strong drink I do not think I would have slept well. It was the quantity I had supped that woke me early and I dressed rather than returning to my bed. I woke the others and we went to breakfast. Arrius was already there. Four guards stood close to the two chests that held my treasure.

The old man smiled, "I thought you might be up early. The other two guards are preparing their horses. When you have eaten, they will ensure that the gates are opened early and you can steal a march on any who have ill intent."

"Thank you. You are kind."

After we had eaten, he said, "Do you not wish to count your coin?"

I shook my head, "I trust you, Arrius, and I do not feel as though I have earned the gold. I will put it to good use but I am not ruled by its glitter."

"And you are wise." I rose and he came to me, "Forgive my impertinence, my lord." He embraced me and I returned the hug. "You have been raised well and you are a credit to your forebears."

The chests were heavy and Arrius had given me a sumpter to carry them. It was still dark when the gates of Caen were opened and with our six-man escort, we galloped north on the road to the river. My men were confused by both the escort and the haste. As we rode I told them the reason.

"But it was not your fault, my lord."

"Edward, you need to learn that some men blame others for their own faults and once that blame is apportioned then everything else becomes easy."

We reached the river and the ferry safely and I gave each of the six men silver coins as a thank you. I knew I needed not have done so for I would never see them again but I had been a pueros and a man at arms. I knew their lives and it was little enough that I did.

I was relieved when we rode into the yard at Fitz Malet. I decided that we would stay just one more day and then head home. Arrius had put dark thoughts and fears in my mind. When we rode north, we would be mailed and armed. We would have to ride as though we were in an enemy's land and keep a good watch over our shoulders. I was glad that I had Jean and Albert with me. They had the experience that the other three lacked.

Chapter 17

Saying farewell to Louis was almost as hard as the one I gave to Carl, Heloise and my people. Louis had saved my life on more than one occasion. I knew that Alain would look after him and give him when the time came, a peaceful end but it was knowing I would never see him again that brought the uncalled-for tears to my eyes. The tears, when I left Fitz Malet, gushed from the normally strong Heloise and I was sad. Had it not been for the fear that my presence might bring harm to them I would have stayed longer. The spectre of Turstin de Corcella drove us north.

We now had two extra men and their horses. I rode Scout, for the first time, and we had three sumpters. I had clothes I had left at Fitz Malet and they, along with spare arms and food were on the sumpters. Aethelstan and Alfred led and guarded the sumpter with the gold. We all rode mailed and armed on the road north. While the others chatted and got to know one another I got to know Scout. He was a clever horse. His ears were pricked and he seemed alert. Alain was right and this horse had qualities that other horses did not possess. I found that he had been well-schooled and I could ride him with just my knees. He responded so well to my touch that I knew the slightest prick from my spurs would start him like a greyhound. I spoke to him as I had been taught by Alain and he responded. I was not one of those riders who believed that a horse was something to take you to battle and be used. For me Scout would become a friend and the journey north began that bond.

We were heading for Abbeville and the crossing of the Somme. With unladen horses, it might have taken just one day but the seventy miles in winter and with the spectre of bandits waiting for us meant that our journey had frequent stops, not least to see if we were being followed. We found shelter. The small abbey at Clais was happy to accommodate a Norman knight, for a fee of course.

The two men at arms were sceptical about an attack, "My lord," I knew it had taken some adjustment from Dick to Sir Richard and 'my lord' was how they now addressed me, "these are brigands. Why would they risk taking on a knight and five well-armed and mailed men?"

The food we ate was a basic stew with more pulses than meat but it was filling and I ate slowly to make it seem better than it was. I paused and said, "I do not have malicious thoughts within me but I met others who have." I was thinking of Sir Durand whom the two men knew. "I do not know what motivates them but until we are back in England I will sleep with a dagger beneath my pillow and assume the worst."

Being an abbey the monks were up and about early. We breakfasted far earlier than normal and headed out on the road. We reached the bridge at Abbeville not long after the sun had made the sky light enough to see faces. We joined the throng at the busy crossing. If we were being hunted then the slow crossing of the Somme would help identify us. We were the only warriors with sumpters who crossed the river. I had feared an ambush just after the river. Anyone who sought us would know that we had to cross the river and Abbeville gave them our route. After that, we could vary it. Despite my fears, it did not seem to affect the others. Albert and Jean liked my three warriors and whilst communication was difficult, Edward found himself translating. The experience was good for all of them. They got on and while I brooded the five of them chattered away.

We made Montreuil safely. We were now in the County of Boulogne. I was luckier than most Norman knights would have been for I had been of some service to Count Eustace. He and King William were now friends but I was wary. I did not know the lord of the manor in Montreuil and so we had to stay at an inn. As with all such places accommodation was not as good as one might have hoped. The stabling was inadequate and the food was both overpriced and barely edible. I consoled myself with the fact that within a day we would be in Calais and there we would be safer. I had one of my men in the room with the chests of treasure at all times. I included myself in the duty. It meant we did not all eat together and I feared that the constant coming and going of one of our party might have alerted any bandit to the presence of something worth guarding. It could not be helped. I studied every face that entered. I knew that I would not recognise any of the de Corcella men but I thought I might recognise

Turstin. I did not see him. I saw suspicious faces but that could just have been the fear planted there by Arrius.

I was relieved when we closed the door on the room I shared with Edward. The other four were crowded into the second room. I had paid for enough ale, cider and wine to ensure that they all slept well. I slept fitfully. Arrius had meant well with his warning but the seed was growing inside me.

North of Montreuil we headed closer to the coast. We had risen early and as the evening food had been so poor we shunned the dubious pleasure of breakfast. Instead, we bought fresh bread from a baker and ate on the road. If we were pursued then I hoped we would have lost them by leaving so early. I rode at the fore as the magpies chattered behind me.

It was Scout who saved us. He suddenly stopped close to the start of a wooded section of the road. I tried to spur him but he would not move. Then I realised he had sensed danger. I drew a sword and shouted, even though there was no one before us, "Ambush!"

Edward, Aethelstan and Alfred had been trained by me. Just as I did, they raised their shields almost without thought. Jean and Albert did not, for it had been some years since they had been threatened in battle, and it cost Albert his life as a crossbow bolt slammed into him, throwing him from his saddle. Four were aimed at me and three of them cracked into my shield while a fourth whirred off above my head. Other bolts struck the shields of the others. I counted on the fact that a crossbow is hard to reload quickly and I spurred Scout forward. This time he responded and took off like an arrow. As I neared the edge of the wood I saw the ambushers. There were eight with crossbows and they were trying to reload them. I saw another four shadowy figures deeper in the gloom of the trees. I was on the eight far quicker than they anticipated and I struck one on the side of the head with the edge of my sword whilst kicking a second in the face. I hurried towards the others. I knew that Edward and Jean would be following me. The sight of Scout's snapping jaws and my sword was making them rush their reloading and in such a rush lay mistakes. I smashed my sword through the skull of a crossbowman to my right and then wheeled Scout sharply to my left to take another in the throat.

Edward and Jean had closely followed me and while the crossbowmen were soon all dead or dying there were four others who were not. I let my shield drop to its guige strap and drew my second sword. I relied on Scout's ability to be ridden by a warrior using just his knees. We wove through the trees. Ahead of me I recognised Turstin. He was mailed and had a shield and a long sword. He was flanked by three warriors. Two had axes and one a pike. I did not hesitate but rode directly at Turstin. He stood for a heartbeat and then ran. I saw horses in the distance. Jean was keen to avenge the death of his friend and he closed with one of the axe men. I rode in the gap between the two axe men for Edward was racing to my aid. Even as Jean slew the first axeman, the pikeman swung his bladed weapon and hacked into the legs of Jean's mount. The man at arms flew from the back of the horse and landed heavily. The axe man and the swordsman raced to finish him off. Edward managed to slay one with a blow to the head and then they disappeared from my sight as Turstin reached the horses and mounted one. I wanted Turstin. He was the cause of this ambush.

"Stay and fight, you coward."

He did not answer. Scout was truly a great horse and even though Turstin tried to shake us off, step by step Scout brought us closer to the fleeing ambusher. Turstin kept looking around in fear and that was his downfall. His horse stumbled and while the man kept his seat it allowed me to close with him. He turned and cried, "Mercy!" It was a trick for he still had a sword in his hand and was merely buying time. The trick did not work.

"You deserve none." I swept my sword and took his head.

Leading the horse with the headless corpse still held by the cantle, I approached the scene of the ambush and saw that Edward, Aethelstan and Alfred were all whole but Jean, like Albert, had perished. The two men had wanted a warrior's end. Had they expected one this quickly? Would their souls regret their decision?

I nodded to the three horses, "Fetch the horses. Leave the crossbowmen but put the others on the backs of their mounts. We will see what the Count of Boulogne has to say." Turstin's body was taken from the stirrups and laid across the saddle.

It was after dark when we reached the castle by the sea and the two sentries at the gate were suspicious of so many men leading bundles draped over saddles. I gave my name but it meant nothing to them. I took off my helmet and dropped my coif, "I have served with the count. Fetch me someone who was there when we took Douvres."

Suddenly one of them grinned and said, "I am sorry, my lord, now I see it. You were the mad young thing with Taillefer. I remember you." He turned, "Open the gate and admit friends." As we passed through and he saw the cloak-covered bodies he said, "And I can see you live adventures yet."

The Sergeant at Arms who greeted us in the outer bailey had heard of me and he recognised me. I told him my tale and he nodded. "I will take you to the count. He is about to dine. Your men and, your cargo," he waved a hand at the corpses, "shall be accommodated. Gaston, find the priest and see to these men's needs."

I was taken, not to the Great Hall but to a solar where the count and a priest were seated. There was a wax tablet on the table and the priest was making marks on it as they spoke. The Sergeant at Arms said, "Sir Richard Fitz Malet, my lord. He was attacked on the road just south of here and he has brought the bodies of those who perpetrated the deed and his dead men."

The count looked angry, "Bandits in my land! Have their heads put on the gates and feed their bodies to the pigs." He seemed to recognise me, "I know you, you were at Douvres. I pray you sit." He looked at the priest who rose.

"I will see to the dead, my lord. They will need to be buried."

I wanted to say words over Jean and Albert but knew that could wait. The dead were dead and their souls, I hoped, were in heaven. My words would be for the living who would be haunted by the deaths until the end of their lives. The three of them were young and Jean and Albert were the first comrades that they had seen die. It had been a silent ride from the ambush and I knew that they had been brooding. I foresaw much work once we were back in England. Their souls were not in jeopardy but their spirits were.

The count nodded to the wine as the sergeant and priest left us. I poured myself a goblet. "Now tell me all."

I left nothing out. I explained the feud that had led to the ambush and the circumstances of the attack. I refilled the goblet when I had finished.

"You have done well then to slay so many and lose but two." He made the sign of the cross, "That you have lost two men is inexcusable but you could have lost your own life. You, from my memory, are a special warrior, Sir Richard. Do not throw your life away by taking such risks."

"I went to fetch what was mine, my lord. I did not expect to be attacked."

He nodded, "And I fear that there is increasing unrest. King William's victory has upset the balance of power in this land. The King of France now sees him as a threat. In addition, there are many men who fought in England and do not wish the heel of Norman rule to be on their necks. Some have fled here and while many find honourable work there are others who seek to cause mischief." He smiled, "You are safe now and this night you will dine with me. I have a cog travelling tomorrow to Remesgat. It is a short voyage and the weather is benign. The ship was travelling to England in any case to pick up some of my men who were wounded fighting for the king in the west. It would be my pleasure to be of assistance to the man who afforded us entry to Douvres."

My squire and pueros served at the table and I was the centre of attention. Some of those who were there knew my name from Douvres and all knew of my relationship with Taillefer. I became Taillefer for the evening, telling his tales and even singing one of his songs. I knew that I did not do them justice but they brought back the memory of Taillefer and, for an hour or so he was alive once more. It expunged, albeit briefly, the memory of the ambush.

We had gained horses as well as some mail, helmets and weapons. Uhtred would need them and they were loaded on the cog. The voyage was longer than the one from Douvres to Calais but we were saved the ride to Calais. I was happy.

As we sailed out of the harbour I stood at the bow with my three men who had said little. As the bows bit into the waves of the open sea I began to speak, "I know that the three of you grieve for Jean and Albert. You did not know them well but you liked them and warriors can form a bond quickly. Their deaths could not have been avoided and both chose to leave a peaceful, dull existence to have the life of a warrior. Death waits around the corner for every man who does so. Let this be a test for you. Do you still wish to be a warrior knowing the risks? If the answer is no then I will not think any less of you and I swear that you shall be rewarded for your service thus far. If you choose to be warriors then do so knowing that there are dangers but the better the warrior you are then the more chance you have of survival."

They were all silent. We had left the harbour mouth and, as we turned, the swell of the sea struck us. Spray came over the bow to splash us. The three seemed not to feel it. Eventually, Edward turned and said, "I know not about the brothers here but for my part I love the life of a warrior. It is just the sudden deaths of the two men that has made me silent. I got to know them and wished to become friends with them. I saw a journey that would see us grow closer."

"You will learn that when you find a warrior with whom you have affinity then you become close quickly. None of you could have done anything to save them. I know you tried, Edward. You slew the two men who ended the life of Jean and even though it was in vain, for he died, I am guessing that he thanks you from the Otherworld for trying to do so. And you two were obeying orders. You guarded my treasure."

Alfred said, "We are like Edward, my lord. The pain of the two deaths is hard. We were young when our father died and we did not see his death. We missed him and saw the grief it caused our mother but this, somehow, was more personal." I said nothing. "We will serve you still and now we can see that we need to improve our skills." He smiled, "I saw a different lord last night when you entertained the men of Boulogne. You are famous, my lord. Why have you not shared your skills with those in Eisicewalt?"

"There I am Lord of the Manor, last night I was Taillefer's squire once more. A man can be more than one person, Alfred. You will see."

We were back in England and the land ruled by Bishop Odo. We were safer than we had been and my name was well known enough to gain us shelter in holy houses. We headed for Eye. My brother needed to know about Jean and Albert and I wished to tell him what I had done. When we rode into the cobbled yard of his castle it was my brother who came to greet me. I smiled at the memory of my early years when I had been treated little better than a thrall. Now I was welcomed like a conquering hero.

"It is good to see you, Richard. I did not get the chance to thank you for your timely arrival in York. The King said that you were going to Fitz Malet?"

I nodded, "And I have much to tell you."

My serious tone took the smile from his face, and he said, "Then let us retire within." He waved over his squire, "Henry, see to my brother's people and their animals."

My brother's wife and his sons listened as I told them of my visit and my decision to leave Normandy forever. William nodded, "I think that I will not be returning home. Our brother Robert has expressed a desire to return to Normandy. I had a thought to give him the title of Seigneur and let Gilbert here be the lord of Shepton."

"I think that Graville and de Caux would appreciate a Seigneur, my lord. They feel abandoned."

"Then it shall be done. And now you head home."

I sighed, "There is more, my lord." I told him about Jean and Albert.

He became visibly upset. "My last men at arms, slain." He shook his head, "I hope, Richard, that you never have to watch your men be slaughtered and butchered. I witnessed it and it was heartbreaking. They kept their oaths and they died."

He was silent and I said, quietly, "And you live."

His eyes widened, "Aye, I feel guilty but how did you know?"

"When Taillefer died I wanted to follow him. I am glad, now, that I did not but at the time the death and the grief almost consumed me."

His smile returned, "You are wise, Richard."

He forced me to stay two days and only allowed me to leave when I told him of my promise to the king to be at the muster.

As I mounted Scout, William came over and clasped my arm, "I am proud of you, Richard, and I am glad that we are of the same blood. Go with God."

Chapter 18

We took the slight detour to York to tell the king that I had returned. He was still celebrating and was with men out hunting but I was told, by Belisarius, to be ready to follow when he passed Eisicewalt in a week's time. I was relieved. I would not have to leave immediately and my two pueros would have time with their mother. I knew that they both had much to say to her. When we neared the village I saw that everyone had worked hard during my absence. Smoke rose from the smithy and there were now houses where there had been burnt-out walls. We were greeted with smiles and waves all the way north from Forlan's farm. It gave me a warm and cosy feeling inside and confirmed that I had made the right decision to leave Normandy. I had chosen my English roots and not my Norman ones and it was good.

We passed through the newly repaired gates and Bergil and Benthe came from my hall to welcome me. Bergil looked approvingly at Scout, "A fine-looking horse, my lord, and he looks expensive."

Shaking my head I stroked his mane, "No, Bergil, a gift from an old friend and, as such, is worth more than gold." I turned to Edward, "Have the chests taken within and then take the mail and helmets to Uhtred. He can take what he needs and then we can distribute the rest."

Bergil said, "I have spent some time putting order into the armoury. The weapons can go there. I will deal with that. It is good to have you home, my lord."

I nodded and then said, "I will get the bad news over now. You remember Jean and Albert, men at arms?"

"Aye, lord. They were left at Graville."

"They chose to return with us but we were ambushed in Flanders and they died. I thought you should know."

He nodded, "I did not know them well, my lord, but we shared a warrior hall and I have drunk ale with them. They died well?"

"Does anyone who is ambushed die well? They died in battle and I think that was what they wanted. They felt as though they were waiting to die in Graville."

"And that is another reason I am glad I wed Seara. I now have a future beyond battle. They did not. I will drink a toast to them and tonight say a prayer. Thank you for telling me, my lord." He turned to go and then stopped, "And that makes me the last man standing. All the others who served at Graville are dead. It makes a man think."

The four warriors who served me had all learned a lesson from the deaths of the two men at arms. Time alone would tell how it changed them.

Father Gregory gushed, as we ate that night, about the new church and the phoenix-like village. "Could you, my lord, ask the Archbishop of York to consecrate our church?"

I said, "Archbishop Eadred is dead, Father Gregory, and we await the appointment of a new one. However, I will ask the king. Perhaps Bishop Odo might perform the ceremony."

Father Gregory was not enamoured of the warrior bishop. He was not renowned for his sanctity and it was said that he ruled Kent with a rod of iron. It was the best suggestion that I could make. We then spoke of the village and its future.

"The animals you secured were distributed well and with the reorganised fields, my lord, we should produce more crops."

"You seem to have a flair for husbandry, Father. Would you act as bailiff until I return from my martial duties? I will appoint a permanent one when we return."

His face lit up, "I would be honoured, my lord."

Once more I mentally thanked Belisarius. He could not have given the village a better priest.

By the time the meal was over I was satisfied with the progress made in my absence. Benthe had joined us along with Birgitte and Ethelred. Bergil and Seara wanted time alone in their new home.

"I will take just Edward, Aethelstan and Alfred with me when I go to serve the king. I believe that this part of his kingdom will be safe but with Bergil and Ethelred keeping watch for enemies I am sure that none will come to any harm."

I saw the slight frown flit across Benthe's face but when she saw the joy on her sons' faces it was replaced by a smile. She asked, "And will this make the whole of the north safe, my lord? The refugees who fled here are fearful to return to their homes."

"And as far as I am concerned they can stay here. As for making it safe? I believe so. The king will build castles. We will make our walls stronger. One day we shall replace the wooden palisade with stone. I have brought my fortune back with me and I will use that to enrich the lives of everyone. We will buy two oxen. I will buy other animals for the villagers to use. I would have horses bred and I want every home to be filled with well-fed villagers. There will be no hunger in this manor."

There was a cheer. Birgitte asked, "And when, my lord, will you take a wife?"

Benthe snapped, "Birgitte, do not be so rude!"

I smiled. I remembered her mother asking the same question, "She means no harm, Mistress Benthe and to answer you, Birgitte, when I find the lady that was meant for me. Your parents found each other. Bergil and Seara were also meant to be together. I am still a young man and one day I will wed but I need to find the woman that is meant to be my wife. Does that satisfy you?"

She beamed, "Yes, my lord, I just want you to be happy for you have brought happiness here. Before you came we were fearful. Now I see hope in smiling eyes. This is a good place to live."

Benthe stroked her daughter's hair, "That makes up, somewhat, for your impertinence now it is time we cleared the table. His lordship has travelled far."

The next day was indeed busy. The improvements that had been made met with my approval but there were others that were needed. I walked with Ethelred, Bergil and Father Gregory as I pointed out each change I wished to make. "We need a good stone path to the new fish pond. In winter it will be well used. We need a much bigger stable. When it is built we pull down the old one and build a bigger warrior hall and each building needs to be connected so that we have solid walls that can be defended. I do not believe that we are in imminent danger of attack but there may come a time of unrest and then we shall need good walls." I turned to Ethelred, "The woods?"

"Teem with game, my lord. When you return it will be time for a hunt. It will be good for the village."

"Then make it so. Bergil, I know you are no archer but we need the boys who were slingers trained to use a bow. I saw at Senlac how effective they were."

"We have archers who are old, my lord, and they can do the training. I will find ash and yew and seek a bowyer and fletcher."

"We now have enough weapons for all the men in the village. Issue the new helmets and swords. The training after church on Sunday becomes even more important. We forged a weapon when Prince Harold came. Let us keep it sharp and honed. If an enemy comes again he will find us a hard foe to defeat."

By the evening I was exhausted. I had not only toured my home but visited with every villager and spoken to them. When I spoke with Uhtred, he told me that he now saw his future with us. "I can make ploughshares as well as weapons. I am training one of my sons as a weaponsmith and another as a blacksmith. When I am too old to wield a hammer they can take over." He smiled, "I am making a sword for you, my lord. It will not be a swift undertaking for I would make one that will neither bend nor break. I will use charcoal and make a fuller. It will be a master piece for my sons to emulate. It will be the last sword I make and it will be the best."

My time at home was all too short and there were not enough hours in the day for me to do all that I wished. The Breton scouts who passed my home warned me that the king would soon be passing. We had packed already and I had chosen Scout to be the horse for this campaign. I mounted him while Edward waited with the two pueros and the mail laden sumpter. I did not think we would need to be mailed until we crossed the river.

The king was flanked by his brother, Bishop Odo, and the Earl of Surrey, Wiliam de Warenne. I would, at least, be seeing Bruno again and I had much to tell him. King William reined in and waved a hand at my walls, "A Norman bastion in this English land, you have done well Sir Richard. Ride with my bodyguards once more and have your squires follow behind."

"Yes, my lord."

I slipped next to three men I knew. As I looked around, I saw that there were newer bodyguards and the older warriors were fewer. Before I could start to chat to the men around me I heard cheers as we passed through the village. The king thought they were for him, and I think that many of them were, but I heard *'Fare ye well Sir Richard'* more and I knew that they were bidding goodbye to their lord. I was touched.

Aimeri was one of the bodyguards and I asked, "Where is Hugh?"

"Like you he was knighted and he was given a manor to the east of York, Ulfketill. King William needed a lord like you to guard the approach to York from the south. It is smaller than yours and he has no men at arms but you know Hugh. He is resourceful."

"And you wait still."

"I fear that I will be knighted soon and given the poisoned chalice of a manor in Northumbria. I think that I would prefer to guard the king."

"And that is a young man's job, Aimeri. Besides, as I have found there are good people in this land."

"You are English, my friend. You were born half English and brought up English by your grandfather. I am Norman. Oh, do not fear, I will make the manor Norman, but I will be far from my two friends."

One of the other bodyguards, Henri, snorted, "First, we have to secure the land. They have had months to prepare for our arrival. I think that we will have to fight for England. They will not give it up easily."

I pointed ahead to where Gilbert Tisson, another bodyguard, now carried the king's standard, "Gilbert has done well."

Aimeri nodded, "And I do not begrudge him anything. He is a brave man and is fearless. Such qualities are needed in the one who carries the King's banner."

We had not even reached the river when we spied the English but it was not an army. The scouts reported the standards of English lords at Aldbrough, two miles south of the river. The scouts said that there were just one hundred men there.

The king took no chances. We were summoned to form a screen and, with the Earl of Surrey and his men close behind we rode to the village. I recognised the standards of the earls Waltheof and Gospatric. Northumbria looked as though it was going to join the king. I wondered if this would be a campaign that was so short I would be home by seed time.

As we rode up to the Northumbrian leaders they abased themselves. Earl Gospatric spoke, "Forgive us, King William. Our people rose and we could do nothing about it. We throw ourselves on your mercy."

The king dismounted and waved forward one of the priests he had brought with him. The priest looked to have been ready for the request and he carried an object covered with a piece of fine cloth. I knew what it was. Before we had crossed to England to fight at Senlac, the pope had sent the king a banner and a piece of the true cross. This had to be the splinter of the true cross.

"You have angered me and caused me much mischief. This is not the first time that you have begged my forgiveness. I am a Christian king and I will give that forgiveness, if..." he waved the priest forward, "you swear on this holy relic that you will never break your word again, on pain, not only of death but also eternal damnation."

The two men held eager hands out to touch the relic and said, almost as one, "We so swear."

"Then rise." He embraced them both and we were dismissed as a camp was made to celebrate this victory that had given us Northumbria and the north.

We were the men who stood behind the king, the bishop and the earls at the feast. We were the first to hear of a marriage to be arranged between Earl Waltheof and the king's niece, Judith. The king was tying the English to him by marriage.

That still left Durham, however, and it was clear, when we crossed the river, that the king still thought he might have a battle to fight. We now rode mailed and helmed. We headed for Durham with its cathedral nestled in the loop of the river. Even as we approached we saw that the men of Durham had burnt their crops and fled. We entered the burgh and found it almost deserted. The handful who were left, the old, the poor and the sick told us that Bishop Æthelwine and his men had fled two days earlier with the holy relics from the church, including the body of St Cuthbert. King Willliam was apoplectic with rage;

Durham, he had thought, was part of Northumbria and now he saw that it was not. Bishop Odo and the Earl of Surrey were summoned.

"I want Durham laid waste as we did south of the river. Any man who is found is to be blinded. I want this land emptied. Warenne, your man Sir Bruno, he is still with you?"

"He is, my lord."

"Then have him take his conroi and find this bishop and my relics." He turned and waved me forward, "Sir Richard can accompany Sir Bruno. The two seem to get on and Sir Richard has special skills which may prove useful." He smiled, "This is his land."

I left with the earl who smiled, wryly, "I see that the king has given you two old friends a needle to find in this inhospitable haystack."

I shrugged, "Bishops with a corpse to protect do not travel quickly and they are carrying holy relics. That means a wagon." I waved a hand at the poor who had gathered outside the cathedral in hope of alms, "Besides, they might well have an idea where they have gone."

"I can see why the king puts so much faith in you, Sir Richard. You have a mind and you can use it."

I bowed, "I will speak with the poor. If you could ask Sir Bruno to meet me at the bridge." Edward had been waiting outside and he had followed at a discreet distance. Now he raced up. "Edward, we leave. You can leave the sumpter here. You three must be mailed and ready to ride. Meet me at the bridge."

Edward was now used to my sudden decisions and smiling he said, "Yes, my lord."

I reached into my purse and gathered a handful of coins. I knew, by their weight, that they were copper. The first of the dozen or so crippled men seeking alms held out his hand, "My lord, alms for the poor. God will bless you." I dropped four coins into his palm and he said, slyly, "Silver would bless you more, my lord."

I nodded and shifting the copper to my left hand reached in and brought out a silver one. The man's eyes gleamed as I flashed it before him, "But for this, I need information too."

He frowned, "I am just a poor man who cannot shift his legs as fast as a man should. How can I help his lordship? I know nothing."

I flipped the coin in the air, and it sparkled in the winter light, "Oh I can see that you are poor but your eyes are sharp." The flight of the coin was followed by the man's shifty eyes. "You sit here each day?" The man nodded. "Then you were here when the bishop left with St Cuthbert."

The man cowered back, "I am still an Englishman, my lord."

I nodded and, catching the coin, moved off saying, "And you will remain an Englishmen with just copper and no silver."

"I pray you wait, my lord." I turned and held the silver coin between my thumb and forefinger, twisting it to catch the light. He hesitated and then seemed to make a decision, "I was here, my lord, when they came out."

I waited and when there were no further words, said, "I know that but I also know that you know where they went."

"How do you know that, my lord?"

I put my face a little closer to his. The stink from his breath and his clothes were almost unbearable. My hog bog smelled sweeter. "I see it in your eyes. Now tell me for each moment I wait makes it less likely that you shall have the coin I hold."

"Lindisfarne, my lord, The Holy Island. Bishop Æthelwine said that he would return it to the saint's home."

I dropped the coin into his hand, "And take a bath."

As I hurried to the bridge I tried to work out where the island lay. I knew it was north of the Tyne and close to Bebbanburg but I had no idea of the distance. When I reached the bridge, I saw that my three men were there but Bruno had yet to arrive. I mounted Scout who seemed eager to be off. I remembered that Edward had been brought up in the north, "Edward, Lindisfarne, what do you now of it?"

"It is a monastery, my lord, in the far north. My uncle once went there on a pilgrimage. It is a holy place."

"And how far is it, would you say?"

He frowned, "I know not the distance my lord. My uncle took a fortnight for the journey but that was from Gilling."

"He was on foot?"

"He was."

Gilling was south of Aldbrough. It could be anything from
seventy to a hundred miles away. At least I had a direction now.
The haystack was a smaller one. I worked out, as we waited for
Bruno, that we would have to head for the bridge over the Tyne
and follow the coast road. It was the way a wagon would have to
travel and, I guessed, the most direct route. In theory, the land
should be at peace. The Earl of Northumbria had sworn
allegiance to the king but I knew that meant nothing. The men of
the north were independently-minded souls and owed more
allegiance to the bones of a saint than to the vacillating words of
a noble.

Bruno wore a scowl on his face and he shook his head as he
rode up to me, "How does the king expect us to find this bishop?
None of us knows this land and he could be anywhere."

I smiled and leaned in, "He is, at most, two days ahead of us
and I know where he is going, Lindisfarne. It is two days of hard
riding away."

"Are you a seer?"

I laughed, "No, but I know how to talk to people and what
they need. Come, we know where they go but we do not know
the dangers that we face."

I led with Edward, and we rode across the bridge and turned
to head towards the Roman Road that was still the fastest way to
travel. As we rode I explained to Bruno my reasoning. There
were forty of us all told. We had just two pueros with us,
Aethelstan and Alfred. They would have to serve as servants and
help Edward and Bruno's squire, Robert. This would be a
learning experience for them but, to be fair to them, they both
looked eager. The deaths of Jean and Albert had motivated them.

The bridge over the river at the eastern end of the Roman wall
was still the best way to cross the river. As we neared it, in the
early afternoon, I wondered if it might be defended. We were too
few in number to force a defended crossing. As we headed north
we asked, whenever we stopped to water our animals, about the
men we pursued. We learned that the bishop had with him more
than fifty men. Not all were warriors but they were all armed. If
they chose to defend the bridge then the fight could gain the
bishop time to evade us. It turned out that they had not expected
pursuit and we galloped, unchecked, over the bridge that was

over eight hundred years old. The Romans built well. We could have headed further east and used the ferry from the place the Romans called Arbeia but that would have added many hours to our journey. We were able to make the hamlet of Dinnington. The people kept within their homes and we camped. Bruno was an old campaigner and his men had brought food. We enjoyed hot food and, as the skies looked clear, we built up the fires and slept beneath our cloaks and blankets.

As we lay there, huddled in the firelight from the fires, I spoke to Bruno, "I thought you would have been in your manor in Surrey with your wife? I was surprised that you had come north."

"The problem we two have, Dick, is that we are too good at what we do. The earl and the king know that they can rely on us. That is why we two were sent on this adventure. From what you told me the king has made mistakes before, as with de Corcella."

"Aye, and that cost my brother two good men."

"There are others like that father and son, Dick. We will be used so long as we are useful."

"At least we know that when we have the relics in our hands the campaign is over and we can return home."

"And for you, that will be many days quicker than me."

We rode hard and crossed the river Aln at the tiny hamlet of Alnwick. There was a bridge and it looked sturdy enough to have been built by the Romans. As we crossed Bruno said, "If I was an earl of Northumbria then I would build a castle here. You could deny the crossing of this river and the site looks like a good one."

"Have you not noticed, Bruno, we English do not build castles. We throw walls and ditches around towns and call them a burgh."

He laughed, "I like that you still call yourself English."

My words almost came back to haunt me as we passed Bebbanburg. It had once been a castle, the home of Uhtred the Bold but, so Edward told me as we passed, the hill fort had been sacked by the Vikings more than one hundred years earlier. I pointed to it. "And there is a site for a castle if ever I saw one. See how the sea laps against the cliffs beneath the ramparts that were destroyed. If King William built a castle there then it would be impregnable."

"Look, my lord." Alfred's sharp eyes had spotted the monastery of Lindisfarne to the north. To my dismay, I saw that there was sea between us and the island. The Bishop of Durham was safe, at least until the tide turned.

We set up, as the sun set, an armed camp by the start of what was clearly the causeway to the island. Bruno set guards and he growled a warning at them to ensure that they were alert. "The last thing we need is for them to come in the night and cause mischief."

We both knew that the tide would turn in the night but we were not familiar with the causeway. When we crossed it would have to be in daylight and the later tide. Our fires told the bishop that pursuers had caught up with him and, as dawn broke, we saw his soldiers hurriedly making a barricade across the island end of the causeway behind which they could fight. The tide was still too high to risk a crossing and Bruno and I conferred to decide on our best approach.

Bruno looked at the sea and said, "As much as I would like to keep my feet dry I fear that the horses might slip on the wet stones. Better that we cross on foot. Your pueros and our squires can watch the horses."

"I agree and from what I can see there are few men with mail. If we meet them beard to beard we should overcome them. I doubt that there are more than a dozen warriors amongst them."

"The problem will be, Dick, that they will fight beyond hope for they are fighting for the bones of a saint. They will fight harder than they would for the earl."

He was right. Edward had said that the people of Durham did not regard themselves as Northumbrians but as haliwerfolc, people of the saint. Edward had explained the word as we had camped by the causeway. It meant we would have a hard fight.

We prepared to cross. Edward helped me to fasten my ventail and Alfred put an edge on my spear. My swords had still to be drawn and were sharp enough to shave with. When we deemed the water shallow enough we marched across, four abreast. Bruno and I had decided on a formation of four men abreast and nine ranks deep. Bruno's standard bearer marched at the rear. We held our shields before us but we were both confident that any arrows the men of Durham had would bounce off our helmets and mail. The haliwerfolc banged their shields and invoked the help of St Cuthbert. I saw the bishop who was standing on the wagon and holding up a cross, presumably also taken from Durham Cathedral. He was seeking divine help.

We in the front rank had the easier task but the march across the salty causeway helped us. We could not move swiftly and our steady approach kept us all in time. The long kite shields would give us all the protection we needed to our left and our spears were better made than the ones that faced us.

"Keep together and push and thrust on my command!" Bruno's commanding voice rang out.

His men all chorused, "Aye, my lord!" He had trained them well. As we neared the other side the water became shallower and we were able to see the crude construction of the barricade. They had little to work with on the holy island and the barrier would not hinder us. The round shields behind were locked but they were just three men deep. Our column of thirty-six men would be a much more powerful force once we gained solid ground.

A few arrows and stones were sent at us but with raised ventails there was no bare flesh to strike. The stones and arrows would cause, at best, a bruise or two but they were largely ineffectual.

Bruno knew his trade and he timed his command to perfection, "Now!"

The front three ranks all had spears which could reach the enemy and we would be the ones to strike. Our shields were locked and the English spears struck them without causing any damage. One lucky spear scratched a line along my helmet but all it meant was a little work for Uhtred's son when I returned home. Our spears had no ventails to stop them and as there were twelve spears all thrusting as one then they were more likely to find flesh. The six men they hit were all either wounded or killed. They fell and the barrier was swept aside as we pulled back and punched again. Already the battle for the body of St Cuthbert was lost but as Bruno had predicted, these haliwerfolc were fighting for a holy cause. Their deaths would ensure that they entered heaven. As we struck again so the men on the sides of the English line had targets. The problem was that on the left they could not pierce the shield wall and on the right they had to endure the darting heads of well-wielded spears.

Bruno timed his next command well. Aware that we were through to the last line of haliwerfolc he ordered, "Break!" Even while the haliwerfolc rushed to attack our flanks we broke ranks and took the battle to them.

His Norman words took the English by surprise and as the men behind us turned and thrust the English defenders of St Cuthbert died. I had never enjoyed so complete a victory. The English lay in a curved line, faithful to the end and the bishop dropped his head into his hands, he had lost. God had not given him the help he needed to overcome mailed Norman knights.

Bruno was aware that the tide would soon turn and did not want to risk being stranded overnight on the island. The bishop had, obligingly, left all the relics in the wagon and Bruno shouted, "Fasten the horses to the traces." As the men hurried to obey him he said, "Would you and your priests give your word not to escape or shall we bind you like slaves?"

Bruno's English was not great and his words were barked out but the bishop understood, "We so swear, Norman."

We barely reached the mainland before the tide had returned and was lapping around our knees.

It took much longer to return to Durham. That was partly due to the slowness of the wagon but also because the land through which we passed had strong associations with Lindisfarne. Knots of men often appeared to bar our progress and we had to force our way past them. Bruno tired of it and after three such attempts to bar our way, he had ten of his men couch their lances and simply charge the men who tried to bar the crossing of the Aln. Five of those men died. As it happened not long before we camped, on a high piece of ground overlooking the sea some two miles from the hamlet of Alnwick, word must have been sent for we were not approached again. Instead, we passed through villages filled with brooding anger. King William had his work cut out. Until he built castles in this land then he would have a populace who questioned his authority.

It took more than five days to reach Durham. We saw the effect of the torch as soon as we crossed into the land close to the cathedral. It was like the land the king had harried further south. Houses were burnt and the villagers had fled to seek winter shelter with others. There were few places in this part of the north where that could be found and I knew that people would starve. When spring came the land would be littered with bodies.

The king berated the hapless bishop, "I am the rightful king. This land, these churches, all belong to me."

To be fair to the white-haired priest, the Bishop of Durham, he tried to stand up to King William. It was painful to watch. "King William, this church is God's and the saint's bones belong to him."

"There you are wrong, old man, they now belong to me." He turned to Bruno and me, "Take the wagon back to York. Sir Bruno, you wait at York with my prisoner, the bishop, until I return. It will not take long to scour this backwater of all my enemies. Sir Richard, when you have delivered the saint and this former bishop to York your service is over. I thank you."

We were dismissed. Bruno was not happy, as he headed south. He would not be able to enjoy any of the plunder from the raids on the lands of the north and he would not be going home. He had a wife now and was eager to be reunited with her. I was happy to be going back to Eisicewalt. The king was hurting the ordinary people. Their lords and bishops might have put the ideas in people's minds but the nobles did not suffer. I did not think that it was right.

So it was that I returned home much sooner than I had expected and that was good.

I bade farewell to both Bruno and the bishop at York and we made the short journey home. Already the castles in York had been rebuilt and the city had a garrison. I knew not the fate of the bishop, but King William was not a forgiving man. One thing was sure; the bishop would be imprisoned, and the next Bishop of Durham would be a Norman.

Chapter 19

King William and his army passed through my village three weeks after my return and he thanked me, from the back of his horse, for my service. He leaned down to speak quietly to me. "This land is mine, now, Sir Richard, although there are some treacherous lords who do not know it. I need time to make York whole. After Easter, we will take the last city that refuses to acknowledge my rule, Caestre on the Dee. I want you at my side when I do. You will join me at York on Easter Sunday. We will seek God's approval and then ride south and west to rid my land of the last of the rebellious canker." With that, he left. I had less than a month to put my land in order. It was not long enough.

I put all thoughts of Caestre from my mind. What we four had learned, in the north, was that there was still unrest. The people of the north would die in great numbers but there would be parts, as yet untouched, that would resent the Norman presence and with the nobles paying lip service to the king I knew that violence could flare up at any time and my village would be a target. The time I had at home, while my farmers planted seeds and cared for the newly born animals, was spent with Bergil, Ethelred and Uhtred, making my lands secure. Where we could we used stone to make the defences at the gatehouse stronger. We made walls to connect my buildings such as my barns, kitchens, chapel, Father Gregory's house and the newly built warrior hall. At the moment the warrior hall held just Edward, Aethelstan and Alfred. We would have more men in the future but until then it would be a refuge if we were attacked again.

It was as we toiled on a door in the wall that bridged the chapel and Father Gregory's home that Bergil said, "I feel guilt that I have not followed you to war, my lord. You have left me behind and I know why, it is because I am married. This is not right."

We paused so that I could check the level of the lintel. "Had you come with me to Durham then the only action you would have seen would have been holding the horses with Edward and the others. Here you trained my men."

"They are still raw, my lord."

"And that is why when I go to Caestre you will stay here. One man will not make a difference to King William's army but you can make a difference here. Your experience and skill along with that of Ethelred, will make my fyrd stronger than any enemy we can expect. We have sent our enemies packing twice and I wish to build on that strength." I smiled. Benthe had confided some news to me when I had returned, "And besides, Seara is expecting your first child. You should be here to witness it."

"How...?"

"I am the lord of the manor and there are no secrets from me save those told to Father Gregory."

The improvements were slow and steady. We also had more refugees seeking a home. There were seven families all told. They came from north of the river in the land devastated by King William. All were emaciated and on the point of starving to death when they reached us. My people were kind and they took in the families. We had food aplenty. Some wished the chance to recuperate and then move further south. They told of great unrest in the north. English nobles were inciting the people to rebellion. Others wished to stay and make a home. I did have land. There were hides south of Forlan's farm and with work, houses could be built and fields cleared. Five families took up my offer of a home. However, I was no fool. I wanted no bad apples to upset the harmony of my village. I had each of the men swear an oath in my newly built church, and before Father Gregory, that they would be loyal to both me and my liege lord, the king. I think they had endured enough of false promises. My villagers had extolled my virtues and I was seen as their best chance of a peaceful and prosperous life.

As it turned out, one of them, Aedgar, had skills that were missing from my village. He knew horses. He came not from north of the river but had lived just twenty miles from us. He had raised horses but Prince Harold, on his journey back to join his brother and uncle, had attacked his farm, stolen his horses and made Aedgar homeless. He hated not the Normans but the Danes. When I learned of this, it gave me an idea.

Ethelred knew my land better than any and I went with my gamekeeper and Aedgar and we found a piece of land that would suit someone who might raise horses. It was in an area we had recently copsed of its trees. They had all been straggly seedlings and we had used their wood for palisades and stakes. It was on a slightly higher part of my land and would not suit crops which needed to be watered. However, it would be perfect for hardy grasses and grazing.

"What do you say, Aedgar, could you live here?"

He nodded, "We would need a home and I have two sons and a wife who are not afraid of hard work." He looked at the ground and shook his head, "But the ground, my lord, does not suit crops."

"And you are no farmer. You are a horse master. What say I give you a pair of goats? They will give meat and milk. I would have you breed horses." I nodded to my paddock, which we could see from our elevated position. "I have two stallions, Parsifal and Scout. Both are warhorses but if we bred them with hackneys and sumpters, while we might not breed war horses the resulting offspring would be better than their dams. When time allows I would have you take some of my coin and buy a better breeding mare. You could have half of any foals that are born. You will not make a great deal of coin at first but we would ensure that you did not starve."

He shook his head, "I care not for coin, my lord, I want a home where my family is safe and I can work with animals."

Ethelred pointed to the nearby woods, "His lordship allows his villagers to trap small animals and birds. If you and your sons are resourceful you can eat well. The forest has mushrooms and there is wild garlic in the spring."

Aedgar nodded his thanks, "I am convinced, my lord, and if you are happy to entrust me with your animals then I shall do my best for you."

"When I go to war for the king, I will leave Parsifal here. We will only need three hackneys and a sumpter. I will take the geldings and leave the mares here. Edward's mare, Marie, is a good animal. Use her to mate with Parsifal. Until you have built your home and your paddock then, perforce, you will need to use my stables for your work. Uhtred's son, Walter, will be your smith if you should need one."

And so it was that we gained, thanks to the mischief of Prince Harold and his Danes, a jewel that would make the village and me stronger. Fate was a strange mistress. A stone thrown into the pond of life had just rippled to Eisicewalt.

The time for us to leave came all too soon. It was an early Easter and as we left, on Easter Saturday, the wind which whipped in from the east chilled to the bone. We had enjoyed wool from our sheep and Benthe and her daughter Birgitte had knitted us warm hats. They had been aided by the two servants Mathilde and Agnetha.

When they handed them to us I saw that Mathilde and Edward exchanged a furtive smile and a brief brush of the hand. It had been a long time since Mathilde had tried to attract Edward's attention. She was now almost a woman and Edward was a man. Nature, it seemed, had taken a hand. With the cowls of our cloaks over them, they helped us to keep in a little of the warmth from our breakfasts. We had said our goodbyes the previous night and we left almost silently. My squire and my two pueros were unrecognisable from the three callow youths who had joined me. Good food, healthy exercise and a willingness to work had made them young warriors who would not be out of place in the mesne of a great lord. When Aedgar had his first animals then the result of the breeding of Parsifal and the hackneys might result in a courser or two. Whilst not as powerful as a warhorse, a courser was the perfect mount for a man at arms and I knew that my squire and pueros would be men at arms.

We were in York within an hour and while my men saw to our horses I presented myself to the king. He was busy and I spoke with Aimeri who was acting as the captain of the guard. "It will be a hard ride to Caestre. We have to cross over the highest part of this land."

I nodded, "But from what my squire has told me there are few people who live there. He and his family came from Earl Morcar's land at Gilling. He said that they were the last outpost before the land rose and only a hardy few managed to eke out a living beyond that manor."

"And that means we sleep in hovels and tents."

I laughed, "Are you getting soft, Aimeri?"

He shook his head, "I do not mind hardship, but I want to fight a battle and not simply burn the homes of the poor who cannot fight back. I am a warrior and would act as one." He lowered his voice, "Some of the others feel as strongly as I do. Perhaps this campaign might bring the honour we seek."

"And that depends upon the opposition. What do we know of Caestre?"

As one of the king's bodyguards, Aimeri would be privy to more information than was freely available.

"Many of the Mercians who served Earl Eadwine fled there and there are Welsh within its walls too. The Romans built it and while it is not a castle such as we might build, it is a strong burgh and fort which is defended on one side by the river. If they hold the walls then we will have to breach them."

"And then that will just leave Eadred at Shrewsbury."

He shook his head, "Your brother has found another enemy. A man called Hereward is causing mischief in the Fenlands. There is no fort there but the nature of the land means that the enemy cannot be brought to battle."

When the king emerged from his meeting he nodded at me, "We have one last push, Sir Richard. When we take Caestre then I can reward men like Aimeri here and my standard bearer, Gilbert, with manors. You, too, shall have another."

"You need not, King William, for I am more than happy with Eisicewalt."

He frowned, "It is for a king to decide what is right and not his subjects." Suitably chastised I bowed an apology. "You and your men will be with the bodyguard. You four have unique skills amongst my retinue. You are English and I might be able to exploit that to gain a victory."

There was a price to be paid for the king's rewards. We might have to betray my grandfather's people. It did not sit well.

We left on Easter Monday having been blessed by the king's newly appointed archbishop, Thomas of Bayeux. The archbishop had been the king's chaplain, and this was the start of the conversion of the church from one run by Saxons to one ruled by Normans.

The ride was a hard one. Ripon gave us shelter and a little comfort before we began the hard ride up the steep road across the spine of the north. A day west of Ripon we found a small settlement clinging to the side of the hills, Bluberhūsum. It was an unexpected place to shelter and even the king thanked God that we had found shelter and did not have to build hovels or try to erect tents. Once we passed the burgh the land descended to the plains of an area that seemed to have few people. The headman in Bluberhūsum had told us that the Vikings from Man frequently raided the west of the land and with few burghs there it was a devastated land. It explained why there was little dissent there. There were too few people to cause trouble.

The flat plain that spread west to the sea allowed us to travel more confidently. We could see any enemies coming from far away. It was the crossing of the Maersea where we had problems. Wallintun was a tiny village a short distance from a ford. The English, perhaps directed by the rebels in Caestre, had decided to dispute our crossing. They had a shield wall backed by archers and slingers. There were eorls on horses and the king estimated that there were more than five hundred of them. The advantage that they held was that we could not charge them at the gallop as we had a ford to cross and we would have to endure arrows and stones. Whilst they would not do much damage to us, our most valuable asset, our horses could be hurt.

When we had returned from Lindisfarne we had told the king how we had defeated the Bishop of Durham and his men. He now decided to emulate us. He personally chose the two hundred men who would make a giant wedge and advance across the river. The Earl of Surrey would be the mounted force that would secure what the king hoped would be the victory. Our successful attack would open the door to Caestre when we had broken the shield wall. We did not recognise any of the English nobles who faced us and so King William took the decision to lead the attack himself. He wanted these enemies to know that King William was a warrior and a force to be reckoned with. William de Warenne managed to persuade him to be in the second rank alongside Gilbert, his standard bearer, Aimeri and me. The earl knew that we would protect him. The men who were in the rank ahead of us were young and they were keen.

We formed up on the north bank of the river. It was a ford but we knew not how deep it would be. The two men at the front of our wedge, Raymond and Jean of Rheims, would be the ones who would test the depths. I did not envy them. I knew, from the causeway at Lindisfarne, how slippery and treacherous the stones underfoot could be. Bishop Odo blessed us as we prepared to move. I never felt that the bishop was close to God and his blessings meant little to me. In contrast, Father Gregory's blessing always inspired me for I truly believed that he was closer to God when he blessed us rather than the king's brother.

Horns sounded and we began to march. I flanked Gilbert and my spear was on the right-hand side of our wedge. Before the four of us were Guillaume, Artur, and Philippe. I watched their feet and moved mine at the same time. Gilbert, next to me, held the king's banner in his right hand and his shield in the left. There was a spike at the end of the banner and, in an emergency, it could be used offensively. If it was then it meant I had fallen. That was a sobering thought.

When we had gone just ten feet the king shouted, "Raise shields." The command was for everyone but Raymond and Jean. They would heft their shields to protect the front of our wedge. The water soon came to just below our waists. It was cold enough to be painful and we would have to endure soggy feet until the battle was over. That would be the least of our worries. When we were halfway over the rain of stones and arrows began. It sounded like hailstones on a slate roof but the storm did no damage and we ploughed on through the water. Soon the level sank to our knees and we had a strange burning sensation in those parts the water had covered.

The king was the tactician and he was peering from beneath the edge of his shield. It was he who saw that we were close to the south bank. He shouted, "Lower shields!"

As we did so our dark world became brighter, and we saw the gaudily painted shields of the Saxon wall. It bristled with spears and with Danish axes. I remembered Senlac. I realised that these were not housecarls. The best had died at Senlac and the rest, it was rumoured, had fled to serve abroad as mercenaries. Even so, the fearsome weapon was not to be treated lightly.

We all knew what the next command would be and we were waiting for it. As the front of the wedge made its way up the bank the king shouted, "Push, for your king, for Normandy and for England!"

We had needed no incentive but I pushed my shield into the back of Philippe. I knew that the end of our column would struggle for the ground was becoming churned up already. As well as pushing with my shield I also rammed my spear, almost blindly. I aimed, as we were climbing, not over the shield but below it. The red and yellow shield was an inviting target and my spear slid under it. The Saxon holding the Danish axe was already swinging it at Philippe when I felt the head of my spear slide into flesh that was not covered by his byrnie. I must have gouged a line along his thigh and then into his groin for the scream he gave was feral. He threw his arms back as his body tried to escape my spear and I rammed it all the harder. He was a big man. His Danish axe clattered into the row behind and his body soon followed. Philippe took advantage and he speared the man behind who had no armour. The body had fallen from my spear and I seized my opportunity. The man next to the dead axeman had just his spear on his right and my weapon drove through the links of his byrnie and into his body.

We had pushed back the three lines and although, in theory, we were surrounded, we had the upper hand for we had momentum and were now on solid ground.

"Break!"

The king's command allowed us all to choose our own enemy. Having punched a hole, I exploited it and headed towards a warrior with a white shield and blue cross. He wielded an axe but his byrnie only came to his waist. He swung the two-handed axe. It was not a smooth swing for he had a shield on his left arm and I easily moved my head and chest back. I rammed my spear at his thigh. It was a good strike and the head scraped along the bone. Before he could react I punched with my shield and he fell. The English shield wall was now in disarray and there were no shields to support him. He fell to the ground. I knew that the wound in his leg was mortal but I gave him a quicker death and drove my spear into his neck.

When I pulled out my spear, I heard the sound of horns as William de Warenne led two hundred horsemen. A solid shield wall might have stood but we had demolished it and the ones who remained were, in the main, without armour. They fled. Some might escape but Norman men at arms with relatively fresh mounts would soon run them down. We had won and, as I looked around, I saw the smiling faces of Gilbert and Aimeri. They had survived too.

Chapter 20

We had to wait until dark for our weary horsemen to return. Some had chased the enemy all the way back to Caestre. The nobles on their horses had led the rout and Earl William told the king that they intended to defend the Roman fort.

Bruno came to our camp. His hauberk was blood spattered but he was in good humour. Alfred had collected a couple of ale skins from the dead Saxons, and we drank good ale. The Saxons knew how to brew. "When I saw you and the king going forward I was angry that we had been left on the other bank but once the horns sounded…Dick, the charge was the most uplifting thing I have experienced. The charge at Senlac was against a solid line of men but these," he shook his head, "they just ran. Had that been me I would have turned and faced. I would have fought to the end."

"Except that you would not have run."

He laughed, "True but if I was cornered and outnumbered I would not simply wait to be butchered. Even if I just had one arm I would fight. That is how a warrior dies, not skewered like some slaughtered animal."

"Did you get to Caestre and its walls?"

"Aye, you can see the Roman fort still but they have improved it. From the mortar on the new walls, I would say the improvements came after Senlac. This might be a hard fight. They seem to like fighting behind walls and there their axes can do more harm."

His squire arrived, "My lord, the earl needs you."

Standing he said, "Thank you for the ale and when Caestre falls we may have even better treasures. I saw golden torcs on some of their nobles. I would have one."

I shook my head, "If you find treasure then all to the good but if you seek it then you lay yourself wide open. The fates do not like such hubris."

He laughed again, the joy of battle was still upon him, "You are like an old woman, Dick."

We rode the next day the few miles south to the fort. The defenders had laid waste to the land around them. All the buildings had been burned so that we had neither wood to build siege engines nor shelter. It did not dismay the king. He had the foresight to have brought some young trees and the squires were set to work building ladders for an escalade. Meanwhile, the army surrounded the fort. The fort was incorporated into the walls left by the Romans. They had been added to when it had been made into a burgh. I remembered Exeter. There we had undermined a tower. Here we would have to attack the walls.

As the king's bodyguards we were privy to the council of war. I saw why Bruno had been summoned by the earl. His master had volunteered to lead the assault on the walls. Like Bruno, the rest of the earl's men wanted the chance to prove themselves. The king agreed. He and his household knights would watch. Bishop Odo and his men would assault a second wall but the Earl of Surrey had been given the gatehouse as his target. I knew from our siege that a gatehouse was always hard to take. There would be the greatest chance for honour.

As we stood waiting for the battle to begin, I heard the king speaking with William de Warenne, "Do not worry if this attack does not succeed. I would not have you waste your men. Know that I have sent for the Earl of Hereford and his men. We will defeat these men and then rid the land of Eadred the Wild. He is playing fox and goose with the earl and I will put an end to that."

I was relieved. It meant that if this attack failed we would have a better chance with more men. I saw Bruno and his men carrying a ladder. The earl and his men had ten such ladders. The men who would be first up would be volunteers. They would be the ones who hoped to catch the eye of the king. They would be men at arms who sought their spurs and a manor. This was a gamble but if it succeeded then the rewards were enormous. I saw that Bruno and his squire would be the fourth and fifth men up the ladder. One disadvantage we had was the lack of archers. Captain Odo and his archers were serving with the Earl of Hereford. Their bows would counter the Welsh and the king's words meant that in a day or two I would see my old friend once more.

With shields held above them, William de Warenne led his men to the walls. Volunteers had filled the ditch with faggots during the night and whilst the crossing would be uncomfortable, the men carrying the ladders would not risk stakes. Arrows and stones rattled against the shields but as with the ford, they took not a man. When the men reached the walls then two men leaned against the bottom and the rest began their ascent. It did not begin well. The volunteer leading the men on the earl's ladder tried to climb with a sword and a shield. He did not see the stone that was hurled to smash into his helmet and throw him to the ground. It brought a cheer from the defenders and disheartened the others. Bruno and his men fared better. As the men reached the top of the ladder so they drew swords to fight for a foothold. It was not easy. I saw men with two handed axes sweep volunteers from the top.

Things went from bad to worse when one of the ladders was knocked to the ground. It was the fault of the man at the top who was struck by a stone. He tried to hang on to the ladder and the result was that he and those on the ladder crashed to the ground. The falling ladder then struck a second which in turn hit a third. Within a handful of minutes, three ladders had been knocked to the ground. As the men lay there they were struck by stones and arrows and they perished. The one bright spot was Bruno. He reached the top along with his squire. Our men cheered but the cheer turned to a wail when the Earl of Surrey ordered a retreat. He had not seen Bruno's success and saw only the disaster of a quarter of his men being hit. The king had said it did not matter if the first assault failed and Bruno and Robert would now be paying the price. Suddenly Bruno and his squire were alone. I know not if he did not hear the horn ordering the retreat or if he simply did not heed it.

I turned to the king, "We must order more men to climb the ladder, my lord. We cannot leave Sir Bruno and his squire to be butchered."

He shook his head, "Sir Bruno is a brave man but I will not risk more men."

I nodded and grabbed my shield, "He is a shield brother and we swore an oath. I will go." Before the king could order me not to, I took off like a greyhound after a hare. The English were too busy cheering the fleeing Normans and they did not see me. I almost ran up the ladder. It was rickety and there was no one holding the bottom but God smiled on me and I made the top without falling. It was as I reached the top that the spearman lunged at me. My shield was on my left and my hand was on the ladder. The spear came for my cheek and I knew that I was a dead man. Suddenly an arrow flew from my right and the spearman was thrown to the ground. My head whipped around and I saw Captain Odo nocking another arrow. The fates were on my side. The archers had arrived and I had a chance, albeit a slim one.

Drawing a sword I leapt over the crenulations. I saw Bruno's squire lying on the stone fighting platform, his head smashed by an axe and a one-handed Bruno had his back to the door of the tower as he tried to fend off two men. There was blood from a wound to his leg. I did not hesitate. My sword swung hard and tore into the side of one man and my hands were so quick that I pulled out my sword and skewered the second before he could react.

Bruno was clearly wounded but he smiled as he said, "You came."

I smiled, "We are shield brothers, why would I not? Now let us take you down the ladder."

He shook his head, "It is not just my arm that I cannot use." He nodded to his calf which had been speared.

I turned, "Then they will have to get through me." I laid my shield over his wounded leg and drew my second sword. I roared, "I am Taillefer's heir. Who is there good enough to face me?"

My English taunts had angered them and a knot of men ran down the fighting platform to get at me. My words had not been pure bravado. At most the fighting platform could only accommodate three men and as two of those who ran at me carried shields then they effectively took up the whole platform. They had swords and thought a man without a shield was an easy target. They were wrong. I did not wait for them but stepped forward striking with both swords at the same time. It is a hard skill to learn but Taillefer had taught me well. One sword, my right one, went into the man's screaming mouth whilst my second caught the other warrior in the shoulder. It was the death of the first man which doomed the second. They both tumbled to the roof of the building below.

Despite my victory, I knew that our position was perilous. The men at the far end of the wall, having rid themselves of their attackers, now looked down the fighting platform and saw a single warrior standing over a wounded warrior. There was a roar and they raced down to slaughter the last of the Normans.

Bruno said, "Help me to my feet. If I am doomed to die let me do so on my feet. I can lean against the door for support."

I put my two swords in one hand and held the other to raise him up. The pain made him wince and I saw the puddle of blood on the stone. It did not bode well. I smiled, "Just like that first time, eh?" He nodded and I said, "And Odo has come. His arrow saved my life so who knows?"

I turned and with Bruno's sword to my right and my two swords in hand, we prepared to sell our lives dearly. The warriors ran at us with spears. These had discarded their shields and that allowed them to come three abreast. They were three tightly packed together but we would have to face three spears and then another three. Our skills, mail and helmets would be sorely tested. The three swords we wielded did not lunge but chopped. The spears outranged our swords but by chopping we could damage them. Bruno's was, naturally, a weaker blow for he was wounded. My swords hacked into the shaft behind the heads. One spear head fell to the fighting platform and the other spear was weakened. It was then that I lunged. Both of my swords found flesh and the men screamed. Bruno lunged and merely wounded his enemy. The man who had the weakened spear managed to stab at me. He was falling as he did so but in that falling he found a vulnerable spot. He hit me below the skirt of the hauberk and the spear rammed into my knee. The weakened spear broke and as the man tumbled to the ground the metal spearhead remained in my knee. My leg screamed in pain and I knew that I could only count on my right leg. I chopped sideways at the last man as Bruno distracted him with a weak swing.

The next bunch of men moved more purposefully towards us. They had seen the folly of a fast attack and the five men who came at us had a hedgehog of spears held before them. They were the smallest wedge I had seen but I knew that they would do for us.

I did not turn around but I said, "Bruno, I fear we are doomed for my left leg is hurt."

He laughed, "Two cripples trying to take a fort on their own. Your Taillefer would make a fine tale of this."

I think it was the thought of Taillefer that gave me hope. He would not have given in. Even when the Housecarls at Senlac had surrounded him I knew that he thought he could still defeat them. That was his way and I was the warrior Taillefer had made. I was his legacy and I would not go quietly.

I could not move my left leg but I had just enough strength to step onto my right to afford the wounded limb some protection. It also allowed Bruno a better chance of hurting an enemy. The five spears came as one and I used my swords like a cross to sweep up. I merely deflected them and they still came at us. One rammed into my ventail. It cut through the mail and into my cheek. A second scratched yet another line on my helmet. I heard a grunt from next to me as Bruno was struck but we still had our weapons. I used the crossed swords to ram at the enemy. If I had been mobile then I might have been able to step forward and push them from the fighting platform. As it was, I managed to slice a sword through one English arm and cut it to the bone. The blood spurted and the man screamed. It was a distraction and Bruno stabbed with his sword at the middle of another. The men defending the walls had little mail and as Bruno withdrew the sword so the man's entrails followed. More men made their way down the platform and I saw, behind the men we were fighting that the rest of the wall and the gatehouse were empty.

The three spears were pulled back ready for another attempt and the next four men were racing to join them when I saw, at the far end of the wall, William de Warenne climb over. Another of his retinue joined him. It would be too late to save us but at least they might stop the warriors from despoiling our bodies. It was at that moment that, closer to Bruno and me, Edward leapt over the wall, followed in quick succession by Aethelstan and Alfred. I had never seen such anger on the faces of my squire and pueros. There were seven whole men between them and us but their swords darted like adders' tongues as Bruno and I swashed and stabbed at them. The seven defenders died. Suddenly we five held the corner of the wall.

Edward said to the pueros, "We protect these heroes. If anyone gets to them it will be over our dead bodies."

I felt Bruno slump to the floor and, sheathing my swords I turned. He was alive but unconscious. I saw that the men following the Earl of Surrey had taken the few defenders by surprise and not only was the wall ours but men were running to open the gate.

"Alfred, find a piece of cloth and tie it around Sir Bruno's leg."

"Aye, my lord."

I put my hand down and felt the spearhead. My movement attracted Edward's attention, "My lord, you are hurt. Aethelstan, tear a piece of cloth from one of the dead."

I took the spearhead and pulled. It came out but the pain made me cry out. I did not want to but the shout rose uncalled for and I fell back to sit on my rump. As the blood flowed, I felt dizzy. Aethelstan quickly tied the cloth above the knee and stemmed the bleeding. I tried to stay alert but, like Bruno, the loss of blood forced my body to do what my mind commanded it not to do. Blackness consumed me.

It was William de Warenne's voice that I heard as I came to. It could have been moments or it could have been many minutes later. "You three did well but these two need a healer. You, Alfred is it not?"

"It is, my lord."

"Make your way back to the camp and there you will find Atticus, the king's doctor. Tell him that the Earl of Surrey commands his presence and his tools on the wall."

"Aye, my lord."

The earl had lowered his ventail and he shook his head. I gave him a wan smile and said, "Have we won?"

He nodded, "They have no donjon here but they are hiding like rats in the Roman rooms. We shall winkle them out. This is your victory, Sir Richard Fitz Malet. It was as foolish a piece of bravery as I have ever witnessed but I thank God that the bond of shield brothers held and you did that which I thought impossible."

"Is the king angry with my action?"

"How can he be? Your action gave him Caestre. He is angry that he almost lost such a knight as you and brave Bruno but God smiled on you this day." He stood, "You two guard the heroes until the doctor has attended to them."

"Aye, my lord."

I realised that while I had been unconscious my men had taken off my helmet and my coif. The air felt cooler. I glanced at Bruno. Aethelstan said, "The bleeding has stopped, my lord and he lives. My mother always says that sleep is the best medicine. If this is the king's doctor who is summoned then he will be the best of healers."

The sounds of battle gradually ceased as the last of the defenders were either taken or slain.

When the doctor came with his assistants, he nodded his approval at the methods used by my men. He said to his servants, "Carry them carefully, down the stairs. This being a Roman fort there will be an infirmary. There will be better surfaces and light." He smiled at me, "You will live, Sir Richard, and you will not lose your leg. King William would not be happy if that happened.".

The carrying was neither comfortable nor pain-free. Every step on the stairs jolted and sent paroxysms of pain coursing through my body. I managed not to shout out. The doctor barked out orders and his men prepared Bruno and me for his surgery. Bruno had more wounds than I did.

I had forgotten the spear through my ventail but, as he tended to it, the doctor assured me that the scar there would be a small one. He shook his head as he looked at the knee, "Your knee, on the other hand, will need many stitches and while you will walk again, when the weather is cold you will feel pain as though you have been wounded again. I am sorry, my lord, there is nothing I can do to prevent that from happening."

I forced a smile, "So long as I can walk then the pain can be endured."

The drug he gave me numbed the pain a little but I felt every stitch as the wound was sewn. The vinegar he used to cleanse out the wound had been painful but despite his efforts to make the sewing pain free it hurt. Bruno was luckier than I was for he remained in a blissful state while his wounds were sewn. He was unconscious. When the doctor was finished, we were taken from the infirmary to one of the bed chambers where there were two cots. Every step jolted and I was glad when I was laid on the bed. With Bruno's squire butchered it was left to my pueros and squire to act as nurses, servants and guards. I slept, albeit fitfully and when I woke, in the dark of night, it was to make water. The pain of standing was the worst pain I had endured but, with the help of my pueros, I managed. I almost filled the urn.

When daylight dawned Bruno woke. I knew his pain as he was helped to his feet and the inevitable visit to the night water urn, but he bore it stoically. While my pueros went for food I told Bruno what had happened. He shook his head, "We were lucky, Dick. Sorry, I was lucky. Others might have left me where I was. I shall never forget what you did for me."

Just then the door opened as the pueros returned and with them was a grinning Odo. He had filled out and whilst still short looked every inch an archer. He shook his head, "I cannot leave you for a moment. It is good to see that you are both still as foolish as ever."

"Thank you for the arrow, Odo."

He smiled, "The Earl of Hereford is due today but my men and I found some horses and reached here just in time to see the retreat from the walls. I saw the crossed scabbards, Dick, and knew it was you. I could not let an oath brother down and now we three are reunited."

"It may well be the last time, Odo." We both looked at Bruno. "My lands are in the south and Dick's in the north. You serve the Earl of Hereford and his lands are in the west. No matter that we have taken the last free English city we will have to be vigilant to hold on to what we have."

While we ate the food that my pueros had brought we shared our experiences of the last years, the first years of the conquest. I think we might have done so all day if the king had not arrived. Bruno and I tried to rise but his face became angry. "Do not move! You need not stand to bow before me." He shook his head, "Richard Fitz Malet, I do not wish you to be another Taillefer. I loved the man but he had a death wish. I want you to live. I need you to be there, in the north as a rock upon which I can depend. You are not only a good knight, you have good judgement and men follow you. When your three young men leapt up the ladder to go to your aid I thought that they were doomed but you train men well. Continue to do so. I came here to tell you that your deeds have not gone unnoticed. Sir Bruno, I give you another manor, Cingheuuella. It is not in Surrey, as your other manor is, but in Essex. The Saxon lord I allowed to live there chose to join the rebels at Ely. Your brother, Sir Richard, slew him. For you, Sir Richard, I give the small manor of Norton. It lies some twenty miles to the east of you. I trust that you will use the income well. And for you, Captain Odo, you are to be knighted. When the call came for you to join me you showed great courage by bringing your men first. To you, I give the manor of Yarpole close to Ludlow." He looked at the three of us. "I remember the pueros who breached the walls in Normandy. You have never let me down and I hope that my rewards will encourage others to do the same."

He left and, along with the bulk of the army, headed south to deal with Eadred the Wild. Sir Odo went with him. We were forbidden to leave until the stitches were removed. One of the doctor's assistants stayed with us.

I hated being incapacitated and I quickly learned how to do things without the aid of Edward or the pueros. When I wanted to get into bed I used my good leg to lift my wounded one. When I rose I learned to stand for a few moments to get my balance and to endure the pain of blood rushing to the wound. I think that my actions helped me to heal quickly. The pain from the wound took a long time to lessen.

When we left, I would not be travelling north alone. Gilbert Tisson who had been the king's standard bearer and was now a knight, had been given twenty men at arms. He was given the manor at Alnwick. The king had never seen it but from what Bruno and I had told him he knew that it would be a good place for a castle. Gilbert had labourers and wagons. They would build a castle to defend the crossing of the Aln. I would not ride home but travel on the back of a wagon.

Bruno had to wait until he was able to ride and so, when Gilbert left, I went with him and I bade my old friend farewell. I did not know if I would ever see him again but I knew that the bond we had would transcend time and space.

On the journey home Gilbert asked me question after question. They were not just about Alnwick but about the north. He would be exposed. The king would appoint a new bishop but until the Earl of Northumbria could be relied upon to be an ally and not an enemy, then Sir Gilbert would be the last outpost in the north.

By the time we reached Eisicewalt, I was able to walk a few paces with the aid of a stick. When I was helped down from the wagon Benthe wept while Father Gregory dropped to his knees to thank God for my safe return. The warrior had returned.

Epilogue

Five months after my return Seara gave birth to a son for
Bergil. He was named Richard and I was honoured. A month
later Edward and Mathilde were married in the now finished and
consecrated church. I had visited Norton and found it to be a
prosperous place. I had left a bailiff in charge for I still had much
to do in my first manor.

Being on the main road from York we had many visitors who
passed and we were kept abreast with news. It was from them we
learned that the king had succeeded in ousting the Welsh and the
rebels from Shrewsbury but Eadred had joined Hereward in Ely.
Earl Morcar and his brothers had also shown their true colours.
Morcar had joined the rebels while Edwin had fled north to try to
get to Scotland. Knights sent by the king found him and he was
killed. Gospatric became the new Earl of Northumbria and that
worried me. The man had changed sides so often that I knew he
could not be trusted. It made me all the more determined to make
my manor safe.

At the end of the year, when the first offspring of Parsifal and
Marie, Edward's hackney, was born, it seemed to me a sign and
the colt was named Taillefer in honour of my friend and
Parsifal's master. Like me, he was half Norman and half English.
He was the future.

The End

Glossary

Bluberhūsum - Blubberhouses
Caestre - Chester
Cernemude - Charmouth (Dorset)
Chevauchée - a medieval raid normally led by knights
Cingheuuella - Chigwell
Coistrel - a wooden or leather drinking cup that could be carried on a belt.
Donjon - keep, keep was not used until the 14th century
Douvres - Dover
Dornwaraceaster - Dorchester
Eisicewalt - Easingwold
Hog bog - a place close to a farm where pigs and fowl could be kept
Jazerant - a padded light coat worn over a mail hauberk
Lincylene - Lincoln
Maersea - River Mersey
Northwic - Norwich
Persebrig - Piercebridge
Pueros - young warriors not yet ready to be a knight
Remesgat - Ramsgate
Socce - socks also light shoes worn by actors/mummers
Tresche - Thirsk
Ulfketill - Elvington
Ventail - a detachable mail mask
Wallintun - Warrington

Canonical Hours

Matins (nighttime)
Lauds (early morning)
Prime (first hour of daylight)
Terce (third hour)
Sext (noon)
Nones (ninth hour)

Vespers (sunset evening)
Compline (end of the day)

Historical Background

A Danish wife was one where a couple married by common consent without a religious ceremony. It was a common practice at the time. It enabled lords to have more than one wife and for those lower down the social scale to be married.

The notion of fire arrows heated in a forge comes from the siege of Brionne in 1092 when Robert Duke of Normandy used the idea. I suspect he would have heard it from his father Duke William. Apologies for allowing my hero to take the credit.

Taillefer is a wonderful character for a novelist. He flashed, a little like Haley's Comet before the battle, briefly across the sky. His only recorded reference was that he asked the duke if he could start the battle. The duke allowed it. Taillefer rode his horse before the English army, showing off riding tricks. Then he juggled with swords, sang a song and challenged any of the English who cared to try to fight him. One housecarl did so and was promptly slain by the skilful Norman. Growing cocky he then rode too close to the companions of the dead housecarl and he was surrounded and he and his horse were butchered. I thoroughly enjoyed making up a backstory for him!

The various battles I describe are, in the main, historical ones but I have added others. The details of the battles are my fiction. I always aim to tell a good story but the historical figures I describe all played their parts. I weave my webs around real people but make up characters to bring them to life.

The Danish invasion and the taking of York was the trigger for King William's revenge. All the Normans in York were slaughtered with the exception of William Malet, his wife and sons. The Danes did leave. They went to the Humber and raided the lands around there. King William paid the Danes to leave. The harrying of the north only lasted a few months and I find it hard to believe that his relatively small army could have destroyed all that was attributed to them. People fled and hid. The Normans took their animals and it was starvation that killed most of the people. It allowed the king to put in place his own knights so that rebellion would not rear its head again.

The English nobles did themselves no favours by changing sides so often. King William is often portrayed as ruthless yet he forgave Gospatric, Morcar and Edwin not once but twice. It seems to me that he did all in his power to incorporate the English aristocracy into his new kingdom.

Many people wonder why in England we still speak English and not Norman-French. The answer is a simple one. The Norman ladies hired English wet nurses and nannies. They taught the young nobles English for they could not speak Norman.

This book ends at the start of 1171. England is still not at peace and Hereward in the fens would continue to be a thorn in the king's side. Scotland too would begin to be a haven for rebels and that too would bring the north of Britain into conflict with the king called, The Conqueror.

The series is called Conquest and the next books will be the story of how the Normans took Saxon England and changed it forever. It will end before the Anarchy series starts.

Companions of Duke William:

1) Robert de Beaumont, later 1st Earl of Leicester
(2) Eustace, Count of Boulogne, a.k.a. Eustace II
(3) William, Count of Évreux
(4) Geoffrey, Count of Mortagne and Lord of Nogent, later Count of Perche
(5) William fitz Osbern, later 1st Earl of Hereford
(6) Aimeri, Viscount of Thouars a.k.a. Aimery IV
(7) Walter Giffard, Lord of Longueville
(8) Hugh de Montfort, Lord of Montfort-sur-Risle
(9) Ralph de Tosny, Lord of Conches a.k.a. Raoul II
(10) Hugh de Grandmesnil
(11) William de Warenne, later 1st Earl of Surrey
(12) William Malet, Lord of Graville
(13) Odo, Bishop of Bayeux, later Earl of Kent
(14) Turstin fitz Rolf a.k.a. Turstin fitz Rou and Turstin le Blanc
(15) Engenulf de Laigle

These are the names of the knights we know who followed Duke William to England. There were others as these were the only fifteen whose names were recorded, I have made the others up.

Books used in the research

- The Norman Achievement - Richard Cassady
- Norman Knight - Gravett and Hook
- Hastings 1066 - Gravett
- The Norman Conquest of the North - Kappelle
- Norman Stone Castles (2) - Gravett and Hook
- A Short History of the Norman Conquest of England - Edward Augustus Freeman
- The Tower of Lundenwic - A L Rowse
- The Tower of Lundenwic - Lapp and Parnell
- The Adventure of English - Melvyn Bragg

Griff Hosker October 2023

Other books by Griff Hosker

If you enjoyed reading this book, then why not read
another one by the author?

Ancient History

The Sword of Cartimandua Series
(Germania and Britannia 50 A.D. – 128 A.D.)
Ulpius Felix- Roman Warrior (prequel)
The Sword of Cartimandua
The Horse Warriors
Invasion Caledonia
Roman Retreat
Revolt of the Red Witch
Druid's Gold
Trajan's Hunters
The Last Frontier
Hero of Rome
Roman Hawk
Roman Treachery
Roman Wall
Roman Courage

The Wolf Warrior series
(Britain in the late 6th Century)
Saxon Dawn
Saxon Revenge
Saxon England
Saxon Blood
Saxon Slayer
Saxon Slaughter
Saxon Bane
Saxon Fall: Rise of the Warlord
Saxon Throne

Saxon Sword

Medieval History

The Dragon Heart Series
Viking Slave *
Viking Warrior *
Viking Jarl *
Viking Kingdom *
Viking Wolf *
Viking War
Viking Sword
Viking Wrath
Viking Raid
Viking Legend
Viking Vengeance
Viking Dragon
Viking Treasure
Viking Enemy
Viking Witch
Viking Blood
Viking Weregeld
Viking Storm
Viking Warband
Viking Shadow
Viking Legacy
Viking Clan
Viking Bravery

The Norman Genesis Series
Hrolf the Viking *
Horseman *
The Battle for a Home *
Revenge of the Franks *
The Land of the Northmen
Ragnvald Hrolfsson

Brothers in Blood
Lord of Rouen
Drekar in the Seine
Duke of Normandy
The Duke and the King

Danelaw
(England and Denmark in the 11th Century)
Dragon Sword *
Oathsword *
Bloodsword *
Danish Sword

New World Series
Blood on the Blade *
Across the Seas *
The Savage Wilderness *
The Bear and the Wolf *
Erik The Navigator *
Erik's Clan *
The Last Viking

The Vengeance Trail *

The Conquest Series
(Normandy and England 1050 - 1100)
Hastings
Conquest

The Aelfraed Series
(Britain and Byzantium 1050 A.D. - 1085 A.D.)
Housecarl *
Outlaw *
Varangian *

The Reconquista Chronicles

Castilian Knight *
El Campeador *
The Lord of Valencia *

**The Anarchy Series England
1120-1180**
English Knight *
Knight of the Empress *
Northern Knight *
Baron of the North *
Earl *
King Henry's Champion *
The King is Dead *
Warlord of the North
Enemy at the Gate
The Fallen Crown
Warlord's War
Kingmaker
Henry II
Crusader
The Welsh Marches
Irish War
Poisonous Plots
The Princes' Revolt
Earl Marshal
The Perfect Knight

**Border Knight
1182-1300**
Sword for Hire *
Return of the Knight *
Baron's War *
Magna Carta *
Welsh Wars *
Henry III *
The Bloody Border *

Baron's Crusade
Sentinel of the North
War in the West
Debt of Honour
The Blood of the Warlord
The Fettered King
de Montfort's Crown

Sir John Hawkwood Series
France and Italy 1339- 1387
Crécy: The Age of the Archer *
Man At Arms *
The White Company *
Leader of Men *
Tuscan Warlord *
Condottiere

Lord Edward's Archer
Lord Edward's Archer *
King in Waiting *
An Archer's Crusade *
Targets of Treachery *
The Great Cause *
Wallace's War *
The Hunt

Struggle for a Crown
1360- 1485
Blood on the Crown *
To Murder a King *
The Throne *
King Henry IV *
The Road to Agincourt *
St Crispin's Day *
The Battle for France *
The Last Knight *

Conquest

Queen's Knight *

Tales from the Sword I
(Short stories from the Medieval period)

Tudor Warrior series
England and Scotland in the late 15th and early 16th century
Tudor Warrior *
Tudor Spy *
Flodden

Conquistador
England and America in the 16th Century
Conquistador *
The English Adventurer *

Modern History

The Napoleonic Horseman Series
Chasseur à Cheval
Napoleon's Guard
British Light Dragoon
Soldier Spy
1808: The Road to Coruña
Talavera
The Lines of Torres Vedras
Bloody Badajoz
The Road to France
Waterloo

The Lucky Jack American Civil War series
Rebel Raiders
Confederate Rangers
The Road to Gettysburg

Soldier of the Queen series
Soldier of the Queen
Redcoat's Rifle
Omdurman

The British Ace Series
1914
1915 Fokker Scourge
1916 Angels over the Somme
1917 Eagles Fall
1918 We will remember them
From Arctic Snow to Desert Sand
Wings over Persia

Combined Operations series
1940-1945
Commando *
Raider *
Behind Enemy Lines
Dieppe
Toehold in Europe
Sword Beach
Breakout
The Battle for Antwerp
King Tiger
Beyond the Rhine
Korea
Korean Winter

Tales from the Sword II
(Short stories from the Modern period)
For more information on all of the books please visit the
author's website at www.griffhosker.com where there is a
link to contact him or visit his Facebook page: GriffHosker
at Sword Books

Printed in Great Britain
by Amazon

37453814R10145